SHARK ALLEY

Paul,
You always inspired
me! You are a
champion and best
of success in your
next phase of life!

Jeff

MONTEREY BAY AQUARIUM

TUESDAY, JULY 4TH, 2017 1800 HOURS

...the pinkish seal intestines were draped over the shoulders, crisscrossed underneath their arms, then wrapped around their waist. It is normal for carnivorous mammals, like seals, to have intestines which are 5-6 times the length of their entire body. So, the intestines from one large seal was more than enough. When the lid came off and was lifted overhead, Miguel and Iovita immediately tried to get up which was nearly impossible in a wet tank, slippery from the seal oil and fat, no shoes and your arms manacled behind your back. Both soldiers were ready for this and a quick rap to their temple, with the butt of their handguns quieted them down.

Miguel would be first. Nielsen and Peterson each grabbed under his armpits and lifted him out of the tank and pushed him face down onto the deck near the edge of the tank. Miguel was prone and stretched out on the deck, his feet dangling over the pool. Nielsen had one knee in the middle of his lower back and the other knee on the back of his neck. He double-checked the duct tape over his mouth, because that was going to be important.

Both soldiers looked up to see whether everything was still clear in the hallway. Peterson had all his weight pressing down on the lower part of Miguel's calves. He reached in his vest and pulled out an X-ACTO knife. He nodded over to Peterson who grabbed a handful of seal entrails. Hovering the razor-sharp blade over Miguel's heel, he plunged the blade into the heel. His foot instantaneously arched from the pain and the scream was suppressed by the duct tape. Blood was pumping out of the slashed foot and dripping into the pool. Simultaneously, the entrails splashed into the water.

The desired effect was to stimulate all the sharks in the water. The inner ears of sharks would register the intestines splashing into the water, then the shark's paired nostrils would be hit with the seals guts, blood from the captive and then finally the big splash and thrashing of Miguel in the water.

Quickly, Nielsen pressed the bloody X-ACTO blade into the other heel and slashed down towards his toes. More blood poured out, Miguel's entire body arched at the pain and he tried to let out another scream of agony. Nielsen slashed through the blindfold and tossed it in the water. Miguel was in so much pain and all he could see was the boot of his captor and a concrete floor.

Iovita was now petrified, she could hear the struggle and muffled screams from her husband. She thrashed and twisted to both sides in an attempt to see who was hurting her husband, but she was held firmly in place.

Several of the seal's organs were tossed next into the pool. Below the surface, there was an immediate chain reaction. All the sharks had caught the scent and felt the vibrations in the water. Bruce was the first to move and reversed his clockwise swimming path. Since his captivity he hadn't been fed any seal, but the delicacy was instantly recognized, and he immediately swam towards the other end of the tank.

Speed was of the essence and all the soldiers knew it. They hoped this human-seal gumbo was going to be tantalizing for the Great White. Each gulped at the thought of facing the beast in his watery home. Each soldier grabbed the lower forearm of Miguel's and pressed up hard enough to give the prisoner another jolt of pain. Nielsen cut through the rope binding his wrists together. With their free hand, they grabbed his upper arms, lifted him up and heaved him into the water with a flailing splash.

There were a few dozen hardcore Aquarium lovers who were ignoring the concert in lieu of having an unhindered time to view the ocean life. There were two levels for the audience to view the Open Sea tank. Those who were watching had noticed an immediate alert in the water when the first drops of blood and seal entrails had landed in the water. From their viewing angle, they couldn't see anything other than the sharks all turning their attention to the left edge and surface.

Nielsen's hand shot into the water with Miguel's phone in the weighted, airtight container. He thought wryly, "This should be a first for Facebook Live."

CHAPTER 1

BANK OF AMERICA, LAFAYETTE, CA
THURSDAY, MAY 4TH, 2017

The bank teller must have thought Mr. DeBoy had won the lottery. The look on her face was just like his...a smile from ear to ear. The check wasn't from the California State Lottery, rather, it was from old Chuck. Charles Schwab, that is. He had closed his stock position in Netflix and what a ride it had been. Back in 2003, Netflix was in the early stages and seemed like a promising business venture. Comparing the overhead of a shipping warehouse to the brick and mortars like Hollywood Video and Blockbuster, it was no contest. Hollywood and Blockbuster and any independents would race to the death of zero profits while trying to maintain thousands of storefronts across America; while Netflix was in a different race altogether.

Mailing DVDs, monthly subscriptions and it was FAST to your mailbox. Convenience. People loved convenience and browsing online—especially this generation—pick your movies, queue them up and they're on their way! Brilliant!

Jarrod DeBoy had always been very thorough; due diligence may have been an understatement. Who was running the company, cash flow, property, future market outlook, hard assets and intellectual property. In his mind, this company really had some room to grow. So many potential customers to gobble up. He had placed his order for 1,000 shares at $12.78 on July 1, 2003. By the following February, it had nearly tripled in value and the stock had been split 2 for 1. He had briefly considered cashing in then, but hadn't held the stock more than a year and there were significant tax penalties. Besides, he felt really confident in the company, the leadership and business model.

After the split in October 2004, the stock price did move down into the mid-9 dollars a share. A bit nerve racking, but that is the game in the stock market. By May 2005, it broke through the 12 dollars a share and it was time to double down. He acquired another 1,000 shares. Now it was time to see how far the momentum could propel this stock. It more than doubled again, nearly breaking into $30. It cooled off in 2007 and 2008, bouncing between $20 and $25. He never really considered selling. Though he had quadrupled his original shares and the second thousand shares had doubled, it just wasn't the right time to sell. His broker had tried to convince him to at least sell half his stake, but he wouldn't hear it.

Fast forward into 2009 and it was time to put the seat belt on. Netflix was on fire! January 1, $36.14,

July 1, $43.94 and by Jan 1, 2010 it hit $62.25 with no signs of slowing down! His investments and fees were just under $26,000. The 3,000 shares now were worth a staggering $186,750. You only have to hit a few home runs in life. In 2010, the stock began climbing at a very steep rate. In June 2010, the stock pulled back a bit and he bought 10 long options for the December strike price of $125. Borrowed against his current stake. By the end of October, the stock was pushing 200 dollars a share and his broker was calling him daily insisting he sell his position. He did and captured a cool $50,000 profit.

For nostalgia's sake, he put the original stake of $26,000 in some bonds and pushed the remaining funds back into Netflix. At $200 a share, it was another 130 shares. Day after day with new all-time highs were making him a bit nervous and the stock market in general was overheated. There were warning signs everywhere. He sold the 130 shares and another 1,000 at $250 and kept it in the investment account. $282,500 minus fees. Both he and his broker felt better.

As the market crashed and burned, his cash position looked better by the month. Netflix had reached $270. By the time the market had imploded, it had dropped back down to the mid-64 dollars a share. Still his 2,000 shares were nearly five times his original investment. And that wasn't including the pile of cash he had on reserve. The market was going to be turbulent for a while. He would pick his moment and use some of that cash to reinvest in Netflix again.

It took nearly a year, October 1 2012, $79.24 and there was enough momentum to begin analyzing the fundamentals again. It could drop back down into the $50s and that would hurt, but it could also be the perfect storm. Blockbuster was going down the tubes and fast. Hollywood Video ceased operations when its parent company, Movie Gallery, filed for Chapter 7 in May 2010. He put a little more than half his cash back into Netflix, which netted him another 2,000 shares. Current status: 4,000 shares and $120,000 cash on hand.

The next few years were nothing short of phenomenal. The chart looked like the flight path of a Discovery rocket. In one year, it had propelled to over $320 a share. He was out of his mind! Yes, this was the moon-shot home run and he was going to savor every minute watching it go out of the stadium! Some of the gyrations in 2014 were very dramatic. In fact, by October 2014 it had jumped to over $390 a share!

December 2014 to January 2015, the stock took off at an unbelievable rate, from 341 to 441 dollars a share! 2015 could not be dreamt any better. The stock was completely out of control. At least twice a day his broker was begging him to sell and completely liquidate. He put in his trailing stop loss orders to prevent losses. By the next day though, they seemed ludicrous and he had to reset them again.

Talks of a split, 6 for 1 or 7 for 1 began in earnest. Even at $500/share so many people were priced out of the market and now that $600 a share was within reach, it only seemed like a matter of time before the split was formally announced. He set his selling price confidently. Intra-day trading on June 9th, Netflix reached his selling price of $650/share.

"Excuse me, Mr. DeBoy," the teller said. "Mr. DeBoy, sir. Excuse me!"

"Oh yes, sorry."

"How did you make $4.6 million?" She sounded flabbergasted. "Oh, I'm sorry, that was very rude. I shouldn't have asked such a personal question. It is none of my business...."

FRIDAY, MAY 5TH, 2017

The drive wasn't far, and they headed a mile and a half West on Mt. Diablo Boulevard. All the boutique stores, Whole Foods and retail establishments indicated an affluent community. There was moderate traffic on the road and as they turned left on a private county-maintained road, it thinned out even more. Gradually climbing, with a few leisurely turns, they drove up the road in silence. Each lost in the next conversation he supposed.

Poor Dad. It seemed like every month he slipped just a little more into the unrelenting grip of Alzheimer's. Jarrod was going to need to place restrictions on his banking account and now it looked like two withdrawals of $500 happened last week. Was finding out where the money went, even worth the questions by innuendo? It seemed like there were so many potential pitfalls that were missing from the books he had read on how to care for your parents in the throes of Alzheimer's disease.

Taking away his debit card two years ago had erupted in a bitter argument. This was certainly the toughest love he had ever been forced to give to his own 82-year-old father. The man whom he respected above all others, who had given him his moral compass, escorted him to the doors of life. He would be as careful as possible trying to discover where these last withdrawals had gone. A charity? Two more business suits? He'd always enjoyed dressing sharply and his quote was burned in his mind like so many others: "Dress for the position you want to be in, not the one you are today."

For the past five years there had been hints of diminishing capacity. At first he had thought Dad was just becoming a little absent minded, slightly out of touch. Less than three years ago, the signs could not be ignored and under the guise of an annual exam, his doctor had extended the appointment to determine if it was Alzheimer's. It was, had tried to prepare himself and his Dad as best as he could. Transferring him to Country Manor specialized elder care facility in nearby Lafayette was easy. He had told Dad, they were going to remodel the wing of his current apartment and he had found a very nice place not too far away.

Because Country Manor had several levels of adult care, his Dad didn't even question it. The amenities made it an easy sell. Dad loved the outdoor benches shaded by the fabulous one hundred plus year-old oak trees. There were also three koi ponds, bocce courts and it was walking distance to his favorite Italian restaurant.

It was time to drive over and take Dad for a walk. They hadn't been up to the reservoir lately. It was a favorite of Dad's. Seemed like so long ago, but less than ten years ago you could find Dad fishing for rainbow trout at the reservoir. He was there at dawn and had likely caught and released every trout in the reservoir. One of his best friends, Travis, had joined him regularly until he had passed away from Melanoma. That tragedy had nearly broken Dad. Only grieving for Mom was longer and more sorrowful than Travis' death; it had nearly bed-ridden him. They had been friends and business partners for nearly 60 years.

SATURDAY, MAY 6TH, 2017

Shark Week, it was advertised everywhere. It must be Discovery Channels' top commercial revenue producer. With over a month to go, he'd seen commercials on the major news networks, sports channels, electronic billboards near the Bay Bridge and even on the sides of busses!

Friday morning, a little past 9am. He'd go over to see Dad now. Parked in his garage, left to right: the current year's Tesla sedan, in electric blue. Next, 2016 Orange U Tempted Metallic Z06 Corvette, then an arctic white 2012 Mercedes G64 AMG and, hidden under a car cover, a car aficionado would see the outline of a Ford GT40. As he slid into the driver's seat of the Tesla, he reviewed the conversation and the possible directions it could take. Backing out his driveway, he nearly missed smelling the freshly cut lawn. The bushes were trimmed, weeds pulled, roses dead-headed and it always looked ready for Sunset magazine.

The gardeners had cut a dozen heirloom roses, three varieties and he was taking them to the receptionist at Country Manor. They would brighten the lobby and cast their fragrance for a few days. Parking was easy, but getting out of the car wasn't. A few hundred dollars given to a charity every so often would actually be fine, but with the empty long-term care account was another story altogether.

Walking across the parking lot, through the automatic electric doors of his Father's Senior Care Facility, he was immediately greeted by Cheryl, this weekend's receptionist. "Hello, Mr. DeBoy." Cheryl's medium length auburn hair was pulled back neatly today.

"Hi Cheryl. How are you today? Here are some roses for the lobby."

"Oh thank you so much for bringing them. I'll grab a vase and set them out. Your father is out near the koi ponds now. We have some bottled water for your walk around the reservoir. Anything you'd like from the kitchen?"

"Thanks for having the water ready. We'll be fine and thanks for the offer. How long has Dad been out?"

"I'd say less than half an hour."

"Ok, great. I think we'll be back by 2."

Straight through the double doors, the lobby was a very nice dark marble with veins of gold and white tones running through it. Off to the left, was the receptionist's desk with a smiling Cheryl today. Directly ahead was the full-service restaurant and open dining area. Square black tables sized for four guests. The tables were always at the ready; silverware wrapped in white or black linens. Glasses and upside-down coffee cups awaiting the patrons. The chairs were medium back, set on legs with rolling wheels. To the right edge of the dining area was the kitchen and you could hear the chef begin his preparations for the lunch crowd.

On the right-hand side of the first floor was a visiting area with tables, couches and chairs lined along the glass perimeter. It was an inviting area, where the residents could visit and enjoy seeing some of the grounds and simply people-watch those entering and exiting. The various couches and chairs were covered in medium dark neutrals, velour and micro-fiber materials. Most everyone had a favorite corner or set of chairs.

The four elevators were just to the left of the dining area and beyond them were the double doors to the koi ponds, benches and garden. He walked through to the doors, waving briefly and smiling to Dad's neighbor, James McInnis. He was just sitting down near the front entrance for his daily vigil. James knew all the comings and goings at Country Manor. He stationed himself there until midway through lunch observing who came to have lunch with their parent or take them out; who had time freedom during the middle of the week.

He watched when hospice was called in to see whether the family would visit more frequently. Were the visits shorter or longer? Tears as they left; grateful to have seen Mom or Dad one more time. James also spied out the reaction to the special of the day. One only needed to watch the reaction to the first bite and how much was left or eaten to know whether it was worth ordering. Overall, they had great meals here, but occasionally the spices were off or it was just a bad recipe.

Dad was sitting on the bench underneath a massive oak tree, which stretched upward to the sky at least 80 feet. It offered tremendous shade. There were several of these trees, native to northern California, sprinkled throughout the property. A concrete walking path meandered through the garden. Dad's hearing wasn't great now, but his senses picked up right away as he approached.

"Morning Dad," he said cheerfully.

"Morning Son," was the reply. "I didn't know you were coming today."

He no longer expected Dad to remember when he had told him he was coming by. "How are things? Thought I'd stop by and see if you'd like to go up to the reservoir or out for an early lunch."

Dad responded, "Is the reservoir still open? I would like to go walk around it."

It was tough to ignore the decline, but he held onto the thought that maybe the progression of Alzheimer's would end right here and not worsen. Because many of his faculties were diminishing, Dad simply wasn't aware of the of what he had lost. At least in this phase, he could maintain a certain level of communication.

"Sure is Dad, and it's early enough to walk in the cool of the day."

It was some effort to get up from the bench, but Jarrod looked around to give him the few extra moments to ease himself up. Dad didn't want much physical help and there was no rush this morning. He straightened himself fairly upright and they walked along-side each other back towards the building. It wasn't a fast pace, but the steps were determined and rhythmic.

"Did you sleep pretty well last night Dad?"

"Oh yeah." He said a little unenthusiastically.

Two steps away from the rear double doors, opening automatically, Dad had an expression of surprise. Jarrod just smiled and looked ahead. They walked past the elevators and James had spotted them. He wasn't coy about his observation and said, "Where are you two going?"

Jarrod said, "We're driving up to the reservoir for a walk and then will head over for lunch."

James responded swiftly as if he needed to approve destination and duration, "That sounds fine. Will it be Celia's for lunch?"

"We'll see what Dad's interested in today. Enjoy your morning James."

They continued walking past James, through the entry doors and out to the parking lot. Dad didn't comment on much today - the car, weather, James or how his morning had gone. Slipping gently into the passenger seat, Jarrod closed the door for him. Jarrod went to the other side and could notice just a little tension building in the pit of his stomach.

It's just two thousand dollars.... but two days. We'd get to that soon enough. "How's your energy today Dad? Want to take 1 lap or 2 around the reservoir?"

"I feel pretty good, son. Maybe we'll get two in this morning."

The drive wasn't far, and they headed a mile and a half West on Mt. Diablo Boulevard. All the boutique stores, Whole Foods and retail establishments of an affluent community. There was moderate traffic on the road and as they turned left on a private county-maintained road, it thinned out even more. Gradually climbing, with a few leisurely turns, they drove up the road in silence. Each lost in the next conversation he supposed.

Judging by the SUVs and minivans in the parking lot, there would be at least two dozen moms and their kids. There should be a few people fishing for local trout and perch. It wasn't going to be crowded at all. They paid for parking at the meter and walked down the asphalt covered walk towards the main walking loop.

The reservoir stretched some 2,000 feet and at its widest point was 300 feet across and the depths ran all the way to 80 feet. There were short walking paths down to fishing decks; usually 12'x12' in size. The first time around, they would walk around it clockwise to have just a little less sun in their eyes. This was one of the patterns he wanted to continue for his Dad and himself as long as he could. Dad wouldn't get out of breath on the first lap, but the second would take considerably longer. In all, the loop was 2.3 miles, mainly flat with slight changes in elevation.

The paved path was about ten feet across with a few scattered signs asking for people to clean up after their dog or to not trample the undergrowth. Pet owners seemed to love this walk. It was safe, and you felt as if you were in nature, not walking through a neighborhood. The dogs loved it of course, because there were other canines, trees and plants to sniff and lots of activity to watch. Even the teacup dog owners came to walk the reservoir. There were benches and seating near the kids' play area and along the walkway.

He wanted to probe about the money here, get it out of the way and then enjoy a nice meal, reminisce with Dad and take him back to Country Manor. The direct approach was his mode in the business world; round-about was never his style. Though, he did see the value in timing of conversations and also preparing the soil, so to speak.

"The kids asked about you this week Dad and how your knee is feeling." I said in a very even, conversational tone. "Is it stiff in the morning or after walks anymore?"

Dad glanced down at his right knee. It had been three months now since the replacement surgery and a year after the left had been replaced. "It feels almost exactly like the other," he said cheerfully. "Dr. Samson is the best." As an afterthought, he said, "There is a little swelling behind it, but only when I walk more than an hour."

"Did you want to have it looked at?" Jarrod immediately asked with concern. Swelling, infection, his thoughts jumped ahead. He knew that was the last place Dad wanted to go was to another doctor appointment. But it was different with Dr. Samson, whom he trusted and appreciated. Two knee replacements and a shoulder repair; they joked about him trying out for the Country Manor football team. All the surgeries had gone extremely well and the recovery, even at his age, had gone even better than could be expected for an 81-year-old.

"Nah, no need to bother the good Doctor. It doesn't really feel painful."

"Ok, well let me know after today." He tried to lighten it up a bit, "We need at least 10,000 miles out of it like the golden Samson warranty states."

The reservoir provided so much to absorb. There was the natural beauty of the trees, foliage and of course the water. There was at least a dozen varieties of birds, squirrels running around and the occasional hawk in the sky. Then the daily visitors. All those adults and kids walking down the path, their voices, the laughter, the parental warnings to the young ones. "Don't put that in your mouth." "Don't pick that up." "Don't get too close to the water."

There were joggers, power walkers, people watchers and always a few baby strollers. It was just the perfect place to go for a walk. Sometimes it did get a little too busy on weekends, but weekday mornings here were nearly always ideal.

He consciously tried not to time his Dad; to not see if he was literally losing speed as track stars would lose speed past their prime. Dad's pace seemed pretty good today and matched his mood. Maybe those were better measuring sticks: his attitude, comprehension and verbal acuity.

As they ambled along, Dad asked if he'd heard from Janelle. In fact, he had, but most of that conversation would be edited out. Recently, their conversations centered more on Dad's Alzheimer's state than anything. Having lost their mom, they were acutely aware of changes. Janelle was four years his junior and quite accomplished in her own right. She ran a very successful paralegal company with offices in Sacramento, San Francisco, Santa Clara, La Jolla, Oceanside and Los Angeles.

"Janelle is doing great, Dad. This week they're in Palm Springs and she said she'd be up next weekend."

"Who'd want to be there in that heat!", Dad exclaimed. "Who needs to golf in a desert?" "There are great spas all over southern California. Why bake in that ridiculous heat?"

Janelle, her husband Trey, their son Grant and his fiancée Giselle were there for a week of golf and spa treatments. Another attempt to bond with Giselle. Attempt number one hadn't worked out as planned, with the engaged couple fighting over wedding location and who to invite. Much of the weekend was tense—these two did not hide their feelings, nor sleep on their anger. Unfortunately, they had saved the last dozen questionable guests to debate about on that weekend.

The second weekend getaway to Catalina island had been another relationship wreck. One of Grant's ex-girlfriends happened to be there the same weekend. Giselle could not be convinced some sort of secret rendez-vous had been arranged. It was three days of turmoil and accusations, not the fun, carefree weekend that had been planned.

"Grant and his fiancée haven't set a date yet" Jarrod added unconvincingly "She seems to be a great young lady."

They kept walking for several more minutes; enjoying the bustle and activity on the trail. Dad had smiled at a few kids and said "Good morning" to some other casual walkers. Occasionally, they would make eye contact with the runners, muted by their ear buds, and exchange nods. The timing wasn't quite right to bring up the account and he was leaning towards not saying the account was empty. He had the means to refill that account several times over. Jarrod definitely wanted to get a little information before lunch. He always wanted to end his visits with Dad on a pleasant, upbeat note.

As they rounded the eastern edge of the trail, the sun was warming up the cool morning air as it continued its arc, moving along the south-to-southwest path. Now that it was behind them, they didn't need to shade their eyes. Trailing them, two brothers were arguing over who got to walk the dog. Ultimately, they agreed to hold the big Lab's leash together.

Jarrod asked his Father if he had taken any walks around downtown or if he had been to the grocery or bank lately. He said he had been over to Ace Hardware to pick up some light bulbs. He was constantly exchanging the provided fluorescent bulbs in his studio with the traditional bulbs. It was becoming more difficult to buy them as the store stocked of the newer energy efficient styles. Dad said they hurt his eyes. I thought he was just having fun with maintenance people.

Dad did say he wondered why the people in the bank changed so frequently. He'd lost a good acquaintance when the last assistant manager had left to run a larger branch in the city. "I really don't like this banking on the internet" and seemed a little befuddled in his next comment "Why can't they pay to put the same people in the bank that are emailing me?"

Dad continued, "I used to only have surveys come to me, but now they're telling me to change pass codes and those ridiculous safety questions and answers." "It seems like last week they didn't have anything better to do than email me."

The alarms immediately went off in my head. "Dad, did they actually email you telling you to change your pass code?"

"Yes, at least they are a little more personal now. Everything used to be from Customer Service, but now at least the emails are coming from someone with a name and title. Good to know their Internet Security office wants me to change my password. Just wish it wasn't so often."

This brought Jarrod's anger back to the surface and he did his very best to hide it from his Father. It wasn't so much that he might have been caught by a phishing scam, but he did not him to feel in any way that he was at fault for letting these thieves into the bank accounts. He'd prod a little more.

"Dad, are you pretty happy with the bank? Would you like to switch back to your credit union?"

"No, I'm getting the hang of internet banking and I can still walk over when I want to talk with someone."

"Did they say why they needed you to change your pass code?"

"It was for my protection," the email said, and that "someone had broken into their master system, so everyone needed to change their password."

This definitely sounded like a scam and he'd have to make a trip to the bank after lunch with Dad. His blood pressure rose a little more as they walked. Stupid criminals taking advantage of his Dad and certainly other seniors or those less internet savvy. They had nearly finished their way around the entire reservoir loop. It didn't seem very cheery now.

He looked over at his father, sad for him as a victim, grateful they could still walk together and have conversations. By his watch, their pace was fairly quick today: a little under 22 minutes. "How are the legs feeling now, Dad? Do you want to take another lap, rest or head to lunch?"

"I'm pretty hungry today, so can we head to lunch?"

This was an interesting statement, so he asked, "How was breakfast this morning? Did you have your standard?" Dad's standard breakfast, for as long as he could remember was a bowl of oatmeal, scrambled eggs: one egg and two egg whites and hot tea.

Dad paused as if to think. "You know, I'm not sure. Don't remember."

He wasn't certain if this was a forgetful moment, but he might have to ask the staff whether Dad was having breakfast. This was one of the most ingrained habits in his Dad's life and if he was missing breakfast, it could mean that the debilitating condition was taking its next step.

"Sure, Dad. I'm a bit hungry myself. By now the reservoir was bursting with activity. More kids, conversation, laughter, dogs and it was a nice hum to watch and hear. More cars had trickled into the parking lot and they headed towards their spot. His mind was drifting a bit towards the concerns brought forth in the last half hour. He needed to focus though and be in the moment with Dad. All the other conversations would be handled after lunch.

He opened the door for Dad, watching his footwork as he stepped off the curb, resting his hand on the Silver Tesla to help him maintain balance. Then he reached out to hold the top of the door window frame and stepped around and sat in his seat. He had considered applying for a disability parking placard and he knew it wouldn't be too long before it was a necessity. Sucks to get old is all he could think.

Dad always had a curious look on his face when I started the electric wizardry of a car and backed up. Of course, there was not even an ignition click that a standard automobile would have. The dash lit up and as the brake pedal was depressed and the car shifted into reverse, the gear indicator moving to reverse was the only visual or audible cue. Once in drive for a few seconds, Dad's shoulders would relax and he'd let out his breath.

The sun sparkled through the trees as they drove westward down Mt. Diablo Ave. The emotions of his Dad at this stage of life paralleled having a child. The concerns were different, but the joys and distress were similar. The responsibility he felt for ushering his Dad through these years was more ominous because of the sad finality.

They traversed over to El Nido Ranch Road. The two-way road meandered along the edge of Lafayette and Orinda. They would take this road to Shelby's.

Jarrod inquired, "Still have a big appetite Dad?"

"Oh yes, I'm ready." He answered quickly.

"I brought along some pictures of Natalia, Clay and the kids. Just saw them last weekend at their house for a barbeque." The few minutes to order the prints was worth it and he hoped it helped him keep the family in his mind. Even if his memory was slipping, the 5x7s would give him something to look at in his apartment during the empty hours.

They made a few more turns and pulled into the driveway of Shelby's. Making it before the noon lunch hour would help with the conversations; less background noise to help his dad's hearing and concentration. There was an open parking spot close to the entrance and they pulled into it. They walked up the old-fashioned, elevated, wood plank walkway to the front doors. The banisters were freshly painted in a gleaming forest green with white vertical spindles. The paint had such a luxurious, glossy appearance it always reminded him of the painted railing and woodwork at Disneyland.

The wooden sidewalk was tightly nailed and left unpainted to prevent slipping, especially in the rainy season. There was a nice sound to their footsteps, unknown in this era with concrete and asphalt everywhere. Opening the door for Dad, they entered and were immediately greeted by the young college-aged hostess. She asked if they were expecting to meet anyone else. They replied no.

"Would you like a seat near the window or out on the back patio?"

"Near a window will be fine, thanks." Dad had plenty of sun today and it would be easier to hear inside.

They were seated and handed the menus. "Ann will be your server today and she'll be right over."

Jarrod watched his dad to see whether he would need the menu or not. Sometimes he remembered his favorite sandwich combination and other times he acted as if it were a brand-new restaurant. He knew quickly what he was having, the grilled chicken on sourdough with light mayo, lettuce and tomato. A side salad and small cup of fruit would take care of him. Dad's favorite was the pastrami on rye or at least it had been most of his days while trading as a stock broker.

He had worked in the city for Merrill Lynch during the 70s and had built quite an extensive clientele, handling millions of dollars. In the summer of 1981, there were some rumblings that the commission structure was going to change. It was to benefit the corporation of course. He, along with half his department brokers, left for other firms or to strike out on their own.

Dad had chosen the independent route. He had planned every detail out thoroughly. In the evenings and weekends leading up to his resignation notice, he had established his C Corp, fee structure, signed an office space lease, joined the chamber of commerce, drafted the account transfer forms, letterhead and business cards. When his April income had been chopped by 40%, he decided to return the favor. His resignation letter would be effective May 30th and he had verbal confirmation that 65 of his accounts would switch over to him June 1st which would equate to $48 million dollars in accounts. Bon voyage Merrill!

"I think I'll stick with my favorite today, pastrami on rye," he said with a cheerful voice. Funny, how these short sentences made him feel so happy and relieved inside. He knew it was only a matter of time and it there would be no "favorites," no "I remember" in his vocabulary.

He had pulled out the picture envelope from Walgreens from his driver side door pocket before they walked into the restaurant. Dad seemed genuinely excited to see who was in the pictures. How big were the great-grandkids now? What was happening in everyone's life?

The first few photos were the standard photos he'd taken of the family in the back yard; his son and daughter-in-law on lounge chairs with one kid in each parent's lap. The smiles were pretty relaxed and natural, which was easy for young children. Their excitement for life and personalities hadn't been chipped away by disappointments in life yet.

"So, tell me how old they are again," Dad said.

"Michael is nearly six and will be starting kindergarten in August. Shelby is four and she thinks she's ready for kindergarten as well." His grandkids brought a smile to his face every time he thought of them. Such an amazing time in life. No preconceptions, the world a great discovery, no responsibilities and the protection of loving parents.

There were a few more pictures of him reading to his grandkids out of Dr. Seuss' Green Eggs and Ham, Shelby's favorite for the evening. Next, a picture showing Michael reading his sight word worksheet. Summer homework requested by his mom and dad from the pre-K teacher. He had worked on the lists two or three times a day all summer long. Reading was the most essential building block in school. "He whipped right through those sheets, Dad. It was common three and four letter words. Seems like he'll be an early reader. Of course, Shelby has heard Green Eggs and Ham so many times, she can nearly recite it!"

The sandwiches came as Dad was finishing the last pictures. "You can keep those; I have a copy already."

"Thanks for printing them for me Jarrod. Wonder if you could take me next time?"

"You bet Dad. Last time you were laid up with that bronchitis. We'd all love to have you there." Finding time in a young couple's busy life wasn't easy, but that was just an excuse. He didn't want to invite himself over so this next time he'd host. Put that on the calendar; have them over for a swim party and cook out. Afternoons would be best, while Dad's energy was at a good level.

Two Army reserves had walked in and were seated next to them. One was his height, 6' and had at least 20 more pounds of muscle. The second was taller by a good two inches. It was clear they were not fresh out of boot camp. They were lean, but not worn-out boot camp lean. Their tan and olive camos were clean and not a touch of dust or dirt on their boots. Seemed a little out of place, younger by at least 25 years than the average patron and you didn't see many dressed military in the town. Though the VA hospital was less than 30 minutes away, there just didn't seem to be many soldiers stopping in this country club enclave of Orinda, Moraga and Lafayette.

The Reserves were talked in fairly low tones and their serious demeanor piqued his interest. Of course, the quieter people talked, the more curious others became. He found himself distracted by their quiet, intense voices, trying to listen to them while holding down a light conversation with Dad. With the ebb and flow of the restaurant conversational noise, he picked up a few phrases. "...trace through their network..." said the taller one and the other replied "...we could find them and set a..."

So much more of today's military had shifted from the ground to cyber, drones, hardening of computer systems and the like. Hearing just these small pieces from their discussion changed his mental image of the soldier profile immediately. Rather than patrols and facing the enemy face to face, these soldiers were a different classification altogether. They went into the Armed Services with a penchant for computer systems or programming; hmmm, well, possibly even a little hacking experience he smiled inwardly. Turn what could have been a detrimental force on the internet into a protector or possibly even attacker to our nation's enemies via the web.

It took a minute to get their waitresses attention. Of course, she was more interested in the younger, fit men at the table next to them. She started to walk over quickly and then slowed her walk; might as well try to catch their eye he could see her think. He had asked for the check and thanked her for the excellent food and service. He quickly calculated a 20% tip in his head and rounded up to the next dollar. Cash. Less work for him and less work for her at the end of her shift.

There were over 65,000 military veterans in the San Francisco Bay Area so it was no wonder they'd run into a few active duty military today. As they got up to walk out, his Dad said, "Hold on one second." He knew Dad would want to say thank you and a quick word of acknowledgement. He said, "Excuse me, sorry for interrupting." The two soldiers immediately paused their conversation as he came within hearing distance. "I wanted to thank you two young men and your willingness to step up and protect our great country," he announced.

Both soldiers looked quite pleased at his genuine thankfulness. In a deep bass unison, they both said, "Thank you, Sir!"

As they walked towards the front door, Dad said, "Those two boys sure did seem serious. Glad they're on our side." Jarrod doubted Dad even knew there was a cyber aspect to war and the military these days. He'd wished he could have soldiers like these watching over his Dad's email! He'd rather have paid them directly than some punk who made off with $2,000. His anger rose just a fraction. Of course, he knew he couldn't stand over his father every minute of the day; monitoring his email responses and internet activity. Nor have someone else.

Jarrod took his mind back to the young Girl Scout, Jamie, and her mom. They had been the last beneficiaries of Dad's increasing senility. Stationed, with their cookies, outside Whole Foods they hadn't known Dad would buy them out. In fact, he told them he would go to the bank and be back in a minute. At a young age, he was certain Jamie had been let down or told a hundred white lies from people who didn't really have the intention of coming back from their car or bank to purchase some cookies.

Dad had walked over to his bank, filled out the withdrawal slip for his account and walked back to the Girl Scout station with cash in his front pocket. Because it was early in the day, they had quite a stock of cookies. He bought them all. He asked Jamie how long she had been in Girl Scouts.

"Almost 2 years now, Sir." She said proudly.

Dad asked, "How many boxes do you have to sell today."

"Our goal is to sell 400 boxes this weekend."

With a big smile, Dad said, "I'd like them all. Can you bring them over to my senior home?"

Somewhat in disbelief, she lost her Girl Scout composure and said, "Mom, did you hear that? He wants to buy them all. Can we do that? Can he really buy them all? What will we sell to everyone else?"

Jamie's mom spoke up, not believing he was really going to purchase them all. "Oh sir, you don't have to buy them all, just a box or two for yourself."

"I'm going to buy them all for the nice people at Country Manor." I moved there and they are the nicest people. A box of cookies will cheer everyone up. So how much do I owe you young lady?"

A bit shocked, the 8-year-old stumbled a little on the math equation and said, "Well 400 boxes, uhm if they are $2.50 a box, but we also sell 5 boxes for $10. And we've already sold some this morning..." The end of her sentence trailed as she looked for help from her mom.

Dad took ten one hundred-dollar bills from his front pocket. "Do I have enough to buy them all?" he said as he slowly counted out $1000.

The little girl's eyes almost popped out of her head and her mouth dropped open. She couldn't take her eyes away from the money to look at the man or her mom. Then she looked quickly at this strange, older man, turned her head to her mother and then back at the money to make sure it was still there.

"I'd like to buy them all, if you could just bring them over to the lobby of our complex."

"Thank you, mister!" Jamie shouted and ran around the table to hug him. "You're the nicest, rich person I've ever met. This money is going to our big week-long camping trip down in the Santa Cruz mountains and also to help feed the homeless."

Her mom was in disbelief as well, but with the cash on the table she immediately recognized the situation. Finish an entire weekend's worth of soliciting in one transaction. Time is money, who cared about the few people who said they'd buy on the way out. Less than half of them really did return to purchase. Was this guy a little old, maybe on the edge of crazy? She'd seen crazier things and if he wanted to buy $1000 worth of Girl Scout cookies, then good for him and their dentists!

"Who do I make the receipt out to?" the mother inquired.

"Thomas DeBoy, please."

"Well, here you are. Jamie and I will start packing them right now and head over. Shouldn't take more than a few minutes." There were only 3 boxes of each flavor on the card table: thin mint, samoas, tagalongs, do-si-dos, trefoils and savannah smiles. They placed them back in the master pack boxes, removed the poster board sign advertising Troop 429 and folded up the table quickly. They were fast, as if the offer would expire.

The mom handed her daughter two cases to carry to the van; while she grabbed three and hurried over to unlock the tail gate. "We'll be right back for the rest," she yelled over her shoulder.

Jamie skipped back to pick up the final two cases of Tagalongs. "Which one is your favorite Mr. DeBoy?" she said cheerily.

"Those Tagalongs that you have right there. I can't wait to see the expression on everyone's face back at the Manor. I'll walk over there now, and you know where it is right?"

"It's that big building across from the Whole Foods parking lot, right?"

"Yes, 428 2nd Street. I'll see you in a few minutes," he said as he headed off down the strip mall sidewalk.

By now there had been a few odd looks directed towards the Girl Scout and her mother. It was fairly early in the morning and they were packing up and leaving.

When they pulled up in their van to Country Manor, they made quite a commotion bringing in case after case of Girl Scout cookies. The ladies at the front desk were taken aback at what to do with all these cookies. They certainly couldn't say no to a harmless gift, but where would they store them all? The shift supervisor came over and assessed the situation. "How many cases did you buy? For everyone? Well, that was quite generous of you Thomas."

Because they didn't want cases lying around everywhere, the supervisor offered to have a case of each flavor taken up to his room. Then he asked the two bus boys to grab the remaining cases and put them in the kitchen's dry storage area. They would stack neatly, and he'd ask that the waitresses offer a complimentary box of cookies to each person at lunch that day. Of course, all the staff were eagerly watching as their favorite flavors were marched through the lobby.

Neither the supervisor, nor the self-appointed lobby keeper, James, had ever seen anything like this and they calculated even with the 40 people on staff, there would be at least 4 boxes of cookies per person. It was obvious the word had gotten out as the lunch crowd began arriving at least 30 minutes earlier than normal. In fact, James didn't wait around to watch everyone eat. He went ahead and quickly sat at his table, knowing at the end of the meal he would claim his first box of thin mints.

There was a definite air of happiness about Country Manor for at least a week. It felt as if everyone there had won a $10 lottery scratcher. There were more smiles at the restaurant with the expectation of the free box of cookies. Everyone knew it would be short-lived; just another day or maybe two. All the jokes had been made about last meals, special 'laced' batches of cookies, local dentists being involved; it was in good fun. Thomas was the talk and certainly there would be Girl Scout caroling this Christmas season.

Whether senility, Alzheimer's or just the thought of good will had provoked his Dad purchasing the bounty for all the residents, at least he knew the $1000 had gone to a good cause…and certainly if one were to stretch it out over the years…. $1000 towards a good organization wasn't anything to begrudge. He too had a streak of generosity and why not? To whom much had been given, much is expected.

CHAPTER 2

This $624,000, extracted by deception from a senior really started to eat into him. Everyone is extra protective of the weak and helpless; whether an elderly parent, young child or someone at a disadvantage. What he wouldn't do to have a few minutes with the perpetrator. He would be considered quite proficient as a user of computers, but he didn't put enough protection up around his Dad to prevent this occurrence. Defense, perimeter, fence, walls, firewalls.... his thoughts trailed off.

He'd rather think about punching someone, exacting $624,000 worth of pain from these internet perpetrators. That $624,000 might pay for legal fees in this type of prosecution—who knew with the international aspect of the crime. Jarrod wanted to teach three individuals a very serious life lesson; don't mess around with my Dad. Do something productive in life instead of hacking into computers and taking advantage of others.

Hacking into computers. Not a line of work he'd considered. He wondered. In fact, his mind started to linger and turn over the thought. Could he hire someone to find the perpetrators? The Lafayette police would be interested, but not trained in this type of criminal activity. Craigslist prostitution, but not cyber criminals. How long would it take the FBI or CIA anyhow for an internet crime? He wasn't taking a chance on it not being a priority.

Independent contractor was the solution. Actually, finding a trustworthy one in a field he knew very little about - that was the challenge. What to enter in as an internet search? Ha-ha, that wouldn't work! Those search words would send off a few alarms and have him monitored immediately. Non-descript phone call and a meeting.

He wanted to keep Dad off his laptop, to maintain the scene of the crime. Who knows? Maybe that was key; having it in the state, as near as possible, to when he was phished. A little white lie or tell Dad the truth? Somewhere in between?

It seemed like Dad had enjoyed the lunch. He was certain any relief from the mundane menu at the Manor house restaurant was welcome. He had tried to savor, sense and taste his lunch, but it was no use. His attention was split between monitoring his Dad's responses and visual cues, participating in the conversation and eavesdropping on the soldiers one table over.

"Dad, can you do me a big favor?"

"What's that son?"

"I'd like you to stay off your computer for a few days. I have a new computer guy looking at my computers for security and I'd like to have him come look at yours. Ok?"

"Well, I'm not on it too often now. Just check emails on Tuesday. I guess I'll check sports and news on the TV."

"Do you turn it off after you're done or put it in sleep mode?"

"I like to leave it on the screen saver; the new aquarium one you found for me. But then it goes to sleep after a few minutes. I don't really shut it off."

"Alright, it should just be a few days until I can get an appointment for him to come out."

It took just a few minutes, street lights and turn signals to make it back to the parking lot. His Dad sat comfortably in the Tesla's rich leather. In his hands he held the picture envelope; mindlessly rotating his right thumb clockwise one rotation and then counterclockwise. Back and forth again. He had a relaxed look on his face. The lunch must be settling and the blood flowing towards his stomach to digest the food. He smiled inwardly: seems like a nice post-meal nap would be in order this afternoon.

As he shut the car off, he noticed his Dad did not immediately reach to release his seat belt. Rather, he grabbed to open the door and got caught by the seat belt. He looked away quickly to save his Dad a little embarrassment. Was he watching too closely? Examining every movement his Dad made? He needed to stop. He was in a great care facility and so what if he tried to get out of the car before unlatching his seat belt.

Dad fumbled a bit with the seat belt and quickly pulled it off, then opened the car door. Lifting his right leg out of the car first and then following with the left he reached up to grab the passenger handle. He then pushed off from the seat with his left hand, was upright and out of the car. He had come around himself and waited near the back of the car. His balance was fine with a light placement of his hand against the rear passenger door.

Dad had left the pictures on the dash, so Jarrod grabbed them and closed the passenger door. Walking next to Dad, he handed the picture envelope to him and said, "Here Dad, you can keep these."

"Oh right, thanks."

The Manor had a van for use on local errands and transporting the residents. It was the familiar white, with burgundy stencil of Country Manor on the driver and passenger doors. It was a larger van, with the standard seats up front. The passenger compartment had a bench seat in the back and two captains' chairs sandwiched the double doors for the wheel chair lift. It looked like Polly and Rochelle had done a little shopping at the Broadway Plaza.

Funny how those two held to their ritual of Friday afternoon shopping. All the other residents and their families pretty much knew the van would be back and forth to the Plaza on Friday. It was a standing request and the drivers knew to write it in the schedule every week. No quicker way to get on the wrong side of those two ladies than to try and book a ride that would interfere with their weekly retail therapy.

From the look of things, they'd been quite successful. The driver opened the rear doors and lifted a total of 7, brightly colored department store bags. They could see the familiar Red Star for Macy's, two vertical striped silver and gold Nordstrom bags, a smaller Tiffany blue, probably a Crate & Barrel or Pottery Barn in there as well. Edward was usually on driving duty Fridays. He knew very well to keep each lady's bags together in one hand as he'd take them up to their suites for them.

These ladies always looked immaculate and were immediately drawn to each other; moving into Country Manor only a little more than a month apart. They were both in their mid-to-late 70s, but you'd never hear them say it out loud. They were mentally sharp, had significant wardrobes and loved to spoil their grandchildren. They were in a cheerful banter as Jarrod and his Dad approached. Dad put on a smile for them both and asked if there were any changes at the Plaza. Were there any new restaurants worth visiting?

"We had lunch at the new place, Toma's. Their food was a little spicy and for a new place the service was quite good. You should visit and try the Chicken Cattiotore or Bucantini all'Amatriciana", Rochelle insisted.

"Thank you for the recommendation ladies. I know you have excellent taste." Even at his age, Dad knew the importance of flattery. Jarrod grinned, "After you ladies." Rochelle and Dana went in ahead of them. Their bags were being handled and they passed by the receptionist to check on any upcoming news, book their next shopping excursion and banter about the service of each retailer.

They stopped at the restaurant to see what dessert choices were available for lunch. Quickly scanning the menu, they noted Pralines and Cream flavored ice cream or Lemon Bundt cake. Neither seemed very tempting and they walked over to the elevator bank.

"Jarrod, thanks for taking me to the reservoir and lunch today." It seemed his eyes wanted to ask when the next visit would be to see him, as they rose up to the fourth floor.

"Remember, Dad, I'll see you again in the next few days with my computer guy. We'll make sure your computer is in good shape. And try not to log on or use it till he can have a look at it." He hated repeating himself, but he said it as evenly as possible. His mind was starting to put some pieces together as if planning chess moves. Wanting to knock out someone in cyber space.

At his door, they exchanged a short hug from the side. Dad wasn't much of the man-to-man hugging type, so this was normal after a visit. "I'll call you when I have a day and time Dad. Have a great afternoon."

Leaving the company of his Dad, he tried not to evaluate the conversations, his Dad's mental and physical state, and just lock in the memory of a nice walk and lunch at two of their favorite spots. His Dad would be fine. He wasn't abandoning him. There were books, the news or friends at the Manor to help occupy his time.

He tried not to appear in a hurry as he waved to the receptionist. "Thank you again for the flowers Mr. DeBoy." The doors slid open for him to the beaming Lafayette sunlight. He strolled to his car and backed out of the parking spot. Less than ten minutes from home and he'd begin planning his crusade.

CHAPTER 3

His home was nestled back from the road. In fact, other than the garage doors, you could only see the path leading up to the front entry gate. The gate was interesting. Covered in a plate of copper, the patina had weathered to a beautiful, dark teal shade. In the center was a raised, Chinese character symbol for the word "abundance."

The house blended beautifully with the landscaping; nestled in through the oaks as it was painted a medium grey hue with teal green trim. The matching double garage door on the left opened as he depressed the button on his car visor. It rolled up to briefly expose the gleaming, polished concrete floor. The Tesla slid in quietly to the bay, closest to the garage man-door.

Stepping out with purpose, he'd been thinking the entire way home. Mentally checking through his contact list of internet and security wizards. Blank. None, but not the end of the road. There were friends he'd kept in touch with over the years with a military background. Making an inquiry like this could only be done in person considering all the government cell phone recording. A simple bike ride invitation would suffice.

Retired U.S. Navy General Simon Delgado. He'd met the General on a 30, 50 and 100-mile ride benefitting injured veterans. These rides were generally very casual; less competitive. But when Simon had risen on his pedals to climb the 5-mile grade, he knew not only was he in top physical condition, but a very competitive, amateur cyclist. He'd been taken a bit by surprise and that spurred a personal best for himself up the grade.

When he caught up with him, they matched their pace and rode together for the final 15 miles through the hills and vineyards of Livermore valley. During the ride, both of them were content with a quick introduction; name exchange, place of birth and some talk about cycling. The finish to the race was interesting as they both knew the grade for the final mile was flat. It would have seemed silly racing all-out down a somewhat busy, major street—this was for the vets and wounded warriors.

They had passed up dozens of riders on the hills, so there wasn't any need to prove their ability and stamina at this point. They actually pulled back on the pace to an even 19 mph. The last few miles in his mind were spent considering the many, many veterans in the area who had been permanently marked by fighting for their country.

It wasn't until the ride was over that they had much of a conversation. Less than a year apart in age, they talked more about life, beliefs, children and hobbies than work. They shared similar philosophies and that is why he would call him first. There was also a high level of trust in place. Simon had risen through the ranks, serving his country well. They talked more frequently in the summer months when they were coordinating rides and events.

He closed the garage door, took the mandatory two steps up and unlocked the door into the house. Automatically placing his keys and wallet on the corner of the kitchen counter, he took a right down the hallway and into his den. Jarrod wasn't much for sitting and he stood at the window facing his backyard; he pulled up Simon and dialed.

Simon answered on the second ring, "Jarrod, how have you been? When are we going riding?" Well, this was a natural invitation and who needed to meet in a dark corner of a restaurant, speaking in hushed spy tones?

"Simon, I'm great and you? Ready for me to abuse you a little on Mt. Diablo?"

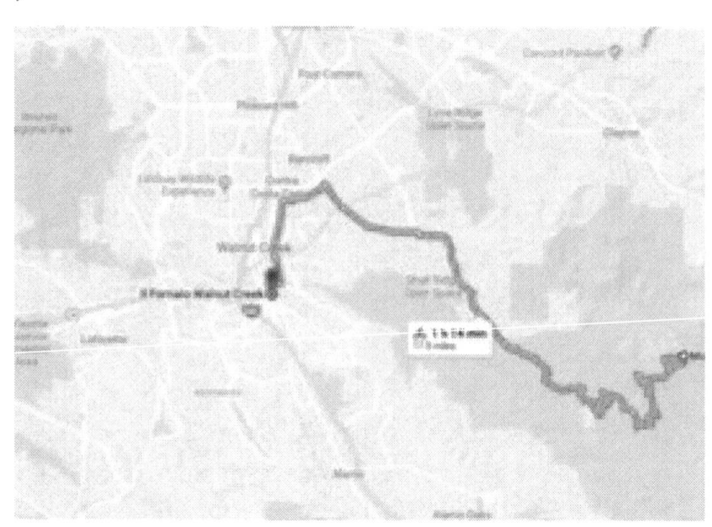

He laughed for a second. "Come on, you know I have bragging rights from the last time we rode it." Mt. Diablo rose 3,957 feet in elevation and was the steepest and most challenging ride in their vicinity. Over the last two years, they had easily ridden it two dozen times. There were two entrances to Mt. Diablo State Park: through the South Gate and North Gate. Each entrance had its own set of challenges and the Tour of California always included a leg which included the Mountain.

"I suppose you're right so now it's my turn to take the crown back. You can even take me to my favorite restaurant afterwards: Il Fornaio. What's your schedule look like this week?" Both were independent of a job or running a business any longer. Using commercial and residential real estate, commodities and stock market investments, they had secured a passive income.

"I can ride tomorrow morning or Thursday afternoon," Simon replied with some eagerness in his voice. They both enjoyed the camaraderie riding together and their similarly competitive spirits.

"Let's go about 9:30. Want to leave from my place?" Jarrod was optimistic about the conversation and wanted to return here so if they needed to plan anything, there would be a little more privacy. Simon had married later in life and his wife Karisa had given birth to twin boys eight years ago. It was a fun and rambunctious house, but maybe next time when there wasn't business to discuss.

Now that the ride was set with Simon, he let a little bit of the anger seep back regarding the scum who stole from his father! In these times of international crime, he had no illusion that he could take them to court here in the States. Could the DOJ or FBI get his Dad's assisted living care money back? Would his request fall into a black hole at IC3, the Internet Crime Complaint Center? In 2013, IC3 received 262,813 complaints of Internet Crimes with losses equaling $781,841,611. The Norton anti-virus company helped law enforcement gain back $5.25 million in criminal restitution which was a paltry six dollars and seventy-one cents out of every thousand dollars!

Even more disheartening is the fact that the Federal Bureau of Investigation estimates that the IC3 only receives complaints for about 10% of all crimes on the web. Jarrod wanted to explore the possibility of hiring his own team to investigate before reporting it to the FBI. If it was international, he was highly doubtful the country would extradite their citizen or replace the money. But maybe there would be another way to hurt them? To steal back the money or take away something of theirs.

Because it was unlikely these criminals were U.S. citizens living domestically, the judicial system his tax dollars went towards couldn't be utilized. He was willing to put some money into a means of justice and revenge. As the situation became a little firmer on whether they could determine the identity and location of the perpetrators, he'd think more on how far he was willing to go outside the law to exact punishment.

The long-term trading profits on Netflix would change his personal taxes for the year, but it also gave him many opportunities. His parents and upbringing in the church had instilled the compunction to give a tenth back to the community; specifically, those less fortunate. Sometimes he would do this through the church and other times he would give directly to charities.

Due to the size of this financial windfall, it was going to take a little more planning. $7 million could be quite impactful to a cause if put to work wisely. The causes benefitting widows, orphans and foster children were always foremost on his mind. These were people who had been impacted by death of a spouse. The children, on the other hand, were affected because their mother or father were addicts or were stupid enough to create life, but not bother taking care of it. Typically, when there was a tragedy and parents died, the immediate families took over parenting responsibilities—regardless of socio-economic status. Not that it happened in every case, but only a small percentage of the time did the family not assume the role.

This could be the year that he would bump up his giving to 20%. Yet this extra 10% might not be reported to the IRS. It might just be given quietly to indirectly help his father and restore a little balance between victims and perpetrators.

The morning of the meeting with Simon, Jarrod woke up as he normally did at 5am with no alarm. Even in semi-retirement he had maintained his life structure and discipline. He consumed 15 minutes from *The Slight Edge* right after waking up. A non-traditional way to start the day. Most were hitting their snooze button until the last possible second and then rushing out the door. No breakfast and likely a quick buzz from the news or Social Media. Ready to sit in a drive-thru line for chemicals disguised as food or a Grande-sized jolt of caffeine and sugar.

His breakfast this morning before their ride wouldn't be much different than any other day. They'd be riding almost 15 miles through Lafayette, briefly touch Concord and into Walnut Creek before they entered the northern gate to Mt. Diablo. Heading up this route was 11 miles and a good 3,875' of elevation climb. He had supplemented last night with an extra serving of pasta. Carbs would be fine; it was just as important to be ready mentally.

The countertop was made from a fantastic slab of flagstone; twelve feet long by five feet wide. A beautiful, deep, southwest pink hue and sealed which darkened the natural color and gave it a sheen. The stone masons were out of this world, he thought as he leaned up against the natural edge finish. His house was designed for entertaining and the same stone had been used throughout the house for built in shelves. The house was full of copper, flagstone and turquoise. Bright white paint in the kitchen and dining area. There were several tones of brown on the other walls.

Feed the mind first and then the body. His breakfast was a cup of steel cut oats sprinkled with cinnamon and a dab of honey. 1 egg and 4 egg whites scrambled for some protein and fat. Half a cup of plump blackberries today for fruit and a steaming hot cup of green and black tea. He took a variety of supplements. Over the years he'd researched and experimented with many brands. Direct sellers, health food stores and online.

His current regimen included a whole food multivitamin, Omega3, palmetto for his prostate, glucosamine for his joints and pycnogenol. Because he was going on a ride later, he would punch in some nitric oxide, guarana and a little creatine. After all, you might as well give your body every advantage when training or cycling up a mountain. It always got competitive towards the summit. The only variable was at what point one of them would rise on their pedals and sprint.

Simon would arrive on time; kids or not. So, Jarrod had his garage door open and, as anxious as he was, forced himself to stick with the routine patterns. His top of the line, high-gloss, custom sunburst orange Trek Madone 9 Series was on the bike stand and he lubricated the chain. He rechecked the brakes, shifters and air pressure just to be sure. Spare inner tubes and CO2, helmet, gloves, shoes, socks, water bottles, post workout powder, driver's license and debit card. He was all set and puttered around the garage anticipating the second half of the duo should arrive any minute now.

The black Chevy Tahoe pulled up in his driveway and Simon hopped out quickly. He only needed to dismount his bike, load up his pockets and top off the air in his tires. His bike was made by a smaller bike manufacturer out of Denver, CO. It was carbon fiber and a subdued custom matte finish in an olive green. Simon was the epitome of efficiency and tenacity.

The cool air of the California morning was still a pleasant 67 degrees. By the time they reached the top of Mt. Diablo, it should warm up to the mid-70s. Fantastic weather to be on a ride. Of course, today's ride would take on a different tone. Jarrod was curious to see what would transpire. Would there be any difference in the pace? Their conversations while cycling covered a broad spectrum of topics and their ride a few weeks ago was no exception. They had discussed elementary school curriculum, how teaching methods had changed, and the ridiculous amount of minimum days this upcoming school year.

Simon and his wife were on the verge of pulling their kids from the public school system. Although their district was highly rated, it was less rigorous than they wanted. Today would be quite different; finding a cyber consultant who would help him protect his father and potentially go after the criminals who stole from him. And the next big question was if they could find the criminal, how could punishment be determined and executed?

"How is life Jarrod? When are you going to replace that tennis court with a 25-yd small bore range," he added jokingly.

"Closed out my position in Netflix and should be able to pay the bills now," Jarrod said wryly. Had my last commercial space get rented out to a national chain. Took Dad out for a walk at the reservoir and to lunch. Have the grandkids coming over for a barbeque this weekend and Candy agreed to meet me at the top of Mt. Diablo today for a little extra motivation to beat you," he smiled and then laughed.

"Well, sounds like a banner week. How am I going to top that?" Simon added.

How are things for you Simon?" returned Jarrod.

"We've put the kids in private school this year; so now I've got them in uniforms," he said with a twinkle in his eye. We're heading off to Tahoe for a few days. I've already had my pre-victory celebration sex this morning, ha-ha. So, win, lose or draw I've already tasted victory," Simon added with a laugh.

They both had a chuckle. Grown men, fully appreciative of life, though in different stages; enjoying their quick life-checks. Their relationship was going to go in a whole new direction after this morning's ride. Jarrod was quite curious about what the next few hours would produce and maybe the next few weeks.

Simon checked his air pressure, the garage door closed silently and they clicked in their shoes - they were off. Jarrod made a point to not turn on his GPS tracker. There might be a few eye witnesses to seeing a pair of cyclists on Wednesday morning, though that wasn't as common during the week; it happened often enough they would blend in with the monthly hum of activity.

As was their practice, they had flipped a quarter for who would ride closer to the traffic. Jarrod lost the flip and would ride closest to traffic with Simon on his right. For riding downhill, the honor of leading was given to the winner of the uphill course. No Gen H pansy everyone wins illogic in place here. As they eased down the driveway, they fell into immediate rhythm.

The gear selection was almost identical the entire ride. Two riders, so equally matched, the odds always seemed to be 50-50 on the ascent up Mt. Diablo. If one showed significant improvement, then the other would be more determined in their training the following weeks to regain the upper hand. It had been like this for over five years; they sharpened each other and were considered in excellent shape.

Their conversation was fairly routine; man speak. Short, information exchanges while pacing through the city streets. As they entered the park, the dialogue would take a sudden leap. Anything could be debated or discussed. In the five years, the breadth of conversation was quite stunning. This was no Monday Night Football banter at half time. 11.3 miles up and they took advantage of the physical stimulation; almost as if the heightened mental aspect elevated the entire ride to another level of communication.

In between breaths and grunts, changing gears and grabbing a drink, the conversation could turn as frequently as the twisted North Gate road. They reveled in their different career paths and exchanged lessons learned. Their life philosophies were similar, and this created an amazing bond.

The route to the North Gate entrance of Mt. Diablo was always the same. 10.4 miles of fairly flat pavement. Just enough stop lights and signs to derail a great rhythm. Car traffic was moderate today and cyclists were few on this weekday morning. From the casual observer, they did not appear to be pedaling very fast, but whenever another rider was near, the pace quickly ate them up and spit them out.

Today Simon seemed a bit more talkative than normal. He was in an excellent mood having made the decision to move their kids into private school. Now he had a better idea of the curriculum and environment. Quality teaching and it was going to push his kids to get up-to-speed with the classmates who had been attending since kindergarten. 2nd and 4th grade, so there was more of a culture shock to his daughter since she had K-3 in the public school system.

Simon asked about Netflix. Normally they did not talk about personal finances, but since Jarrod had brought it up, he was curious. Jarrod didn't close out of a stock position often. He began, "Netflix has run its course and made me a small fortune. For the last month, the technicals were right in the mid-700s and now I've got some time to reallocate the funds. Might even have lunch with the founder, Reed; thank him for his beautifully run company and vision."

Whizzing down South Broadway, one of the annoyances of cyclists came upon them. A public transportation bus, coughing out plumes of diesel exhaust. Why weren't these things electric already?

Jarrod's only comment was, "Nice" in a very sardonic tone and Simon tried to hold his breath as it passed by.

At first, he thought he saw an advertising on the side of the bus for the Monterey Bay Aquarium, but no, there it was, another ad for Shark Week. A Great White's jaws agape, teeth ready to bite into anything and the gills visible. Now that was an unfair fight; shark against nearly anything in the ocean—especially an unsuspecting surfer.

Jarrod wanted to shift the conversation to family and asked Simon, "How's your brother doing? Is he still stationed down in San Diego? Living the dream?"

"Steven's great and just earned another promotion. Now he's a Captain, another bump in pay. Yeah, he's living the good life down there. He'll be sailing out soon I expect. They don't let them get too comfortable." Then he added, "In another 4 years, he'll have 25 years of service, Lord willing and retire."

Jarrod heard the "Lord willing" and was quite surprised. The one topic they had skirted was God and religion. He knew what he believed, maybe the subject would come up. As they were approaching the next intersection and stop sign, there was no traffic and they coasted into and through it. As expected, Simon continued the family theme and asked about Jarrod's father. They had talked briefly about the onset of Alzheimer's and Simon could tell it was a real struggle for Jarrod seeing his dad's battle.

Simon kept it light and asked, "How was the reservoir and time with your dad?"

Here we go, thought Jarrod. "He was having a good day. Good conversation and he kept a decent pace on the walk. It was just a single loop. I'm a little more worried about his decision-making skills....", his voice trailed off.

Simon didn't want to pry, but also was genuinely interested. Seemed like more frequently, he was hearing about a friend who had an Alzheimer's parent. He wanted to pick the right words and tone of voice, then with a mixture of seriousness and concern said, "More donations to the Girl Scouts?"

Jarrod had told him the story of the $1000 for Girl Scout cookies so it was a reasonable question.

Normally, they could have laughed about it, but if this was another lapse in judgment, then of course it wasn't a laughing matter. Jarrod's demeanor changed considerably as he recalled his initial response when he had discovered that the $7000 had been phished out of his father's bank account. But when Jay determined the linked account had been completely pillaged; that put him over the edge. Stealing from his dad, a senior citizen with diminished capacity, really clawed at his heart.

"Well, I wish it was more Girl Scout cookies. You know I monitor his bank account and I noticed two withdrawals over three days," his jaw and voice tightened. He thought he was going to compress the handle bars he was squeezing so tightly.

Then he relaxed as he put himself in the moment of approaching the topic at the reservoir. "I asked Dad and he starts talking about this email he's received from his bank. Oh, I started to get angry, but didn't want to show Dad. Anyhow, long story short, Sunday and yesterday he was phished - $7000! Really pisses me off.

Simon hadn't been expecting this type of a story and could feel his friend's outrage. "What the .... Aw and to your Dad," his voice was full of anger, disgust and sympathy. "Man, I'm really sorry about that. Did you go to the police or CIA? Do you need a contact?"

"You know Simon, I haven't reported it to anyone yet. Not even the bank. I'm still kind of mulling it over in my head and I think I'm going to try and catch the criminal."

Simon looked over at him. They were at a stop sign and hadn't noticed cars were waiting on them to cross the intersection. "Let's ride and talk."

"I know if some criminal is smart enough to hack into Sony and all these government agencies that someone equally smart can find out who did it. My Dad hasn't touched his computer or accessed email the last few days and will stay off it for now. I've only told him that we are going to have a computer tech come over and make sure he has all the latest patches, etc.... before he uses it again. I really don't want to embarrass him that he's been phished twice."

Simon's mental wheels were spinning. Rather than asking the obvious questions about how he was going to find a trustworthy computer expert and did he really think a cyber-criminal would leave a trace? He mentally leapt ahead several chess moves and steered his bike even closer to Jarrod. Their hands just two inches apart. Simon looked dead serious and asked, "How far are you willing to take this revenge for your Dad?"

Jarrod paused for half a moment and said, "I'm willing to find the right resources and pay to see this through to the end. I want justice and don't think for an instant that Lafayette PD, FBI or IC3 are going to chase down this damn thief. I have the finances to make a move and bring on some good old-fashioned justice." He was a little surprised at his own comments, but at this stage of life and happening to his own dad—he was ready.

They had turned on North Gate Road and begun the slight incline towards the park entrance. The grade wasn't too noticeable for these two and they were less than a mile from the park. Their pace had imperceptibly skipped a beat when the ultimatum was asked and answered. Now they were right back into rhythm and their hearts beat just a little harder.

"Simon, do you know any ex-military computer guys who can track this type of person down? Or do I need a sergeant first?" Jarrod inquired with earnest. Now that he'd committed to capital punishment, he needed the first players on the team.

"Yeah, I know a handful who can track down your phisherman for you," Simon replied in a steely voice. "Let me do a quick check and select two. This type of operation could cost you..." his voice trailed off.

"I've built in some offshore accounts over the years. No need having everything taxable and in my name. It's in the seven figures." To be exact, it was $3,458,786 in various accounts in another name. Dad had taught him well; then he'd simply adapted and refined the strategies over the years. Cash was always king.

Simon replied, "Good, this type of justice can get expensive in foreign countries. We can talk more about how to pay these soldiers later on. They all could use a pension boost." They passed the pay booth and began the ascent automatically. They had been training their bodies for years. Unconsciously, they dropped down to the smaller front sprocket. Their minds intuitively commanded and bodies executed the required changes for the grade.

The scenery was a combination of the fairly worn asphalt, patched as needed, or orange road cones warning travelers where the repairs hadn't caught up with the deterioration. Great oaks, pines and brush were clumped together. At the lower elevations there wasn't any shade provided, but as you moved beyond 1,000' elevation there were patches of the road covered with shade to offer them a little respite from the sun and heat.

At this time of the year, all the undergrowth was dry and brown. Fire watch was a serious task in the surrounding hills and lower residential neighborhoods. This was the best time of the week and day to avoid car traffic. In general, there weren't many cars, but on some weekends, it could be a fairly constant stream up and down.

"How do you want to be involved? Do you want to call the shots? Being at the scene is pretty risky."

"I want to work with the sergeant in the planning, but once it goes live, I only want updates or the final disposition. I'm not a trained soldier nor do I need that type of rush in my life." Simon added as a matter of fact.

They kept their pace pretty hard. Whether to test their focus or portray two competitive friends, they were hammering out the climb. Much of the ride would be up, out of the seat, standing on their pedals to grind out the next twisted incline.

Simon was intrigued by his friend. He was curious to see how far out he had planned the revenge. "Once these wheels are in motion, there will be a point of no return. No communication, black out and no stopping the maneuver."

Jarrod said with firmness, "I have resolve. It's time to make a statement and to deal with people who are harming the innocent and weak. I'd like to get any money that can be recovered back to the people who have been phished. I'm betting they've got active accounts they are stealing from and it's possible they have records of all they've stolen from."

"What do you mean, 'make a statement'?"" Simon gave a friendly wave to the white Honda Civic as it passed them cautiously on a straightaway. There looked to be two people coming up for a hike. He wondered why so many people came here, drove to the top and just hiked around the peak. They could park at the base for free and walk in or even select a lower parking area and hike up.

"I'd like hackers to start looking over their shoulders. Have a little fear when they hear what happened to their fellow-con. Wake up in a cold sweat. I don't mean to take out families of the perpetrators, just take them out in a manner where they reconsider what they're doing for a living." He had started to formulate his plan for the style of execution, but for now he wasn't going to divulge any details. Soon enough.

"Well, we've got to find them first. The art of tracking someone through the internet almost takes another hacker. After lunch, I'll make a call because we do need to move on this quick. The con could get spooked and may not even come back for more. The clock is ticking so how fast we can get him to your Dad's pc is very important."

"Let's ride!" They were in agreement on the initial steps and the ride became a little more intense. Jarrod felt he could focus more on his form and breathing now. Simon had the same reaction. They both liked to think things out when riding. Wheels were cranking on the pavement and their minds were racing even faster. There was definitely a surge and Jarrod almost regretted having turned off Strava. He would have loved to have seen the comparison segments and watt output. Neither took a ride up Mt. Diablo leisurely, but there was certainly a distraction while feeling each other out on today's topic.

Simon would have his watch running of course, so there would be the gross time from leaving his house to the summit. The ride downhill didn't change much these days. They picked their lines appropriately for speed with a pinch of caution for oncoming cars, branches and dirt on the road. There was a little pedaling involved for the last quarter of the descent, but even there they rode equally hard.

Jarrod was the first to rise up on his pedals for the final 2 mile climb to the Visitor Center. They weren't looking at the scenery and the background music from their pedals and chains was muted by their hearts pounding. Pushing each other constantly. Simon immediately rose up as well, blocking out the potential mission for a few minutes and recovering a bike length on his friend. They were side by side, pressing the pace up the hill. Had there been onlookers, they would have thought a significant wager was at stake and not just a lunch tab.

They both knew the hill extremely well, cycling up and down it dozens of times in the last 2 years. Two more switchbacks, another 800 feet and they would be at the Wall. They had both decided the civil engineer had purposely set this in place for cyclists. To separate the amateur from the semi-pro, to crush the will of those unprepared and to test the mental strength of the experienced. Coming upon The Wall, if you weren't in the correct gear it was all over. It could only be 3 gears. For those professionals who entered in the Tour of California, they would be in 3rd, semi-pros would be in 2nd and those just beginning to conquer The Wall would be in 1st. And, when you saw someone take The Wall in 4th, it was time for a urinalysis.

Today, with the adrenaline they both were in 3rd and straining their arms, torso and legs in a rhythm up the 13% Wall. The beginners approached The Wall and immediately unclipped to walk their bikes up. There was no shame, it was The Wall and only the top 5% of cyclists would ride up it. By the time an amateur rode up the 3600' elevation from the North Gate entrance, it was too difficult an obstacle to overcome. Looking straight up, it resembled the steepest grades of streets in San Francisco and back handed the novice. For those more experienced and conditioned it was the test. The test of mental strength and willpower. The mind had to see it and push out all thoughts of difficulty.

It was exactly 38 pedal strokes of agony and could only be completed at an extreme angle. Their legs were straining, but their minds were racing as they continued to crank down on their bikes. Each pedal stroke, accompanied by a shift in body weight of the upper torso. The arms and shoulders being called to shift the weight of the body; in sync with each breath and down stroke of the pedal. There was no need for either of them to look to the side. This was not the finish line at a local race where guys were jockeying for position and slinging their bikes along at 25 mph.

A jogger could beat them up this incline.

With the final five agonizing pedal strokes left, Jarrod was just ahead by the front wheel of his bike. Today, the fire engine red Trek would have bragging rights and the dark green Fusion steed would be buying lunch. The great part about this finish is you earned it; someone had to take it because The Wall gave nothing. Who had a little more mental focus and carbs left to burn? Champion for a day, bragging rights until the next time and lunch to the victor. Those were the spoils of this hour long ride up Mt. Diablo.

The crest of the hill was their imaginary finish line which led to the parking lot atop Mt. Diablo and the visitor center. Today's parking count was pretty high for a mid-morning weekday - 8 cars. The parking lot was in the shape of a gently squeezed circle with parking on the perimeter and another dozen spaces in a double center row. There was an asphalt sidewalk around the circumference of the parking lot and, at 2 o'clock, there was an opening in the steel handrail with steps leading down to the restroom.

The visitor center and lookout point were at the Eastern end of the parking lot. Both riders took two leisurely laps around the parking lot and then unclicked on the north-facing side of the lot. They lifted their carbon fiber horses up onto the sidewalk and rested them against the rail. Breathing was pronounced after The Wall and even the most conditioned athletes would see a big spike in their heart rates. When they had their heart monitors in place, they would typically measure 140 bpm at the finish of The Wall.

Jarrod was a supplement addict and his second

water bottle held a recovery drink with everything a serious athlete would take after an intense workout. He slowly squatted to keep the blood flowing in his muscles, stretch the hamstrings out and guzzled the 20-ounce chocolate drink in about 10 seconds. The ride down to the entrance would be no effort at all on his legs except for one half mile stretch. Best to get the BCAAs, protein and vitamins in now; nutrient timing was crucial for recovery. He'd always believed in doing everything possible to restore his body.

As Simon was stretching, he commented and grinned, "Great strategy to distract me, Jarrod," taking a swig from his water bottle as well.

"Hey, anything to get an edge and free lunch out of you," Jarrod looked over and smiled back.

They both finished their stretches and mounted back up on their bikes, clicking in. Simon said, "Lead the way yellow jersey."

CHAPTER 4

Jarrod made a few pedal strokes and they started down the mountain. For the ride down, they could match and exceed the speed limit signs. Of all the things in life, descending down this mountain and playing with his grandkids made him feel his youth. The wind in his face, he recalled his youth and riding down the hill next to his house on Shattuck. This was quite an extended ride and it could be dangerous if you weren't keeping an eye out for the occasional pine cone, dirt or branch on the road. The contact surface on these skinny little road tires was half the width of a dime.

There wasn't much time to enjoy the views or scenery on this descent. In fact, it was a great workout on the triceps and lats. Something about going faster than the cars could made the ride down fun. He had to remember to keep his legs moving. Blood flow through the muscles was important lest you wanted to completely lock up your quads with cramps. Jarrod was making fairly aggressive lines on his turns and Simon kept back about 2 bike lengths. There was no race down nor risk of miscommunication, which could end up in an accident.

For the past 15 years in May, a race up and down Mt. Diablo was held. That was the opportunity to let it all hang out. They were typically in the top five for their age bracket and not far off the pace of men half their age. In cycling, your prime racing years were 30-37. Armstrong and the like continued a little beyond that, but not much longer on a team with a major sponsorship. According to Strava, the top riders this year made it up Mt. Diablo in 48-50 minutes. Today they had come in a shade under 52.

On the descent, there was time to think about their conversation. Jarrod had taken a big step and he felt the sense of focus and determination to repay the criminal who had stolen from his Dad. Most of the process would be out of his control, but he started the ball rolling and would be influencing the route. Simon, in similar fashion, immediately began assessing the tactical situation. If it had been anyone else, he may have suspected some sort of set up, but not with Jarrod. He was not an actor and his body language, voice inflection and demeanor matched exactly what he'd be like under similar circumstances.

As they snaked downhill, they only encountered two cars coming up and two other pairs of cyclists. They would wave and smile at the fellow bikers who were leaning into their bikes, riding their own races against time that morning. It was quite a spectacular clear, sunny day in Northern California. There wasn't a cloud in the sky as the occasional hawk soared above.

The golden colored hillside sped past, with the interruption of oaks and pines, some scrub brush and the darting ground squirrels.

Simon mirrored each movement by Jarrod, leaning into each bend of the road. The ride down took nearly 25 minutes. This was one of the great rewards from Mt. Diablo. Cycling 25 minutes in the Bay Area with no stop signs was to be savored. There were some other hidden, desolate back roads scattered throughout, but none as challenging for the hour ride up. This one would also lead them to great outdoor dining, where they could keep their bikes within arm's reach, enjoy the fabulous weather and people watch the hustle of downtown foot traffic.

Today, he felt like Italian for lunch. They might have a few private moments to talk more about plans, though it was a bit early in the planning. Il Fornaio at the corner of Broadway and Main would be the spot. They had an extensive outdoor patio and it was early enough to not have to wait for a table. He could already see the menu, feel his legs relaxing at the table and his toes breathing as he kicked off his cycling cleats.

As they approached the North Gate entrance, a half dozen juvenile buzzards were pecking at a small carcass. They slowed with the rutted and cracked asphalt and could see what was likely a house cat being stripped of its fur and flesh. It had wandered too far from home and now was filling a void in the food chain. The buzzards were either brave, starving or accustomed to bikes because they didn't even move away from the cat. Each bird participating in the feast of fresh cat.

Once through the gate and onto the public streets, there was a little more elbow room and Simon slid in beside Jarrod. It was a more leisurely pace now. They knew a few neighborhood streets to speed up the trip into downtown Walnut Creek. Simon, always thinking a few steps ahead, said he'd really like to get his contact over to Jarrod's Dad's place today. It seemed like these phishing cons like to hit and run. Not risk a chance at hitting an account multiple times. Hopefully, this would be an overconfident or inexperienced criminal. He wanted to find out today.

Riding through the neighborhoods, the age was apparent by the design architecture. The city had not planned beyond ten years when planting these trees along the sidewalk. There was no dwarf elm species and many of these sidewalks were being lifted here and there by the tree roots. The mature trees offered excellent shade and based on the upkeep of the front yards, this was an upper middle-class area. Likely two incomes.

They slowed down at the stop signs and continued on until Rudgear road. This was a more heavily trafficked road, but the quickest route to the restaurant. Now they would need to be more aware of their surroundings, cars and the idiots texting or simply not paying attention. Crossing the four-lane street at the intersection, they would be heading south. Cars opposite them were barely slowing down to make a right-hand turn against the red light. No cop, no stop.

A driver in a stunning orange, late model Lexus coupe was paying attention and was courteous enough to stay back from the cross walk, making eye contact that he saw the riders and was giving them plenty of space to finish crossing. It was a far cry from the ride up Mt. Diablo.

A casual observer would have only seen two fit cyclists waiting at the edge of the sidewalk. Looking closer, you might think they were middle weight class powerlifters. They weren't gaunt with a narrow profile similar to the marathon runners. Years of running the body for 3, 4, 5 and hours at a time, eating away at the muscle. Fueling as best as you can while straining for the next 8-minute mile. Simon and Jarrod were not particularly tall, but with their V-shaped physiques sculpted by years of weight bearing exercise and countless days in training they could step into a spray booth and compete on any given day in a natural physique contest.

They both had ingrained the discipline of daily fitness in their lives and it showed in their ride today, but could also be seen bulging through their skin-tight cycling kits. Simon was a better natural runner with his years leading fitness in the military. Jarrod had no particular desire to run, but would put in a few miles every week. His cardio exertion was heavily biased towards his road bike. They often joked about mountain biking off into the sunset at a national park, never to be heard from again.

It was effortless cycling on these flat city streets, but they could still push themselves and maintain a 20-mph pace. They'd lose ground to the cars and then just see them as they coasted to the next street light. The drivers enjoyed their mindless freedom from exercise while Jarrod and Simon enjoyed the freedom from another box and pushing their bodies physically.

They were less than five minutes from the restaurant and just like the automobile statistics with the great percentage of car accidents occurring near the destination, they remained alert to the traffic and pedestrians. Seemed people couldn't walk and talk without their eyes glued to their smart phones. At the last possible chance, they eased their bikes from the street to the sidewalk, carefully picking a gap in the pedestrian traffic.

The façade of Il Fornaio was standard faux Italian with the name written vertically on a thirty-foot-high outcropping. The sign was not so impressive during the day, but at night it could be seen from quite a distance. Large, ornately carved wooden double doors were propped open to welcome the lunch crowd. The manager, Philippe Foggiato, was an amazing host and made it a point to meet and greet his lunch guests. He was one of those individuals with an amazing capacity to learn and retain names. If he couldn't, his Italian welcome was certainly warm.

"Buona signori giorno" which was good day gentlemen in Italian. And who was the victor today? Was there a little more at stake today? You look a little tense. Come, relax, enjoy my gnocchi and drink a bottle of wine for your successful race," he said with the biggest smile. Philippe was so personable and within one sentence put you at ease, ready to sit and spend the day consuming all he had to offer.

The greeting made them recognize their external countenance was affected by the seriousness of their conversation. They immediately reflected his smile, felt the muscles relax as they wheeled in the bicycles. The checkerboard, black and white marble flooring was particularly loud underneath their cleats. Phillipe directed his hostess, "Please seat them at table 44 and open the umbrella. The Giro d'Italia have arrived. They have had challenged our Mt. Diablo, conquered the summit and descended into the valley below. Celebrate with us today."

Simon and Jarrod both said thank you for the greeting and knew Philippe would place his hand on their shoulder or grab an arm during their welcome. It was no wonder they'd seat and serve over 300 guests during their 2-hour lunch peak. How could you not pick Phillipe and Il Fornaio for lunch? The hostess gave a warm smile and said "Please come this way" as she slipped in front of them. Her raven black medium hair curled out at the bottom to touch the top of her shoulders. She was average height and stood stock straight with a tiny wiggle in her walk. Jarrod thought she had been their waitress in the past or possibly at another restaurant.

As they led their bikes to their seats, the rhythmic clicking of the gear cassettes identified their approach. It wasn't such a strange sight and a few of the patrons simply nodded as they walked by. "Here is your table gentlemen and your server today will be Gio. She'll be here in just a moment." In the bright sun, the table umbrellas were a nice relief. The outdoor seating of Il Fornaio was approximately 60 feet by 100 feet and the tables were covered in white linens; the silverware bundled for the moment placed next to the heavy china. Their table was on the perimeter of course and they leaned the bicycles up against the wrought iron fence.

The fence merely served as a visual barrier and kept non-customers from walking through. At thirty-six inches high, it could easily be stepped over. Simon sat at their table and bent over to release his shoe buckles. A little breath of relief came out as he rotated his ankles and let his toes stretch out. He sat upright and headed to the restroom to wash up. Jarrod had unbuckled his shoes as well and set them next to the rear wheel of his bike. He pulled out his keys from the left kit pocket and Samsung S6 phone from the right, placing them on the table.

He held the button on to power the phone up and a few seconds later the phone was ready for the security code. Jarrod didn't enter it right away. His cell phone was a tool and not an addictive gadget to be fondled all day long. A quiet beep indicated a voice message had been left during their ride. Nothing urgent happening in his life at the moment so he resisted the urge to pick up the phone. He was more interested in follow-up to their conversation. Was Simon calling his contact now?

Simon had spent a few minutes at the urinal and wash basin. With his socked feet, he had been more than careful where he stepped and stood in the bathroom. He also had taken a moment to look up his contact's work number and powered off the phone. As he left the restroom, the restaurant was still pretty uncrowded. He expertly scanned the room, looking for an out-of-place person or someone who was trying not to catch his eye. Il Fornaio had a bustling 'to go' business on top and had a small counter situated across from the bar.

He smiled and put a look of need on his face as he approached the 'to go' cashier. "Ello, chap. My battery seems to have died and I was hoping to make a quick call," he said with a smile and a British accent.

Simon gave a quick nod and smile as he approached the table, "We have an appointment at your dad's 5:30 pm tonight."

Jarrod had been getting up as Simon approached and smiled quickly, "Perfect, thanks. Be right back." And he was off to take his turn at the lavatory. He had taken off his shoes as well. He walked in his socks quietly and confidently, weaving through the tables. Being a little more observant than usual, scanning while not looking like he was purveying the crowd. The early lunch crowd was beginning to build in downtown and a group of a co-workers had walked in. Someone quickly approached the hostess asking for their reservation for two under the name of Williamson.

Jarrod maneuvered his way past the group, while a few glanced briefly either at his socks, ripped muscles or bike kit. Into the restroom, he'd take a few minutes to relieve and wash up. In the washroom, he'd perfected the art of not making eye contact. There was the infrequent occupant looking for more than a pit stop. Thankfully, today, there was no one to avoid.

There were three sinks and Jarrod chose the one

closest to the door. He scrubbed his hands in the raised, beaten pewter-looking wash basin. The counter top and 10-inch backsplash were a white acrylic compound, which was a nice contrast. A spotless oval mirror reflected his bronzed face briefly. He wasn't any different looking today, though he'd started a hunt less than 2 hours ago.

He shut off the water and flicked water droplets off his fingers. There was a wire basket with a stack of pre-folded paper towels. Three, was how many he grabbed. Straightening up and drying his hands, he grabbed the door to walk out into the lobby. The lunch party was heading outside and he paused, looking over the room. Business was good, the food smelled wonderful, lots of conversation and smiles.

Jarrod turned his head back to the group. He picked up out of the corner of his eye a smashing woman walking through the door. He found a reason to pause. What could he look at in her vicinity to steal a more thorough look? Just from the milliseconds, his eyes had captured the brilliance of fire red hair in a professional looking low chignon. Skin tone was just a shade or two lighter than his and sensuous lipstick to match her hair tone. Absolutely gorgeous! He knew he'd had a thing for redheads his entire adult life.

It was almost as if discovering a rare gem. He'd Googled it once, and the gene for red hair is recessive, so a person needs two copies of that gene for it to appear. In the world's population the odds were .5%, or 1 in 200, that you would have red hair. Even in Ireland, your chances were only 10 percent, even though about 40 percent of the Irish carry the recessive gene.

He smiled at the trivia. Time to move his legs and get back to business. With any luck, she'd end up eating outside and thoroughly distract him. Pulling his mind back and refocusing, what had really caught his attention was the confidence and grace in the few steps he'd seen.

What the mind and eyes could capture in a split second was absolutely amazing. He managed to move his right leg and turned his head a quarter turn in her direction. Why not have a better glimpse? This wasn't high school or a job, where you'd see the same person day after day. This was a moment and you had better live in it fully. She had paused for a brief moment to look over the room - likely looking for her lunch date.

Very well dressed was his immediate impression. She wore a white knee-length skirt and matching jacket with a sheer jade green blouse. Glimmer of a white gold watch on her right wrist. Hey, a lefty wearing a proportionally sized watch and not those gaudy monstrosity sized watches. She also had a black leather portfolio tucked under her arm. White heels and before he knew it, she walked right past him to see the host.

Phillipe had glanced down at his seating chart and reservation list, then said, "Ciao, senorita Williamson. Would you like to be seated inside or outside? You have a guest arriving?"

"Outside please and I'll wait here," she responded evenly.

Jarrod heard her voice and he felt just the slightest glance in his direction as he walked past her. He would have loved to have seen her mouth phrase those words. This was turning into an intriguing lunch. Heading through the doors to his table, he did need to refocus on Simon.

Two more tables had filled up and he must have had a pretty silly smile on his face. Simon chuckled and said, "You must have seen that amazing redhead. I spotted her the second she got out of that white Range Rover across the street." He had a pretty satisfied look on his face as if he'd just had a conversation with her in his mind. Then, in his normal Brigadier voice he said, "Let's order and we've got a few things to go over."

Their table had four chairs and they both sat with their backs to the short fence. Simon was seated furthest from the main restaurant with Jarrod on his left. "So at oh-five-thirty we'll meet our computer whiz at your Dad's complex and after introductions can you take your Dad for a quick walk?" He then added, "It shouldn't take more than 15 minutes and he'll know whether we are going to be able to track this guy down."

"Sure, no problem. We'll go out back to sit outside. He might not have that much energy at that time of the day." Jarrod began formulating the phrases he'd be speaking to his Dad about just a quick little walk while the technician was working on his computer.

They had both decided what menu selection they were having for lunch. Today, their server was Sandra, a middle-aged brunette who wore her hair up in a bun. "Hello gentlemen, what a beautiful day for a ride. Where did you go?"

Jarrod offered, "We rode up Mt. Diablo today."

"Well, my name is Sandra and I'll be serving you. That's quite a ride. I go hiking there sometimes and see people riding up and zooming down." Her voice and eye contact showed she was a people person. Not somebody who was only interested in the next tip. She recited the specials of the day and added that her own lunch favorite was the Salmone Con Spinaci.

Jarrod decided to venture out from one of his standard dishes and go with the special - rainbow trout on a bed of penne pasta in a light sauce. Feeling a bit hungrier than usual, he also ordered an appetizer of their amazing meatballs. Simon chose the lasagna and grilled shrimp as an appetizer.

"And what would you both care to drink?"

They both chimed, "Water is fine." After years of drinking sticky sweet sports drinks while riding, the pure refreshment of water was quite welcoming. Once the meal started, their taste buds may ask for some vino or ale.

"I'll be back with some fresh bread and bread sticks. Please let me know if you need anything else."

The conspirators just smiled at her, ready to move into conversation. Simon started immediately in a quiet, firm voice, "I trust this techie guy and when you meet him, we won't be using names in front of your Dad. Go with 'Jay' if your Dad asks his name. Really, he just needs to be on the machine for 15-30 minutes. You'll give him $200 today and hopefully we can start to track down this…" Simon's voice stopped abruptly as two people were being seated at the empty table closest to them.

He smiled and winked at Jarrod. "Now we're going to test your skills of concentration."

Jarrod had also heard the hostess bringing over more people and the unmistakable sharp sound of high heels, accompanied by a pair of dress shoes. He didn't glance over immediately, but knew Mrs. Williamson would improve the view immensely. Focus now and peek later he told himself, smiling back at Simon, "Luck of the Irish?"

With a devilish smile, Simon said, "Ha, I think you'd take anything with this Irish. She's got a friend, but he's got nothing on you in those $500 dollar shoes and custom suit. You've got your favorite spandex suit on, best eau de Mt. Diablo stank cologne. Go bust out in a physique pose."

Simon always brought up women when he was around Jarrod. He had an unbelievable wife, family and marriage. Though Jarrod had his time freedom as a bachelor, make that a wealthy and successful bachelor, the deep one-on-one relationship was a void in his life. He did not divert his eyes from Simon, there was plenty of time to glance over at the table. "You're absolutely right," Jarrod continued with the joke on himself. "She might just ignore me based on the company I keep."

Grinning for another second, Simon brought them back to the matter at hand in a quieter voice. "How accessible is your cash? If we are going to run a long-distance op, there will be expenses."

His Dad had taught him a few tricks with money. An interesting turn, now that some of that would be used in order to bring about a certain renegade justice. "I've got $400,000 in cash that is not in the banking system. I've moved it around over the last 15 years."

"Looks like we're ready to hire then." Simon added with a smile, "After this is all done, I'd like to learn a few of those cash strategies." He knew his friend was successful, but this was a little surprise. You never knew people's pasts or who was planning for what. His thoughts immediately went to illicit dealings…who has that kind of cash on hand? But knowing the character of Jarrod these past five years and the fact that he wanted to have his own stash not under the purview of the government was pretty appealing.

They both reached for their water and expected their waitress should be coming soon with their lunch selections. At some point during the meal, Philippe would come out and ask for their opinion on the food, staff and restaurant. He was the most proficient survey collector; gathering real-time data from diners on the spot. Jarrod would ask about Mrs. Williamson, rather Ms. Williamson. Might as well keep the background fantasy running while he could.

Their waitress came prancing to the table, her face beaming with pride as if she had just made the dishes from scratch herself. As she was coming, Jarrod looked up and back a little to take in a little more of the scene at Ms. Williamson table. No wedding rings for either of them. If he were to guess, they were meeting to review some sort of legal documentation because each had their own billfold with a half inch of papers.

Didn't mean they were together and without a ring all was fair in the pursuit of love.

Both were somewhat stiff, as if representing two opposing sides of a legal matter. Their lunch would be leisurely, as neither had a clock to punch back at a j.o.b. He wanted to see the finish to their lunch and maybe a few spot checks. Hey, he might even catch her looking his way.

Their waitress offered fresh parmesan cheese to grate onto their plates and both accepted. Another chance for Jarrod to take a peek. He felt a bit sophomoric and decided to just hold his gaze there, not under the pretense of looking at the server. They both thanked their waitress for bringing their course. The aroma was to die for. As was their tradition, they raised their glasses in a toast. Jarrod spoke first when their glasses chimed, "And justice for all."

Simon replied, "Yes, and justice for all." Each took a healthy drink of water and commenced to reach for their fork.

The Cannelloni Al Fornaio dish which Simon ordered was unique in that it came from the cities of Bologna, Parma and Modena. It came stuffed with spinach and ricotta, had the tomato sauce underneath and a *besciamella* sauce covering the top. He had ordered it many times and it always pleased his *appetite gastronomico*.

As a patron of Il Fornaio, you could ask your server and they would know many details about the dish, preparation, herbs, spices and region. They wouldn't give everything away, but the restaurant was consistently rated in the top five places to eat in the East Bay. Neither had an interest in spending hours of preparation for a meal, but they certainly had learned to appreciate excellent food.

Jarrod had named Ms. Williamson dining partner Mr. Smith. Their luncheon was certainly business - exchanging documents, making notes on them and a few terse statements. This was quite alright with him. He'd had a chance to take in more.

Simon interrupted his thoughts, "So what is your intel on your long distance beau over there?"

"Not married, a wedding ring would need to be at least 3 carats to properly outshine those earrings," he chuckled. "Business review of sorts and my guess is a transaction on a piece of property, something with little emotional attachment—business transaction. Or maybe you hit the jackpot and she's not an emotional roller coaster gal. She is either self-made or had a huge settlement." Jarrod spoke in a very natural tone, but his eyes held a very particular interest. After half a breath, he added, "Left-handed and she'd look much better in your seat than you." And they both had a quick laugh.

"You failed to mention," Simon looked up and added with a devilish grin, "she may come with more than the factory options."

"Pretty good study there. You're having a good day overall. Now what plan have you conceived so this isn't just a fantasy till the next striking red comes within 20 feet of you?" Simon was curious. Men were always looking for tips, pointers and strategies. Copy what works best.... It wasn't that Simon was looking—just wanting to hear the plan and see if he'd execute it. You have to do more than talk in the romance part of life.

Jarrod took another glance across as their waitress brought their meals to them. He opened his mouth to answer Simon and on queue Philippe strode quickly to their table and asked, "Mes amis, how are you finding the selections today? Is the execution magnifique?"

Simon had a mouthful of penne and rinsed down the bit to reply, "Excellent and please give our thanks to your chef."

"Oh, I will! Henri has been with me for over 4 years now. I stole him away from cooking school... And how about you mesieur Jarrod?"

"Please pass on my compliments to Henri as well," Jarrod patted his flat stomach. "He is restoring my energy as we speak."

"You are both so kind and where else will you be riding today? What dessert can I tempt you with on this beautiful day?" Phillipe genuinely wanted to know both answers. He did have a unique habit of asking the second question before you could respond to the first and they weren't always the same subject.

Jarrod was the first to speak this time and leaned towards Phillipe and lowered his voice one notch, "What help could you give me on Ms. Williamson? Is it Miss?"

Philippe beamed immediately, "Ah, mesieur Jarrod. You have seen the prized gem of the day and you are in luck, it is Miss. Of course, you can only meet such a princess here at my Il Fornaio. It is true! She is your type; you think? You like her confidence or her red hair? No, no, she must be admired from across the table, not across the room. That is not possible right now. How will you like to meet her? Let me think. She will not be ordering dessert in the afternoon. That is only with her evening meals. You must leave a moment before she leaves and take your bikes over to her car; the white Range Rover. That is your best plan today. Take her to the Art & Wine Festival."

"She will not chit chat with the attorney, their business is nearly complete. There will be no parting kiss. This is what you must do. Wait for her and pour a moment of your soul into the chow. If only you knew Italiano, it wouldn't matter what you said because you would sweep her away. This is why everyone needs to learn to speak Italiano, to start the romance of a lifetime. Il Fornaio, of course you found love here." The ebullience, energy and love in Philippe's voice was contagious. The expression on his face would have challenged Napoleon's portrait for austerity.

"Grazi, thank you so much Philippe," Jarrod was impressed and amused with Philippe. In this case, it was ok to be a step behind Philippe and his wedding vow vision. He had waltzed off to attend other guests, Jarrod could hear him singing an Italian love song in his surprisingly clear, deep baritone voice.

Simon looked over to Jarrod and said, "Well, I think there was a plan in there, but basically you are to grab her at the curb and propose to marry her at the Art & Wine Festival. Is that what you got?" He laughed and then got a little serious. "No pressure buddy, now

Philippe and I will be watching intently –just execute the plan."

"From the looks of things, we better wrap up and get the check." He added sarcastically, "Can't have that holding off the royal marriage."

Jarrod thought Philippe and those of his ilk were amazing, spontaneous and so emotionally raw. He, on the other hand, was a planner and thinker by nature. Spontaneity was something he'd needed to work on his entire life. He was fine with that. His character traits had served him well; maybe not so much in romance and relationships, but in life all the personalities made the world spin 'round.

Before either could finish their last two bites, their waitress came with more water and to ask about dessert. There was still a residual energy lingering in the air from Philippe. What a dynamo. In his single years, he probably had his choice of dates every weekend. Simon looked over, raising his eyebrows and asked with sincerity, "Dessert today?"

"Nah, maybe when I beat you two times in a row. Could we get the check please?" taking a jab back at Simon.

Their waitress went to retrieve it and returned within two minutes. Looking across at Williamson and company, they still had a two or three-minute lead. Simon finished off his last bite and with a satisfied grunt, intertwined his fingers and stretched his arms overhead for a few seconds. Jarrod had a nervous yawn, smiled and rolled his neck in a circular motion. This was a different type of pressure or more aptly put, anticipation.

As he was writing in the tip amount and signing the check, Simon was smirking and said, "This is quite a day for you. Beat me up Mt. Diablo, turn into an international financier and taking the victory celebration lunch and turning it into a proposal on the curb to a woman you've never met."

Jarrod smiled back, "You're right! Use you up the hill, get into your little black espionage book and free dating advice from Philippe. I've still got half the day to make more happen." And then in a more serious tone, "Joking aside, I do really appreciate your help. As for Philippe and Ms. Williamson, that remains to be seen. It could be my most embarrassing moment of the year or something to celebrate the next 50 years."

They rose in unison and the timing was great. Williamson and company were just looking over their separate checks. They picked up their shoes and Jarrod noticed she definitely had taken a look at him. The bikes clicked quietly and they walked them single-file towards the restaurant doors. Just as they pushed through them, Philippe came rushing over and grabbed Jarrod's hand vigorously with both of his hands. "Good luck mesieur Jarrod, your princess awaits your invitation."

"Thank you again Philippe, for everything. I'll see you soon and let you know how it all worked out."

They carefully steered through the lobby crowd, drawing a few looks. Most weren't riding their bikes on a Tuesday, let alone to lunch. Stopping at the hostess station, Jarrod asked if he could make a reservation for two, on Friday at 6p. The hostess asked for the name to put it under, "Jarrod is fine."

"Hey Mr. Confidence, I hope you'll be able to ride home and watch the road," Simon teased. They still had a minute advantage, at least on Miss Williamson et deux.

"It'll give me something to talk about," Jarrod laughed lightly.

"Lead the way Romeo or are you going to get on your knees here in front of everyone?"

Jarrod ignored that jab and did lead the way outside. Their four wheels combined cost the same as a new Honda Civic he figured. On their right, down the sidewalk was a four-way light and crosswalk, so they walked down there. This may not appear totally natural, but at this point who cares? There wasn't time for dress rehearsal, let alone a long a shower. Looking across the street, her Range Rover was parked on the curb, four cars down. All the parking spots were metered, and the city was doing a nice job of keeping the streets clean.

"What's the plan? Need me to fake an injury? Want to stage a fight? What's the pitch? Any way I can embarrass you?" Simon was enjoying the moment. This reckoned back to his old high school dating years. Might as well have a little fun and break the tension.

"Actually, we're just going to conveniently stretch for a minute right next to her shiny grill, I'll introduce myself, you'll try not to drool, I'll get her name and number, we'll confirm dinner and be on our way," Jarrod wanted to keep it simple. His heart was beating just a tick harder than while making the reservation. What a funny feeling to have now in life; a little anxiety to ask a complete stranger out.

They walked up to her car and began stretching out. Touching hands to toes, reaching for the sky, arching backs, bending side to side and he could pick out her heels walking across the sidewalk. T-minus 20 seconds Jarrod and don't forget to smile his self-talk began. It would be awkward if he were straddling his bike or the bike were in between them, so he made sure when he'd started stretching to be closer to her driver side door than towards the front of his bike. Simon was doing the same at the next parking meter.

As she approached, white heels clicking on the sidewalk, Jarrod pulled himself fully upright. He'd guessed right on height, plus heels, that she was 5'6". What a walk. Measured pace, one foot in front of the other, straight and confident. You could see she was assessing the bikers and her car. Simon was taking a drink from his water bottle and Jarrod had put on his best first impression smile.

She looked at him, the handsome stranger at Il Fornaio, and a brief smile crossed her face as she approached her vehicle, looking at his bike and him.

Jarrod rested his right hand on his seat, two steps, one step, his eyes and mind capturing milliseconds of her walking towards him. They made eye contact and his smile caused her to smile. "Good sign…, continue" Jarrod told himself. He had already cleared his throat when she'd stepped from the sidewalk to the corner. Tilting his head just slightly, he smiled wider and said, "Hello" in a nonchalant, engaging voice.

"Um, hello to you," Miss Williamson matched his tone and smile.

Body language, intonation, smile, eye contact, warm, friend or foe…all these things she'd read before his next words came out. "My name is Jarrod," as he slowly offered his hand to shake. For a moment they looked at each other's left hands to confirm again no rings and to firmly extend their hands to shake.

"And I'm Lorrie," she said evenly with two brief shakes as they moved half a step closer to each other. Neither stepped back.

Cut to the chase he said to himself. Don't put her in a corner, compliment, compliment; quick! Smile. "I noticed you across from us at the restaurant. You're quite stunning." Keeping eyes locked in; they were a dazzling turquoise blue. "You have an amazing presence about you, confidence and I would like to meet you here for dinner; Friday at 6."

"Well, thank you for the compliments," smiling back. "Are you married?" She was direct, heaven in a woman.

"No, I'm not. Divorced many years ago. And you?"

"Divorced as well." She returned with an even voice. And after a half moment, she let out a quick, cute laugh. "Alright Jarrod, I'll meet you here at 5:00. You're cute, bold and your timing is right."

He wanted to ask 20 more questions, but knew to keep it simple. Find something intriguing to say, man. "Magnifique" rolled off his tongue, in his best Philippe impersonation. "6 o'clock it is Friday. Have an amazing day," he said inserting some joy into his voice. They both paused. It wasn't the moment for a hug, nor a handshake. Quick waves by both and she flashed a brilliant smile, remarkable! He automatically grinned back. They both took half turns, Lorrie towards her Range Rover and Jarrod to grab his water bottle. Each of their necks trailing behind to keep the eye contact a second longer.

As she opened the door, Jarrod adjusted his helmet and quickly put on his fingerless, biking gloves. Her car door shut and Simon immediately let out a quick, low, congratulatory whistle. "Romeo, you got the date. Good job throwing in the Italian. A Philippe in training," he laughed. "Now, let's ride. We've got a few more details to work out at your house."

CHAPTER 5

Lorrie pulled away slowly from the curb, looking over at Jarrod she waved again and was off down Broadway. Jarrod and Simon put their bikes on the street, threw legs over their bikes, clicked in their shoes and pedaled off slowly in the same direction. At the intersection, they slowed, but didn't stop and turned left down Pine St. It was lunch hour and they cautiously pedaled and coasted the next two blocks. They kept pace with the slow traffic and made themselves visible to the drivers.

Jarrod felt a sense of accomplishment and relief. He believed had he not asked Lorrie, there would have been regret. It was so simple, to speak a few sentences, yet challenging with strangers. In this case a ravishing one. The dinner would be the reward. In his youth church group, he recalled the simple and poignant dating advice. "There are a lot of women and you'll never know about them until you ask them out. Keep asking and you'll find the right one," from their youth leader.

To take the spotlight away from him, Jarrod asked Simon about his kids. Maddie was a spunky little 6-year-old in 1st grade who thought she should be the principal. Miles was an 8-year-old miniature of his dad and ready to go to war at a moment's notice. They had both recently transferred from public to private elementary school and their parents had hoped it would delay some of the negative social influences they had seen the children bringing home.

Despite living in the highest rated school zone of Walnut Creek, they had made the choice to move the kids last summer. Private schools were a curious process and the time commitments for the parents were non-negotiable. The tuition was a hefty $750 per month for each child. The price was worth it to Simon and Mariela.

On the ride home, Jarrod felt his mind was a three-channel receiver; Dad, Lorrie and the conversation. He was listening to Simon and having ridden so many miles over the years, his body was on auto-pilot. Scanning for obstacles on the pavement, watching for cars and joggers, shifting gears, braking, breathing and carrying on a conversation. Then he had his Dad and the imminent life changes to plan and adjust around. And now, a new and unknown prospect of a date this Friday with Ms. Lorrie Williamson.

It wasn't that dates weren't available, but he had turned off the romance, relationship and sexual side of life for some time. He had plowed his energy into his family, investing and business interests. He had wasted some time dating in the past. Maybe 'wasted' was too strong. He enjoyed himself and people were always interesting, but it seemed the end game to a relationship was a permanent relationship.... he had determined by date one or two that it was a 'no go.'

Some people would stay in the relationship if 70% of it seemed worthwhile. Ha, many stayed in it just for the sex. He didn't have that interest in trading one objective for a lesser one. In his dating life, he had kept it pretty simple and over the years had figured out how to accelerate the sorting process. It could have been perceived as judgmental, but time was so valuable and you're sorting anyhow before you even consider a prospective date. He knew he hadn't made it through other people's sorting mechanism.

"Yo, Romeo!" Simon called to pull him out of his mental loop. "Focus. I know you have a lot churning through the old noggin. I asked whether you had a grand at home."

"Sorry, yes a lot running through my mind. I do have cash on hand," Jarrod was immediately back in the conversation. He needed to keep his head in the moment and not drift. His pace had also slowed down and he quickly kicked up the pace.

Simon commented, "That's more like it. Get the body and mind engaged. What about the other cash? Is it easily accessible this week?" They were only a few minutes out from Jarrod's home and this certainly was one of the more scenic routes; winding down El Cerro Canyon. The wildflowers sprinkled throughout the landscape. Brilliant orange California state poppies. Lavender to contrast against it.

Jarrod answered back, "Yes, I have cash money here

and in Europe if we need it."

Simon raised an eyebrow, "That might come in handy." Looks like his cycling pal had taken some precautions. "Any changes to your home security system?"

"Nah, it hasn't changed since you checked it over a year back. Buttoned up pretty tight." Jarrod was actually grateful that someone other than a salesperson had input on his home security system. Simon had taken a few hours last year to help him sort out the options.

Traffic lightened, the closer they came to his home. One of the many reasons Jarrod had purchased this lot and had his home built. His 2-acre lot was backed by state park land and if someone wasn't driving to his house, they wouldn't be on this street. The road had a slight rise and fall, the trees and foliage were very mature. Oaks, Bays and Buckeye trees had grown to their full height in this part of Lafayette. When he had bought the lot, there were more than a dozen oak trees with a trunk diameter of 4 feet.

The sprawling 4,400 square foot, bi-level home may have seemed too large for just one person to live in, but he loved the space. He had two architects submit plans and the end result was a very livable space, open for entertaining, yet private from the street. They eased off the pedaling and coasted up onto the half-round driveway; the three single garage doors hiding the fact of their double car depth.

Simon had dismounted from his bike at the back side of his black Denali, changed into tennis shoes and began securing his bike to the hitch-mounted bike carrier. Jarrod had unclicked as well near the far-left garage door where the security pad was affixed to the house. He slid the panel door up and entered the ten-digit code, 2-4-8-0-7-1-3-5-8-9. Most home security users had a four-digit code; typically, ascending sequence which was easy to break. The code would never be changed, the keypads would show the repeated contact and in short time more wear because the other buttons were never even pressed.

A thief looking at the keypad could usually guess in one or two attempts the correct code. Not this code. And he'd change it at the end of the month.

Simon's demeanor had changed; transforming from a cyclist with a full stomach to an infantry quarter master. In a military staccato, he said, "It's 12:35 now. I've got a few things to take care of at home. Park off Second street and walk up to your Dad's place. The tech and I will meet you out front at 16:30. Have the $1000 and we'll see if we can sniff out a little phisherman."

"Yes, I'll see you then, Simon," Jarrod replied in a quiet, low voice. The gravity of the situation was taking hold. Acting to catch a criminal and possibly taking the extremely illegal action of hiring a hit squad for his Dad and possibly for the any other innocent people that had their money stolen in similar fashion.

Jarrod had to admit he felt a little jumpy, but he followed his routines as closely as possible. His shoes were placed in a little cubby shelf on the wall. After any ride, he wiped down his bike very thoroughly, went through all the gears and checked the chain. His garage was immaculate, and the Trek had a mount up on the right-hand wall, next to the Corvette. Their colors were picked, not to match, but rather for their own distinct beauty.

Both gleamed under the incandescent lighting of the garage. Sunburst orange covering the sweeping lines of the Corvette with the dazzling chrome 5 spoke mirror cut lip Cray Scorpion 20" rims. You would not be missed driving down the road from the color or the low, throaty growl from the modified V8. Just as striking, up on the wall, was the 2016 Trek Madone 9.9, fire engine red to catch the eyes of distracted drivers. There wasn't any trendy, matte black finish in this garage.

Jarrod closed the garage door down behind him as he entered the house. He felt a little more relaxed having performed the habitual post-ride tasks. He needed to wash up, check his phone for messages and maybe do a little reading before taking off for Dad's. Dad… his mind began to churn through the gears. Such a fall in life, from an outside observer. Family man, successful stock broker, investor and highly intelligent. Now, Alzheimer's chipping away at his mental capacity and distorting who James Phillip Washburn, his boyhood hero, was in this life.

Jarrod still dressed as a younger man, not succumbing to the complete Docker's wardrobe. He enjoyed being physical and active; why not look the part? He slipped on a pair of comfortable, dark blue boat shoes with white stitching. Khaki 5-pocket, hiking shorts and a baby blue Polo shirt. He laughed in the mirror for a few seconds as if a close friend had just mentioned an inside joke. It was going to be a pretty serious day so why not break the tension before it begins?

He strode from the bathroom to his den. He set aside three, thirty-minute blocks for emails. 7a, 11a and 3p. Their ride had pushed out his late morning email slot until now. Jarrod pulled his laptop out of the wall safe, powered it on and went to get a glass of water. His email folders and subfolders were prioritized top-down in order of priority, not alphabetically. Dad had the top spot and then his commercial and residential properties were listed in order of monthly cash-flow. Inevitably, a property might temporarily have a potential legal matter and it would be moved up accordingly.

Very few decisions had to be made or approved by himself personally. Jarrod had elected to go with an individual, rather than a property management firm. He had managed them on his own for almost ten years and once the income stream from the properties justified the position, he was more than happy to hire it out. After dozens of interviews, he had decided on a senior accountant, who didn't fit the corporate mold, and trained him in property management.

Today he scanned the preview of new emails in his top ten folder; there were none of any consequence. Two he forwarded to his property manager Thomas and the rest were marked read. Looking below to his opportunity folders, properties and areas he was looking to own real estate, there was one agent who had agreed to his proposed terms. There were two condo units a family trust was looking to unload at Sun River, Idaho ski resort.

Rental history had been provided and though it

hadn't been leased in over 18 months, the cash flow it had provided was in line with the ratios he required. It was likely the family owned the property outright and just lost interest in managing it. The title search and inspections were complete, and the combined price was $690,000. It had taken 20 days for their reply, which was an improvement from their first emails which weren't even replied to at all. He replied to Natashia, his most productive agent and countered at $649,000 which would expire on midnight Friday.

This set of condos would be his seventh and eighth in Idaho; each were at a ski resort. They had been brought to him by one of his favorite RE agents, Natashia. She excelled in discovering properties locked up in trusts that families were trying to unload. The other six were in town and these were bought with the intention of renting to those vacationing. In 5 years, he would see which units performed the best.

With email completed, he shut down the laptop and secured it back in the safe. Intentionally, he left his cell phone on the kitchen counter. It was so easy to be sucked into the world where people couldn't go for five minutes without a swipe, scroll, like or text. He had seen the benefit of smart phones and always owned one, but as a tool, not as a security blanket.

After he had come in from the garage, he had intentionally left the ringer off. Leaving the den, he felt like some music and went to the living room. Each room, except the den, was connected to the audio system. From XM satellite, 90s Rock sounded good today. He was in an upbeat frame of mind. Fantastic bike ride, the plan was moving forward for Dad and he had a date with who appeared to be a business savvy woman who was also drop-dead gorgeous.

The message light on Jarrod's cell phone wasn't normally blinking, but it was now. He picked it up, then set it down. It could wait a few minutes because he was hungry now. His kitchen had two Sub-Zero units, the 22 cubic feet one on the left was for freezer and the twin on the right was for refrigeration. He pulled out a 6 oz. filet mignon that he had grilled Monday. Spinach, baby kale was the base and he'd top it off with sweet yellow and red bell peppers.

The steak went onto a plate and he placed it in the stainless convection oven for 3 minutes. Fork and steak knife and plate for his salad; he had about 2 cups of greens and sliced off pieces of the crisp peppers. He was in a pretty serious groove with his food the last two weeks. Completely eliminating the starches from his groceries and choices at restaurants.

Eating alone there was the tendency to be distracted or entertained. He made it a habit to not watch the news, his computer, phone or even a good book while eating. There was plenty of time for that. He would rather be turning challenges inside-out in his brain. At a restaurant, this was even more challenging. However, with an engaging server, one could have an interesting conversation. You didn't have to sit at the bar to talk with the bartender or watch a game.

Jarrod enjoyed people and yet, sometimes he really loved solitude, being alone in his space and mind. He loved the activity, vibrancy of the parenting years and seeing his children develop right before his eyes. Yes, there was the no real preparation for the work involved in raising children, but what incredible memories and to think he was a major influencer in two human beings' lives. It could have been easier with a cohesive marriage.

Relationships were good and bad, healing and hurtful, give and take, then eventually it had to end. Enough of this thinking. He had processed the marriage and divorce a hundred times over. His house was that of a single grandparent and he was grateful for his life. Nearby in Walnut Creek, his daughter Chelsea, her husband Grant and their children: Brett and Alanna. Just a little further south, his son Clayton, his wife Natalia and their children: Luke and Madison. They were less than 30 minutes away.

Jarrod had finished eating and moved his plate, steak knife and fork to the dishwasher. Now he'd check his phone and go take a look at the mail. The green message light blinked as he slipped it in his short's pocket. Let's go check the mail. It was warming up nicely and felt close to 80 degrees on this cloudless, blue Wednesday. Walking to the end of the driveway he consciously made himself breathe in the aroma of the roses. His parents had taught him to not miss the little things in the day.

Easing open the mailbox, he reached in and pulled out a single item, a carpet cleaning ad. It appeared again that his phone would win the day for most interesting messages. He looked out on the front landscape, inhaled the richness of freshly cut grass, pulled his arms and shoulder blades back for a stretch and walked back up the driveway.

Through the front door and to the right he sat on

his favorite couch. Jarrod felt invigorated with the day it had been. He swiped his phone and entered the pass code; this month it was a +1, -1, +1, -1 pattern for the last four digits of his social security number. Since he had taken care of his emails earlier, his phone only had 2 purposes - text and talk. He had one phone message, one missed call and text from an unknown user.

Voice was always first. In this day and age, if anyone called or left a message then they got first priority. They were seeking to communicate with him; whereas texts were good for little pieces of information. Not that you'd notice that from most people's texting their life story. Natashia had called to make sure he had received her email and that the sales conditions were correct. She had fantastic follow-up. He listened to the entire message and nothing else was covered that wasn't in the email. He had confirmed, and the message could be deleted.

Next, the missed call was from his Dad's primary physician. His first thought was shaped towards what could be wrong and then he changed it; everything has stabilized, and Dad's appointment confirmed that basically everything was the same as six months ago. But they only left a cursory message to call their office. Doubt tried to creep back in. Calling them back was the only way to find out good or bad.

He dialed immediately before any more doomsday thoughts could enter his mind. The doctor's office greeted him with a perfunctory female voice, "Thank you for calling Dr. Rosenal's office. How may I help you?"

Jarrod replied in the most neutral voice he could

muster, "This is Jarrod DeBoy, returning your call about my father, Thomas DeBoy."

"Oh, Mr. DeBoy, one moment while I pull up the Doctor's instructions."

The inflection of her saying "Oh" and pause after it wasn't very reassuring. He replied, "Sure." As if there was another option.

"The only notes I have here is that Doctor Rosenal would like to speak with you, today. He's with a patient at the moment. Is this the best number to reach you?

"Yes, it is."

"If he cannot reach you during office hours, can he call you afterwards?"

"Yes, most certainly." This wasn't easing any of his doubts or questions. How is my father? What is so important now that you have to call me today?

"Thank you, Mr. DeBoy, he'll be in touch with you today."

"Ok, thank you. Good bye." He couldn't really feel the phone in his hands and practically dropped it after she hung up. Jarrod placed it gently on the counter. He hadn't even realized he had gotten up off the chair and walked into the kitchen. He thought better in stressful situations when he was pacing or at least fully upright.

He was in turmoil, trying to direct his thoughts and not have them run rampant. He reached back for his phone and made sure the ringer was up. The green message light was still flashing at him. Was this the time to get religious? He was feeling a little helpless. Maybe he'd wait on the doctor's call and then decide on asking for God's help. How serious could it be? Was it stage 4 cancer? Could it be an inoperable condition? "Stop it!" He shouted out loud and startled himself.

He needed to refocus his mind or at least distract it to pull his energy away from these thoughts. Messages. There was another message he could check and he grabbed the phone. He wasn't in a calm mood and it wasn't from a number he recognized. Was it spam, a wrong person?

Jarrod clicked to open the message. Hoping for a novel, anything to take his mind away from the Doctor's message. The message and picture jumped out and grabbed his full attention. It was a professional quality image of his date, Lorrie! She had sent him a message.

Jarrod,

I'm looking forward to our dinner on Friday. Hope you're having a great day!

Lorrie

This was the most incredible unsolicited message from a stranger, ever! He could hardly believe her face was right there on his phone. He quickly rotated his phone to landscape in order to see her image fill the screen. The photo must have been recent and this time her hair was down, shining in its radiant red; magnificent. Her makeup was similarly subdued, and you could see just the collar of a blouse.

Well it had been sent when he was working in the

den. That would have completely stopped him in his tracks. What amazing timing. His emotions had gone from despair and anxiety to kindness and excitement in the millisecond after opening her message. Now, of course, he had to reply as a 51-year-old and not with the impetuousness of a young teenager. A selfie was out of the question. He'd send Lorrie a picture giving her a second dimension to layer on top of the cycling Romeo. He chuckled to himself. Team Romeo Cycling. He'd run that by Simon and get a laugh. He'd have to ask how she got his number. Likely, Philippe! He'd have to thank him later.

Scanning through the pictures on his phone was enlightening. At least half of the images on his phone were centered around cycling. His friends and the great vistas from the rides. She had already seen that aspect. Women. Back to the basics, Jarrod. Women gravitated towards family and relationships in a conversation. Earlier in the summer, he had attended his niece's high school graduation and they'd gone out to dinner afterwards at Wente Vineyards.

The waiter had taken a group photo of his family with the vineyard backdrop. His brother's family and his own. Shawn was there with his wife Alyssa, their graduating daughter Kayla and older son Kyle. Jarrod's grown children, along with his four grandchildren, made a great family event photo. This picture would put his best foot forward. "What to say," he wondered aloud.

"Dearest Juliet, wherefore…," he smiled. He hummed Ray Orbison's "Pretty Woman" for a little inspiration and was glad he had indeed met the Pretty

Woman. Too bad he couldn't acquire a sexy French accent in 2 days. Come on already, make it short and sweet.

Hi Lorrie,

Your message and picture made my day.

Or should it be reversed? Picture and message? And it has to be more than 7 words buddy. Alright, picture and message it is, we're all a little vain about our image and pictures. Let's add a tiny bit of Jarrod in the message and send it already. Quit over-thinking and analyzing to the 100th degree.

Hi Lorrie,

Thank you for the great surprise - your picture and message truly made my day. I'm looking forward to dinner as well. Here's a family pic at my niece's graduation back in May. Hope your day is great.

Jarrod

There it is, not over-thought and to the point. In an instant, she really had turned his mind completely away from the stress and uncertainty of the unknown in Dad's situation. With the sexiest grin he could muster, he scrolled up in the message to see her face one more time and clicked Send. Keep your expectations in check buddy and be grateful she even sent you a message.

It was pretty amazing how the simplest things could make or break an entire day. He wanted to tell Simon or Shawn or anybody about Lorrie; how she had put an immediate smile on his face and pulled him out of the moment. Relax, he told himself. Dinner one wasn't for another 52 hours. He saved her in his contacts, and was glad his host prodded him to ask her to dinner.

More important now was the meeting with Simon and his internet guru buddy. Could he really trace down the person or group who stole from his Dad? Would they know without a shadow of a doubt the computer and person who had phished the $7000? It was a little uncomfortable knowing how vulnerable his Father was and that anyone, including himself, could be traced via email to their residence. It seemed like there should be an impermeable barrier between the Internet Service Provider and his email account.

Jarrod finished cleaning up around the kitchen and it was nearly time to go to Dad's. He wanted to arrive at least 15 minutes early and gauge his energy and clarity. The idea was to take him out to the backyard grounds, for 30 to 60 minutes, in order to be out of the way. Well, let's get over there and see. It was impossible to quantify what his Dad meant to him.

Not only was his Father his first hero figure, he had helped raise, protect and nurture him. His parents had also been there for him as an adult; going through a divorce, starting his real estate investment trust and on and on. For a few years now he had become the provider, protector and confidant. Jarrod was grateful to have the time and live close enough to give those back.

As much as possible, they were trying to keep a low profile. That meant he'd be driving the Tesla again. He really needed to take his Corvette and blow it out soon. He set the home alarm and stepped out into the garage. Jarrod reached to press the garage door button and felt a little tension in his upper back. The magnitude of the day was building.

Jarrod slipped into the driver's seat and silently started the deep blue metallic Model S. The dashboard came alive, he placed his foot on the brake pedal and shifted into reverse. The garage closed behind him and he started his quick drive to Country Manor.

Here we go, the understatement of his day. There were no traffic snarls at 3:30pm, though there was a definite increase in the number of cars; schools had released. It wouldn't be long now, and he would meet the first member of his anti-cyber terrorist crime team. Jarrod had the utmost confidence in who Simon was selecting for this job. It had to be someone with experience doing the same type of internet back-tracking. He parked on the curb of 3rd, which wasn't more than an asphalt finger two blocks south and one street east from his Dad's place.

The solid *whoomph* sound of his car door shutting behind him acted as his starting gun. He did his best to walk at a normal, nonchalant pace; though in his mind it felt like he had one foot on the accelerator and the other on the brake. The cross walk made him stop to wait for the cross-traffic to stop and the light to change in his favor. He was counting the seconds, one-one thousand 29, one-one-thousand 30, one-one thousand 31 and ding. The vision impaired audio chirps along with the white pedestrian light signaled he could walk.

There was a young mother and her two children walking hand in hand towards him in the cross walk. The kids were shy, but Jarrod and the mom exchanged brief smiles. They were all brunettes and the kids 3 and 7 by his estimation. Mom was in her early thirties. No cars in his peripheral view and he allowed himself to naturally walk a little faster as he approached the curb.

He headed west one block and made a right on Moraga Boulevard for the Country Manor elder care home. It was only another block. Just a few minutes and he'd be walking through the double sliding glass doors. Jarrod was almost to the door and his phone beeped with the incoming text message tone. The bright sunlight and glare wouldn't allow him to see much, so he'd take a look once he was inside. It was hit or miss how many people would be in the dining parlor.

Retirement changed the clockwork urgency of eating meals and care homes actually brought the residents back into the daily regimens. It was also for the efficiency of the restaurant. You weren't paying for a 24-hour buffet! But, if you missed a meal, the staff made a note and if you missed a second that day then the on-staff nurse would come check on you within the hour.

He entered the lobby, took a few steps to the right and away from the reception desk. His text was from Simon and confirmed they would be here in 25 minutes. He knew Simon would come, but it was reassuring to see the text. The front desk was busy helping a woman; likely the responsible child of a resident here. Jarrod was able to get by with just an exchange of waves. One less person to remember him being here, he thought.

He walked briskly over to the elevator bank and as

soon as he pressed the up arrow, it opened for him. Dad was on the 3rd floor with the preferred view of the garden grounds out back. Preferred, and of course, there was a slight premium for the view. The elevator ascended swiftly up and released him on floor number 3. Jarrod stepped out and took a right down the hallway; his father's room was the 8th door down. The corner suite also had the advantage of the stairwell, which was great in the event of a fire or if someone needed to remain a little less conspicuous on their visit.

Jarrod would spend a few minutes with Dad, reminding him why he was there and that two computer technicians would be coming to take a look at his machine. He strode up to the door and gave 3 moderate raps on the door. It did not take his Dad much time at all to open the door. Jarrod always paid particular attention to his Dad's response on seeing himself or anyone for the first few moments. For the last few months, it had been taking his Father just a few seconds to recognize and associate the person with a name.

This afternoon, when his Dad opened the door, the facial recognition took a full 3 seconds, "Well, hello Jarrod. Come in." He did his utmost to not change his facial expression until Dad recognized him.

"Hi Dad." Then another few seconds and he said, "You're here to fix my computer?"

"Yes, I'm here for your computer and I'll have another 2 technicians in a few minutes." Jarrod hated the timing of everything. It wasn't fair. What if he had just awakened from a nap? He wanted to find good reasons why there was a delay on his Dad's part. They walked over to his couch and recliner and sat down. Jarrod had brought over some furnishings, books and artwork for the walls from Dad's old house to the apartment. Otherwise, it felt too much like an extended stay hotel.

Next to the coffee leather recliner was a small, round table that his mother had made. She was so gifted in arts and for the most part, self-taught. This particular table had a black, wrought iron base and the circumference of the top was made from the same material and color. She had edged it with white gloss mosaic tile squares. Each piece had been hand set; mom was meticulous in her placement of each piece.

The top was an intricate mosaic tile, featuring two hummingbirds hovering at a lush purple Butterfly Bush. The stained glass was held underneath by a metal grid. Jarrod could still remember the day when his Mother had shown it and two others to Dad, his sister Janelle and himself. She crafted three with the intention of keeping one and giving the other two for their children. Mom had made these for the holidays and typically let the kids select first. On this particular Christmas, before Mom could even say a word, Dad had immediately inserted himself between the tables and his adult children to choose this table.

Dad had stated, "Phyllis, this is stunning, and I know the exact place for it - next to my recliner." And there it had been for the last 15 years. Whatever book Dad was reading was placed on this table and he made it a point to showcase the table to anyone who came into their house. Jarrod and Janelle were amused and surprised that day because of Dad's instantaneous attachment to the table.

The background glass was pieces of medium to darker pieces of purple stained glass. There were tiny swirls of white marbling contained in the purple. These hummingbirds were shades of white, grey and flecks of amber in their bodies. Their beaks were a perfectly straight, single line of the grout. Today, there was no book on the table, but he did have the photos Jarrod had given him at lunch.

The frequency for Dad to start a conversation had continued to decline over the last 2 years. Jarrod was not particularly verbose; he was quite comfortable with the non-conversational moments. Here now, he made it a point to create the dialogue with his Father. He wanted to take advantage of Dad's limited time with Alzheimer's draining the drops of water from his clepsydra clock.

"Dad, did you notice the landscaping crew is adding new flowers and shrubs in the northeast corner of the garden today?"

"No, but I do remember reading it in the newsletter. I'm glad to see that wretched ivy yanked out. Good for nothing except rats," his Dad said with disgust.

"While they're working on your computer, maybe we'll go take a look? I'm going to head down to the lobby and bring them up here. Ok?"

His Father had walked to the window for an overhead view of the gardening work. "Sure Jarrod."

Jarrod glanced over at his Dad. He'd need to move an extra chair over to the desk for Simon. Overall, his Dad still kept a pretty tidy place. Jarrod opened and closed the door behind him quietly, not wanting to wake any potentially napping neighbors. Walking down the low-pile carpet, he noticed his footsteps could hardly be heard. They used a shorter carpet intentionally, for ease of use with walkers, wheelchairs and just general walking for the elderly. He was certain they had used an excellent grade of padding and maybe an extra sound barrier.

There hadn't been much activity in the Country Manor elder care home and it must have been the residents' resting time. The evening meal was served between 5:00 and 6:00 pm; preparations were underway in the kitchen area. Jarrod exited the elevator and figured it would be best to let the front desk know he had 2 guests arriving. Walking over, he received an immediate smile from Sam; Samantha Josephson. She had been here the last time he had dropped off the roses.

"Hello, Mr. DeBoy. Is everything ok with your Father?" she asked with genuine interest.

"Hello Miss Josephson." He chuckled. "Remember, it's ok to call me Jarrod. And, yes, Dad is fine, thanks. Though his computer may have a virus, so I've got a technician coming soon to check it out."

"Oh, I'm sorry to hear that. Seems like that's happened to a few people lately."

"Really? You mean here?" A faint alarm was sounding off in the back of his head. Could this be some inside scheme to the elderly, well-to-do residents here? Or were the cyber punks specifically targeting senior care homes?

Sam lowered her voice, looked to both sides before speaking and said in a confiding tone, "Yes, 3 people in the last week. Plus, your Dad, that makes 4." The alarm in her voice went up a notch with the *'makes 4.'*

Jarrod tilted his head slightly to the left and raised his eyebrows; the right brow higher than the left side. "Is that so?" he said as he was checking the time.

"The tech should be here in a minute, so I'll talk with you later Sam. Have a great day." Jarrod walked the 30 feet over to a padded arm chair with a view of the front door. He'd mention this to Simon and the tech in case it mattered. Relaxing for just a few minutes and looking through the windows, he spotted Simon and his companion. The tech had a purposeful gait like Simon, laptop bag slung over his shoulder and across his body. Both were wearing jeans and polo shirts. Jarrod smiled at the jeans. When he thought of Simon it was always in a cycling kit or exercise shorts.

Simon could have easily passed for a man 20 years his junior and the tech appeared to be in his early thirties. Jarrod immediately got up and took a few steps towards the doors which would be opening for the two guests. The two friends immediately shook hands.

"Simon" and "Jarrod" were the only words exchanged and then Simon said, "I'd like you to meet Jay." Simon had told Jarrod, this was the type of introduction he'd receive for several obvious reasons: precaution and to set the chain of command.

"Pleased to meet you sir" the tech said formally.

Jarrod responded with, "Thank you for coming Jay. I'll show you to the apartment." He knew the tech would see his father's name when examining the emails and could simply put two and two together to trace down Jarrod, but there was no team without a certain level of trust. Simon trusted Jay and depending on what was discovered in the next few days, the plan would stop abruptly or move forward.

Jarrod made it a point to not look in the direction of Sam the receptionist. She was aware of why his guests were there and had inadvertently given him some very interesting information. In a few short steps they were at the elevator doors. Pressing the button, the elevator ding came immediately and when the door opened there stood the resident watchdog, James McInnis.

The three quickly stepped aside and Jarrod gave a quick "Hello McInnis, we'll get out of your way."

An inquisitor by nature, for some reason he did not ask why and just replied with a "Oh hi Jarrod."

Jarrod knew he'd be making some mental notes and possibly even ask Sam if she knew the reason for the visitors. Sam wasn't the most close-mouthed receptionist, but it wasn't really a concern at this point. Computer virus was about all he'd find out and he'd only seen the guests for a brief second while at the elevator door.

As the door closed shut on them. Jarrod spoke up, "In talking with the receptionist today, she volunteered that 3 other residents here had what she called a quote, unquote 'computer virus' within the last week."

Jarrod and Simon glanced over at Jay to read his reaction. In a measured tone, he said, "I'll look into that as well." No real emotion was Jarrod's first thought. Then, of course, he's trained and just received a piece of data to investigate.

They exited at the ding of the third floor and the elevator closed to wait for its next instruction. Jarrod led out front, with Simon and Jay a step behind. At the door Jarrod knocked and said "Dad, we're here."

His Father opened the door and stepped back to let the guests inside. "Dad, here are the techs who want to take a look at your computer." He'd decided to not introduce them formally. For an instant Jarrod wondered if his Dad might recognize Simon from any cycling pictures. He knew this was the first time they'd ever seen each other in person. At this point, he didn't think there would be any recognition. Most pictures that he showed his Father were family and to a much lesser degree, Jarrod's activities.

"Here is the computer. We don't have a password, but I'll get you logged onto Dad's email account. I'm guessing the activity would have been less than 3 days ago." The technician waited while Jarrod typed in the email password. The password was accepted, and he got up from the desk so Jay could use it. As the tech sat down, Jarrod brought over another chair for Simon from the small dinette set.

Simon replied stiffly, "Thank you Mr. DeBoy. It should take us 30-45 minutes to go through the diagnostics."

"We'll be out walking in the garden and be back in 30 to check on things. Thanks. We don't want this to happen again." The DeBoy's walked out and closed the door behind them.

CHAPTER 6

Jay immediately piped up and said, "I hate this acting crap."Simon didn't bother to respond, they were getting paid to do a job and a few minutes of acting didn't matter. "Let's see what you can find," he said with the tone of his voice equally stating it as a challenge and directive.

"Yes sir." The tech went to work immediately, previewing each email for content and hovering over the email headers to see the receiving and sending email server. The tech pulled out his own laptop, flash drive and four wireless USB cards for internet connectivity. In Notepad, he copied the email headers from three emails along with the date and time received. Those were saved on the flash drive.

Next, he went to the Sent email folder and again went through each email for the last three days. Jay looked over to Simon and said, "Well Mr. DeBoy gave his personally identifiable information twice, which would have allowed the access to his online bank account. Step 2 is to see the sending email server which will determine the IP address and associated Domain."

Simon, ignoring the cyber mumbo jumbo said, "I want the flash drive and Notepad file when you're done."

"Yes sir. Step 3 The Domain is registered to a network provider, who I will access." The word *access* made Jay's steel grey eyes glint as he grinned. The tech pulled his flash drive and inserted it into his laptop. Simon watched intently as he copied the links from the Notepad file into his browser. He bet the software running on this laptop wasn't available through Amazon.

Steps 2 and 3 were completed and Jay copied more information onto the Notepad file. Next he pulled the wireless modem and handed it to Simon with the words, "Hold this and we'll destroy it after." Simon put it in his pants pocket, agreeing with word selection. Jay put in another type of wireless modem now. This one looked very similar to those offered by his cell carrier. "We're going after the first hack. The domain is registered to a network provider and that's where I'll find the IP address this email was sent from."

Jay typed in a command, copied another link from Notepad and pressed the enter key. He sat back and watched as the program generated 8-digit random numbers as fast as the 6th Generation Quad-Core Intel processor would compute. "You either find the back door or brute force it. And believe me there is always a back door."

"I believe you; as much of this stuff going on out there." Simon agreed.

Jay's laptop screen flashed for a second and a new

window appeared with what looked to be a DOS type directory listing. He moved a little closer to the screen and a smile began at the corners of his mouth. Jay muttered under his breath, "Motherfurbererer, I'm getting you now." Faster than Simon could assimilate, he watched the tech blazing through the commands and scanning the output scrolling down the page.

"Botswana, got you now Mr. X1." Jay took a breath and looked over to Simon. "Ok, Mr. X1 is in Botswana. I'm going to do the same and find X2. Then swap modems for the final step. Accessing the ISP, find who the equipment is registered to and then the address." This all came out in one breath and Jay pivoted his head back to his laptop. "It looks like there's a second account that was accessed." His brow furrowed even deeper and he gasped, "Criminal bastards! This guy yanked $300k last night from account ending in 6343!"

Simon jerked his head over barely controlling his voice "Did you say $300,000? Not just $2000?"

"Sir, yes sir. $2,000 emptied out account ending in 2806 last week and then he jumped into a linked account 6343 and transferred out three hundred freaking thousand!"

In disbelief Simon said, "Lord have mercy. I don't think our client knows that yet. You're certain?"

"Yes, sir and I will copy the transaction numbers into Notepad for you."

Simon replied with contempt "And there's a second phisher?"

"I'm gonna nail you next X2."

Simon was glad Jay was on his team and not someone else's. He made a mental note to hire him for his own internet security advice as soon as this job was completed. If this guy could do it, then there were hundreds more out there practicing the same craft—most likely with bad intentions.

The tech was back in his cyber zone and going through the commands, copying to Notepad and back to the laptop. This went on for a few minutes and he abruptly stood up. "One second," Jay directed at Simon as he walked over to the window. He closed his eyes and rotated his neck side to side, then arched his back and inhaled. "Ok, X2s a little more buried than X1." He got back in his seat, pulled up what looked like another program and proceeded to enter the commands while copying links from Notepad.

It seemed like another 5 minutes passed by with only the keyboard clicks to break the silence. Jay sat back again and said "Finally" as the 8-digit random codes began to generate. He began humming Metallica's "For Whom the Bell Tolls" with his head moving slightly with the rhythm and thumbs playing the beat on the desk and mouse pad.

The thumb drums became a little louder and then the screen flashed. This screen looked more like a Windows based administration screen. "Ooh, nice. Here we go." Jay commented on progress, not the play-by-play, which was fine with Simon. The tech clicked, tabbed and typed while moving from screen to screen. "Not there" and closed the window out. Shaking his head from side to side and stretching his fingers on both hands; another rapid progression of clicks and typing. "Bam!" Jay exclaimed and clenched his right fist.

Simon smiled, he liked the tech, but did find this so different from the battle preparation he'd performed over his career.

"So, this X2...You're not going to believe it. He's down in Palo Alto! Looks like he got in a day prior to Botswana X1. He used the same maneuver. Grabbed $5,000 from the smaller account and went all in to transfer freaking $317,000!" Thieving Peninsula prick. Probably some Stanford grad student or drop out. Looks like they were racing against each other to pull out as much as they could." He copied a few more lines from the laptop and pasted into Notepad, then pulled out the 2nd wireless modem. Simon was still shocked and wondered how the bank and Jarrod had not been alerted about these two accounts being wiped out of $624,000! He placed the last wireless modem in his pocket with the other one.

Jay looked at the two remaining wireless cards and said aloud, "International or Domestic? Let's travel to Botswana why don't we?" Do you know anyone who can speak Setswana? No matter, most speak English as well. He shoved in the bulkier of the two cards, let it register and began typing away. While Jay was performing his magic in cyberspace, Simon began to plot out Botswana and Palo Alto. Interesting where life took you; he'd been sent halfway around the world to Botswana, but never visited Palo Alto an hour away!

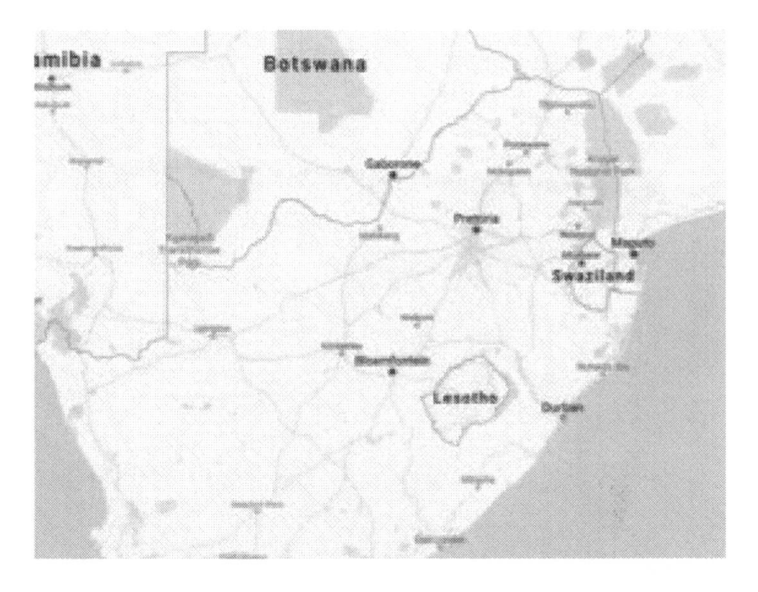

Recon work would be much easier in Palo Alto of course, but what if Mr. X2 was being watched by the FBI already? Might as well ask. "Hey Jay, can you find out if either X1 or X2 is already being watched by our government or Botswana's authorities?"

Jay knew what he was thinking. Nobody wanted to be nabbed while making a nab of their own. These guys weren't playing around. "Yes, but not from here with this equipment. That is way outside the scope of this proposition."

"How much time and what's the price?" Though Simon was simply the middle man in this transaction, he was 100% responsible for the lives of two teams he'd be sending in after these cyber criminals. Not only was there the likelihood of their personal protection, but they could be part of a crime syndicate. "What are the odds they are working independently or a part of a team?"

"Botswana is almost certainly part of a syndicate who would be involved in every type of extortion, fraud, etc… Palo Alto…hmmm more likely an independent. Learned his trade and probably building his own nest egg." His looked up for his carefully measured response to Simon's initial question. "I can get the intel on whether the Xs are being watched by midnight tomorrow. Two stipulations: I will not be observed or followed from the time I leave here. It will cost $20k unmarked, small bills of course."

"I'll let you know by 1800 tonight." Simon wasn't going forward without this information, so now it was just a matter of Jarrod's commitment level on seeking retribution.

"Per your instructions, I'm going to have you type in a few commands and the registered address for the physical device will come up on the screen. I don't want to know any of it. Up to you if you want to put that in Notepad or not."

Simon responded, "You'd know it anyway with any type of keystroke tracking software on your laptop and looking again later."

"True, but I have a feeling these are not two names and addresses that I'd want to be found with on my person."

"I'm ready when you are" Simon replied.

Jay got up and walked across the room towards the window. "Mr. DeBoy isn't going to walk in on this, right?" The tech kept his face turned away from Simon. He didn't have an uneasy feeling in his gut, but these names and addresses would most certainly go in his 'When I die' folder. He'd never been a part of this type of non-military directed hit; not on active duty and definitely aiding and abetting a possible 1st degree murder; as serious as it could get in either country.

"He won't be back till I text him."

"Alright. Then from Notepad you will see X1 account and the number next to it. Copy that account number and paste it into the window I have open: Republic of Botswana ISP Administration. Halfway down the page on the left, paste that into the customer account cell and click enter."

Simon pasted the entry and clicked Enter. A pop out window opened with the device's model number, serial number, account activation date, balance due, payment due date, first name: Raul, last name: Soares city: Gaborone/Metsimothabe, address: Lot 1941 Mogoditshane. Notes: L4 Apts A-D. Simon typed on the keyboard: Ctrl-A, Ctrl-C and Ctrl-P to paste it into Notepad. "Gotcha X1. I'm gonna see what's behind door A, B, C and D; then you'll see my kind of phishing."

"Ok, do you want me to exit from Botswana or what? Do you need to back out of your access or what?"

"As long as you've got the address copied, you can close out the customer service window. Now navigate to the XFINITY window and the same process."

Simon copied the account number from Notepad and pasted it into the XFINITY account portal. As the account information opened up, he felt the adrenaline course through his body. He hadn't directed a mission in over four years, but all the patterns were falling into place. Capture or kill? This seemed like the latter. Although, now that an American citizen might be involved, who actually lived here on American soil, Jarrod may reconsider.

Miguel & Iovita Sarmento

535 Arastradero Rd. #22

Palo Alto, CA 94306

Home: N/A Cell1: 713-243-3133 Cell2:408-905-4522

Interesting names was Simon's first thought. They may not be US born. Well, they'd definitely need to find out more. Their work here today had gone exceedingly well, and they'd wrap things up here. Now it was up to Jarrod and what he wanted to do next. Simon knew what he'd do if someone had stolen that kind of money from his papa!

"We're done here right Jay? If so, I'll send the text to have them come back."

"Yes, go ahead and X out of XFINITY, then I'm going to shut down a few things, delete some network access log files and we'll be wrapped up."

Simon double checked the Notepad file contents and the information was there for both targets. XFINITY was closed and he pulled out the flash drive. "Can I take out this last wireless card?"

"Sure, we're going to destroy them here in just a minute. Wait another minute on the text." Jay sat down to close out the remaining apps, powered the laptop off and shut the lid. From his laptop bag he removed what looked like a portable blender.

"Wireless card please." Simon still had the last one in his hand and handed it over. Jay unscrewed the half-dome lid on the portable blender. Next, he broke off the flat antennae portion of the device and dropped both pieces in the blender. He screwed the dome cap back on, set the speed to high and pressed the On button. There was a fairly loud crunching, cacophony of breaking plastic bits as the blender efficiently cut it up into pieces between 1/8" and 3/16".

He unscrewed the cap and poured half the contents into one Ziploc bag and the remaining half into another. "You can do it again at your home in the sink garbage disposal." Simon just smiled. The three other wireless cards were ground up and poured into bags; each of them now had four bags.

"Now you can send that text." Jay put the laptop back in his bag and the portable blender in a side pocket. The case was zipped, and he pulled a pre-printed dummy invoice out of the bag. Both men pushed their chairs back from the desk and waited for their hosts to arrive. There would be time for small talk later, both men were drained and charged emotionally.

From outside, they could hear Jarrod and his Father in conversation. Then the front door knob turned, and they reentered the apartment. The senior went right to his recliner and let out a breath. Apparently, they had walked quite a bit and it had taken a toll on the Father. Jarrod spoke up immediately, "Well, how did it go? What did you find?"

Simon stood up taking the center of attention. "It's as you had supposed, but we actually found two very interesting viruses from completely different sources. So we identified them and now you can decide whether to fully disable them, reimage the machine or buy a new one just to be safe." The inferences were immediately grasped by Jarrod and he could tell they'd need to have a discussion; possibly with or without Jay.

"Well, thanks. We both appreciate you cleaning it up and I'll take your advice on what to do with the computer. What do we owe you?"

Jay handed Jarrod the invoice, "I've got an invoice here for you. Just drop a check in the mail unless you have cash."

"Jarrod's always carrying around cash," his Father piped in. "Loves paying in cash ever since I can remember."

Jarrod smiled as he looked at the invoice. Continuing to act in character, he frowned a little at the bill and said, "Well, I guess that's what virus removal costs these days." Taking out his money clip, he removed two $100 bills and handed them to Jay.

"Can you write 'Paid in Full' with today's date on it?"

Jay took the invoice back and wrote it out. Handing it back, he said, "I can recommend a few good desktop models and the software I'd recommend to prevent this from happening again."

"Sure, that would be helpful." Turning towards his Dad, he said, "Let's go ahead and not use the computer again. We'll get a new one set up in a couple days for you Dad. Is that ok?"

"Oh, sure son. I don't really use it too much these days."

"I'm going to walk them out and we're still on for the barbeque this Saturday. Clay and the family are coming over. I can pick you up around 11:30." Jay collected his laptop bag and pushed the chair back under the desk. Simon had moved his chair back to the dinette.

"Uh, right. Yes." His Father replied with a little uncertainty.

"I'll call you Saturday morning Dad; for a quick reminder."

They all headed to the door and Jarrod let the technicians out before him. With a quick wave, Jarrod said, "Bye Dad. Love you and I'll see you soon."

Looking at the techs, the senior DeBoy said "Thank you gentlemen and have a good day." Then moving his eyes to Jarrod, he said, "Thanks again son and I'll see you later."

Jarrod twisted the door knob lock and shut the door behind them. "Well, that seems to have gone very well. What are our next steps?"

Simon looked back over his shoulder, "We'll need to sit and discuss a few options. Your house?"

"Yes, that'll work."

They arrived at the elevator and once they entered it, Jarrod reached into his inside pocket to retrieve the remaining portion of the cash payment. $4800 made a nice, thick envelope. It was unsealed, and Jay opened it briefly, thumbed through the 100s and was satisfied that it was the agreed upon amount.

Jay looked at Jarrod and told him, "Thank you. Maybe we'll work together again soon."

They all exited the elevator deep in discussion about the upcoming Giants and A's baseball series that weekend. McInnis was there making a mental note of them. There was only one other family at that time in the lobby as they stepped on the weight sensor tiles, which opened the front sliding doors. Back out into the bright sunlight; each person heading to their respective car. Simon looked nervously over his shoulder to Jarrod and said, "I'll see you in about 20 minutes."

"Yeah, see you then." Jarrod replied while his mind began to click through the sequence of the day. He altered the route back to his parked car, taking a more circuitous route. He wondered if he was being over the top melodramatic. Would anyone be looking for him? Had Jay tripped any alarms, and could he be traced through him?

CHAPTER 7

He jumped in the car and gripped the wheel very tightly with both hands. His white knuckles stood out as a reminder that he needed to relax. Did they accomplish what they had set out to do today? It seemed that everything was falling into place, but he couldn't be sure until he talked with Simon in 20 minutes. Until then, he needed to distract himself and not worry over questions that would be answered very shortly.

It was an uneventful drive home and in the ten minutes of driving his grip had lightened considerably. The garage door opened and he slid the silver Tesla rocket into its place. He decided to leave the garage door open and putter around in the garage—maybe clean something. That always relaxed him. Cleaning things up was enjoyable and then having the satisfaction afterwards.

He opened a cabinet in the corner of the garage and pulled out his bike vice. It was a necessity with his bikes not having a kick stand like his childhood bikes.

Taking his Trek off the wall, he always admired how incredibly light and balanced it felt in his hands. Placing the center vertical tube in the bike clamp, he gave it two full turns and it was locked in securely.

Jarrod had installed an 8-foot-long workbench along the backside of the garage. The top of it was a Corian surface with grey, white and black shaped pebbles. He found the lubricant for his chain and grabbed the combination wrench to tighten up his brakes. He went through each of the seven gears, while adding 2-3 drops of the chain oil directly onto the rear sprocket. He'd turn the pedals with his right hand for 5 full rotations to ensure it was covered completely.

When the chain and gears were finished, he replaced the oil and went to the garage sink to wash his hands. He checked the clock and had successfully killed 10 minutes. He dried off his hands and returned to the bike. Jarrod made slight adjustments to the front and rear brakes and took a mental note to get new brakes pads the next time he was at the bike shop.

With the brakes tightened, he took out a light cleaner and rag to set about wiping down his bike. The underside of all the tubes were where most of the road grime stuck. He methodically cleaned each tube and smiled. The fireside red paint was dazzling now after the cleaning. The rims were the last things to address, but Simon pulled up directly in front of the open garage door. The rims could wait.

Simon hopped out of his black Tahoe and said, "Cleaning the orange beast ay?" He carried a laptop bag with him into the garage. He admired the gleam as it was such a contrast to the matte black finish of his bike.

"Yeah, a little grimy after my last victory," he said jokingly. "Go inside?"

Simon replied with a smile. "Yes, let's lock up little Star Trekky here."

Jarrod closed down the garage door and they went through the mud room and into the kitchen. Simon asked him to turn on the TV in the family room. A little background noise wouldn't hurt, and you couldn't be too cautious for what they were about to discuss. Simon pulled out the 4 Ziploc bags of wireless card debris and waved it to his friend. "Jay was really on top of his game. Mind if I run these down your garbage disposal?"

"Go right ahead. What were those?"

"He used a separate wireless card for each type of system he was accessing. These bags have half the ground up portion of each card and he has the other half."

With the water on, Simon poured the bits and pieces into the disposal. The noise generated was just loud enough that neither of them could hear the news. It was a young reporter who looked to be in her early 30s. She had a unique multi-cultural look about her. The bone structure of her face indicated some strong Asian traits, especially around the cheeks and eye sockets. They could only see that she was in Monterey and there was a group protesting behind her.

Once the grinding halted, they could hear her clear, articulated voice over the protestors, "...this is the second time the Monterey Bay Aquarium has had a full grown great white shark. A crowd has gathered here demanding its release back into the Bay. The scientists haven't determined how it was injured, but they think it was hit or cut up by a propeller before being caught in the commercial fishing net. Their goal is to nurse it back to health and then release it back into the ocean."

The cameraman panned the small gathering, which was hardly more than a dozen people. Signs reading "Animal Cruelty", "Fish Prison", "No More Sad Endings."

The reporter continued, "They have placed this 18-foot Great White, weighing approximately 4100 lbs into a special million-gallon tank. You can visit the Aquarium and see this amazing creature for yourself. Is it a man-eater? Are they profiteering from the rescue attempt? Is it truly endangering the shark, or do they have its best intentions at heart? This is Jenna Lee, Channel 7 news, Live from the Monterey Bay Aquarium."

Simon responded to the TV, "Pretty good timing if you ask me. I've seen that Shark Week advertised everywhere for the last few weeks. Now they've got the most adept killing machine around and they'll sell a million tickets. You're a goner if that guy gets a hold of you. I looked it up and a single bite from a Great white can take in up to 31 pounds of flesh and they can also consume a few hundred pounds of food at one setting!"

"So, we need the TV on for noise?"

"Doesn't hurt if you have any nosy, high tech neighbors. What kind of heavy metal music you have around here?"

"I can put on Pandora." Jarrod turned on the audiophile music system and found an appropriate head banging station. Channel 7 news with Rage Against the Machine playing "Bullet in Your Head" as an accompanying music line seemed somewhat appropriate considering their subject matter.

"I can leave the garbage disposal on as well, No?"

Simon looked over and raised his voice above the noise, "Not necessary."

They both seated themselves at the flagstone slab island in the kitchen. Simon pulled out his laptop from the case and thumb drive from his pocket. The awareness level in the room elevated several notches and Simon unlocked the machine with his pass code. Next, the flash drive needed another password. He entered it as the directory appeared. With a dead serious look in his eyes, Simon and Jarrod met each other's gaze.

Simon was always abrupt and to the point. No need to change his approach here. "Jarrod, you know this is much worse than you told me. You must have only looked at one of your Dad's accounts. The account ending in 2806 had $7,000 stolen. But then they phishers got linked to account 6343." The words were sticking in Simon's throat.

Jarrod's face turned ashen and he said hoarsely, "Nooooooo! The long-term care account 6343 funded for the next five years of Dad's assisted living care expenses." He looked over furtively at Simon and groaned, "How much?"

"They wiped it out, $627,000. I'm so sorry buddy. If Jay or I can help you get it back....." and his voice trailed off.

Jarrod was in utter disbelief. $627,000 was gone! How could he have not noticed? Why hadn't the bank stopped the transfers? They had set up a special account and estimated $3,500 a month for the next five years to pay for Dad's assisted living care expenses. Auto-scheduled recurring transfers moved $3500 from 6343 to 2806 on the last banking day of the month. Then on the first banking day of the month Country Manor pulled the monthly rent from 2806. Now it was gone. Wiped out!

Jarrod seethed with anger. The audacity of these crooks invading his father's bank accounts and stealing every penny. Were the other residents at risk? He wanted to punch somebody's face it? He wanted to do more than that. He wanted these people hung or shot by a firing squad. Hell, he wanted to do it himself. "Does Jay think he can get it back?"

"He thinks there's a possibility if he can get back in there fast enough. I'd like him to find out whether these guys are working with someone on the inside of the bank or if they are a part of a syndicate. He'd be willing to go back in for that intel. Cost you $20,000 in small, unmarked bills and he won't have anyone standing over his shoulder."

"Do you trust him."

"I said no results, no pay. I saw what he could do in

ten minutes to uncover X1 and X2; so yeah, we have the right guy. I trust him."

"Jarrod. Before we go any further; you are absolutely certain you want to see this through to completion?"

"Yes, I'm not lying down while someone walks away with my Dad's life savings! It is time someone went after these criminals."

"What if the perp is a woman or a couple? What if it is an American? Does that change anything?"

"I guess we assumed it would be some evil man in a foreign country, thousands of miles away." He paused. "No, it really doesn't change things. There are evil men and women in the world. All things being equal, the punishment shouldn't change based on any physical characteristics."

"Good, I just wanted to check. I felt the same way when we went after any target." Simon opened the Notepad file and highlighted the contact information of the target in Botswana. "We will refer to this guy as A1." He scrolled down to the couple in Palo Alto and highlighted them. "Until we determine whether they are working together or not, the male will be PM1 and the female PF1. No names, ever. Got it?"

"Yes, A1, PM1 and PF1." Jarrod knew this was Simon's end of the business and he would be leading from here on out.

"Being that PM1 and PF1 are here domestically, this leads to another type of concern. In Botswana, you get in, make the hit and return to the safety of home sweet home. PM1 and PF1 are here in our backyard, so it is our best interest to find out whether they are already on a watch list. It may also help us determine whether they are working together or not."

"That type of information isn't going to be found in the White Pages, so I asked Jay what that would cost. He would pull that information for $20k and for our own safety we need to have it done. I won't be stepping into an FBI sting with what we're executing here. He's expecting a message from me by 1800 tonight and he'll have the intel back by tomorrow 2200 at the latest. Jay said we could not observe him accessing the systems and information."

"You trust him completely?"

"Yes, I've trusted him with my life before and I still do."

"Do you want the money right now or wait for tomorrow? How much more information is Jay going to need about the project?"

"I'll get the money before I leave today. If he's watching the local news, he's going to tie PM1 and PF1 with reasonable cause to us. A1 would be more difficult of course. Either way, he's supplying the mission with information we need and linked to us. Let me text him." Simon pulled up his messages and found his last exchange with Jay. He typed:

You are a GO for 20.

"While he's in there checking watch lists, history and such; is there anything else we need? I don't imagine he wants to be poking around more than he has to be."

"If the FBI or another government entity is watching any of these three, he'll take a look at their background and history for any organized crime associations, terrorist groups, etc.… and let us know." Simon's phone chirped, and he saw the reply from Jay,

Got it.

"How soon do we have people start to watch them?"

"Good question, that was my next topic. I had one team of four on standby and they were expecting to travel on short notice. We'll call them Bravo Team, for Botswana. Now we need a second team, locally, Papa Team for Palo Alto. I'll meet with Bravo Team tonight to give them travel and operations money. We need to be in and out in a few days."

Simon had already estimated that it would be $40-100k to fly the team in and out of a non-friendly country. Botswana wasn't like North Korea or Syria, so $50k to be conservative. Living expenses and incidentals for a hit could run up another $50k. Each member was receiving $40k; 20 before and 20 after whether the mission was 100% successful or not. He had felt this was very fair. They were putting their lives at risk, but how else could you earn $40k tax free in a week? And it wasn't like they could use these highly trained skills anywhere else in society.

There were tens of thousands of retired military, but there were only 2,500 or so active duty Navy Seals—Simon felt confident in their training because he had completed it as well. He had known about 100 while serving and had kept in touch with two dozen. These were the men he trusted. While he didn't know if the government was tracking them for certain types of activity or travel, these were the men he'd trust and choose.

"Up front, I'll need $180k for Bravo Team travel, incidentals and that includes the $20k per man. When they get back next week, Lord willing, another $80k and they'll return any of the unused funds. I'll take my $30k as well. So Jay, Bravo and I total $230,000 today."

"Ackh" was about all Jarrod could say and then he quickly corrected himself. "Your $400k ballpark was pretty good. And for Papa Team? No war reparations I guess here?"

"Right, the city of Palo Alto isn't going to pay us to take out their trash and Botswana won't be sending you a thank you note either. Papa Team will be much less for travel, so make it $140k."

"Since we're running up the tab. Can you ask Jay if he can get the money back that these guys have been stealing? Not for me, but to trace back and return the money to the people who have been bilked?"

"I like the idea of getting all the money back, but, I'm not sure that most of those accounts won't have been closed by now, but at least get a list of those who were phished. Then it would be up to you to figure out how to get them the money back. That might take Jay accessing several banking institutions depending on where they've put the money. We can hope they've got it all on hand under their mattresses."

"Check with him. Maybe he'll do it gratis as operation Robin Hood." Jarrod said with a smile.

"I'll run it by him when I give him the 20k tonight."

An idea had begun to form and develop in Jarrod's mind. Thinking aloud, he said to Simon, "You know, I'm doing this for Dad, but I'm really wanting to make a statement to the hacking and phishing criminal element. Seems like most believe they won't be caught, they're doing it outside their borders and believe they wouldn't be extradited. I did some research and it only costs $500 to set up a phishing scam targeting a bank and 50,000,000 emails. F-I-F-T-Y M-I-L-L-I-O-N!"

"But you and I know now that this type of phish can be traced back and yes there is the right to 'privacy' the ISPs will proclaim, but this is criminal activity. If Jay can get us names and addresses, what is our fabulous government doing about the problem? Nothing." Jarrod was agitated, which was something new for Simon to see and hear.

"Yeah, there's a lot of information out there not acted on by our government. You would think $627,000 from your Dad is worth a minute of time from the Feds. It would be to Lafayette police, but they don't have expertise or time to track down cyber criminals. So, it falls through the cracks of law enforcement, but on an aggregate level I'm sure it totals in the millions. If not tens of millions per year. What statement do you want to make, Jarrod?"

"Well, public flogging, guillotine, firing squad and hanging are out of fashion these days."

"Unfortunately," Simon said wryly.

"We need media coverage to make a statement. Bravo and Papa are 8 highly skilled and former Navy Seals. I've got an idea now…and I know it complicates things. Instead of busting in the targets' homes and taking them out, I'd like them removed and transported. Papa would need to travel 90 miles or so and then set up the fatality. Bravo is going to need a flight. Might be an hour; certainly, less than two. Let's look on your laptop at the logistics and I'll explain how we're going to add some fear into the phishing community."

CHAPTER 8

THURSDAY, JUNE 29, 1745 HOURS

Two hours later, the cycling friends had a completely new awareness about each other. The tension had been building and this new bond felt like an emotional cable between them. The steel braided cable able to withstand nature's strongest storms. Their minds were locked in on the purpose and mission. It wasn't the high five type of energy, but more releasing an energy force. In a physical sense like arm wrestlers grabbing each other's right hand before the match. Then gripping with all your might and pulling in to each other's body as a show of strength for the other; locking eyes and knowing this bond was solid and steadfast.

Simon laid out the teams. Each soldier he knew personally and kept tabs on their physical and mental health. Some were more gainfully employed than others, but they were all still capable of executing a mission. Bravo Team had a general awareness that they would be heading out of the country for a quick termination and then back home. He would be meeting with the team late tonight to fill in the blanks.

BRAVO TEAM

Shawn Neilsen: squad leader. Al Loomis, Corey Peterson and Rob Roman were all Navy Seals who Simon had worked with personally.

The newly created Papa Team were also soldiers he had fought with previously and they also maintained an excellent readiness state. The type of short-notice jobs they had picked up over the years were typically reconnaissance or protections. Being caught on this type of mission meant federal prison if you were lucky. If you were caught in an unfriendly country or neighborhood, the price was torture, death or both; thus, the price rose accordingly.

PAPA TEAM

Richard Chew, squad leader. Johnny Senoren, Kendrick Daniels and CJ Lee.

Jarrod had brought up the thought of a single team executing both missions. Simon gave him several reasons why that wouldn't work. These missions were going to hit on the same day to enhance the media storm. Additionally, if there were an injury or worse from the first mission, another soldier or several would need to be brought in, briefed on the mission and valuable time would be lost. It was much easier to have both teams in place from the outset. Simon would be meeting with Bravo Team tonight at 2100.

They both were a little tense and exhausted from the planning session. Jarrod said, "Let me get the money now. Do you have a duffle bag or backpack, or can I give you one?"

Simon answered, "I've got one out in the Tahoe, so I'll go grab it." He got up from his barstool and noticed the crushing chords of "More Human Than a Human" by White Zombie.

Jarrod got up also and headed down the hall to the den. His desk in the den held a fingerprint enabled gun safe. He felt a lot better having his Smith & Wesson .40 tucked in his waistband since he was pulling nearly a quarter of a million dollars out. He had four of these in the house - the den, master bedroom, downstairs in the game room and another in the garage. It wasn't like you could stage where you'd be if an intruder forced their way into your home.

He pushed the Gould & Goodrich brown leather holster and Sig into the small of his back. Next, he opened the den safe and tucked neatly in the back were five banded stacks of hundred-dollar bills; $10,000 a bundle. The thought crossed his mind that he better get to work to replace this cash. He headed downstairs to the game room for the big safe. Game room was a bit of an understatement.

The room was nearly 1,200 square feet and set into the naturally sloped edge of the lot. The wall where the stairs were placed faced the inside of the house and sat against the earth. The north and south walls had windows and the front right corner held a mud room for anyone leaving the pool dripping. There were two sets of French doors leading out to the pool and Jarrod pulled down the blinds over them and the other windows while he accessed the safe.

There was a massive 8-foot copper brown leather couch with recliners built in and it faced the northern wall and state of the art big screen TV. A few feet to the left of the TV was a door for the audio-visual equipment. The small room held two amplifiers, satellite receiver, Blu-ray and universal remote receptor. The door opened inwards and was practically the depth of the small audio cove. Rich walnut paneling lined the interior walls. There was only a two by three-foot square area to stand, but that was the only place to stand, the swinging door closed from the inside out in order to access the panel and safe behind it.

This was also an emergency hideout for one person or two in a pinch. The door hinges were not accessible from the outside and the special door had a fire rated outer shield. A massively thick steel plate was placed in the core and capable of stopping anything short of a LARS rocket. The surrounding walls and ceiling had the same plates welded to surround the audio closet. There were two small horizontal vents on each wall, one-half inch by three inches with heavy gauge steel grating.

The walnut panels were joined at the inside corners by a half-round strip of trim, which could be slipped off. The longer wall panel was divided in half vertically and by an ornately carved, half-round piece of trim. Jarrod appreciated the details in the trim-work. There was also a carved grapevine sub panel which was at eye level. Measuring from the floor, it started at the 60th inch and was 12 inches high. This was the panel which covered the keypad for the safe.

The walnut paneling was glued to the safe door and if someone were tapping the walls, listening for a hollow sound, they would only hear a very solid note in return. The steel plate on the longer wall gave a very similar sound back. The carved panel covering the safe keypad was actually cut in a manner to slide up and down, allowing the combination entry. The keypad was programmed to allow only one entry every 3 hours.

He had recently changed the code, so he had to pull out his phone and look at the keypad. This safe combination was always a word, translated into a number, which was why he had to look for the number to letter conversation on the keypad. It was CHESIRE, but backwards 3747342. Why not? He should smile when opening his safe.

This safe held $450,000 in cash; you never knew when you were going to find a treasure. Cash always talks and he could flip art fairly quickly now with his sister's help. He had contacts who would come to him when they needed to move an object. But this wasn't like a simple pawn broker. The items could be quite expensive, could be appraised and the seller was in dire need for cash. Jarrod counted out the stacks he needed to get this mission launched. The bound stacks of $10,000 and $20,000 in $100 bills had considerable weight in the rucksack.

Glancing for a moment at the shelves and contents,

everything was in place; even the exploding dye packet between the cases of mint condition coin sets from the early 1900s. There were a dozen ingots each of gold, silver and platinum and pre-IPO stock certificates.

He closed the safe door with a solid *thunk* and pressed the * key on the keypad. When you pressed the * key, it activated the lock immediately. If you did not, there was an extra 5 seconds to pull the door open before the locks engaged. Next, he pushed down the small panel covering the keypad. He looked at the wall with admiration, fine craftsmanship. The joints were spectacular, tight and true. He stepped back in order to pull the audio room open.

Simon would be patiently waiting upstairs for him. He closed the door and strode across the entertainment room towards the stairs. Taking the stairs, two at a time, he found his General seated again at the island counter. Sipping on water, Simon glanced up and set his glass down. Jarrod set the mini fortune on the counter in between them and began pulling out the stacks of bound $100-dollar bills.

Placing them in stacks of $100,000, there were four stacks and the remaining $50,000 next to the last stack. "There it is, a little travelling money for your boys."

Shaking his head, Simon said, "Remind me to review your home security when this is all done. And I'd also like a few cash money-making strategies as a gift to a friend."

With a small final shake of his head, he said with slight amusement, "Who has this kinda loot in their house?"

Jarrod ignored his final question and said, "Ok, what's next?"

"Do you want to do some recon in Palo Alto with me tomorrow? It'll look more natural if two of us are riding or running together. Probably not riding, your bike stands out like a beacon. We'll go pound some pavement for a few miles around the location. We need to see what's on the ground and make some plans about how Papa Team is getting in and out."

"Ok, I'll at least be your alibi. Want me to drive or get a rental car?"

"Better if you can you take your car in the shop and get a loaner. Any recalls or work coming up?"

"I'll find something on the Tesla. Their loaner will blend in better in Palo Alto. What time do you want me to pick you up?" Jarrod inquired.

"Come by around ten hundred hours," Simon replied as he eased up from the bar stool.

Jarrod got up as well to walk out to the driveway with him. Ironically, AC DC was playing "Dirty Deeds Done Dirt Cheap". The grinding chords playing and the monologue came on Jarrod quickly sang inserted, *"Great White"* as a method of death.

Simon opened the door and smiled; looking at his financier, employer and cycling partner. "See you tomorrow as a runner."

"Yes, ten o'clock and ready to run. We've got to be back by 3pm. I've got to pretty up for a hot date."

The double alarm chirp of Simon's big, black Tahoe sounded as the driver door unlocked. The car seemed to gleam a little more as if it knew it would be transporting a significant amount of cash this day. He backed it down the half-round driveway and was off to start their private counter-cyber-attack team.

All the tension of the last few hours had given Jarrod the intense desire to exercise. He hadn't lifted weights in 2 days and this would be a great time for back and chest. He found exercise a great way to slow down time, his mind and muscles forcing movement on the barbells and gravity. He would put his subconscious mind to work on challenges he was about to face. Lifting also took the focus from the problem and diverted it to the task bench pressing or squatting; it really helped with the stress.

When he had the house constructed a secondary building was included as a gym studio. No waiting for equipment at the gym any longer. The room was 20 x 30, with the longer side parallel to the swimming pool. It sat back about 30' from the pool and the entire wall facing the pool was covered in glass. Jarrod threw on some gym clothes, took the stairs double time down to the theater room, out the rear French doors, down the sidewalk on the edge of the pool, then opened the door to the gym. He started solving the problems of the world on the incline bench with two 70-pound dumbbells.

CHAPTER 9

THURSDAY, JUNE 29, 1900 HOURS, 501 SILVERADO DR., LAFAYETTE

In less than 24 hours, Bravo Team would be flying out of SFO and on their way to Botswana via Munich and Johannesburg, South Africa. He had to admit, he felt more like a character in a Marvel Superhero movie than Robin Hood. Who didn't want to get the bad guy and be a hero? He couldn't do this indefinitely, but these two missions he was sponsoring should bring about some justice in the world.

According to Jay, their techie hacker, he might be able to recoup and refund a substantial amount to those who had been phished. Any extra money this guy had lying around he'd must be returned. But if he didn't receive a single dime back, he'd be at peace defending his Dad and seeking retribution for all those others Soares and the Sarmento's had stolen from these past years.

Tomorrow was going to be a time constrained day. He'd be driving down to Palo Alto with Simon and jogging for an hour or two. The drive back would be 90 minutes for sure. Jarrod was no military scout and knew he wasn't doing much more than taxiing Simon and maybe offer an alibi as a jogging partner. It was going to be interesting nonetheless. Tomorrow night was the big date with Lorrie. He hadn't had a meaningful date in months. Ha, probably more like 2 years. Better figure out a few good questions to ask.

Jarrod wanted to go into the night with as few preconceived notions as possible. He wanted to be relaxed and just enjoy a dinner and conversation with what he hoped to be an intriguing woman. Of course, he had judged her by external appearance. Her business suit, hair, physical features, white gold Michelle watch, diamond earrings, diamond bracelet and the Land Rover. There was always a physical judgement and bias. Every person he'd met had a bias or preference. Tall, petite, brunette, blond, leggy, rumpy, busty, glasses, athletic and the list could go on and on.

It was time to show some interest and reconfirm. How to be interested, yet not too interested. Better yet, quit over-thinking and just call her to confirm. He was reminded of the quote yet again in moments like these: If you have the slightest doubt you're over-thinking or procrastinating, you are. ACT NOW! He pulled out his phone and dialed, without scripting his words in advance.

Ring-ring, ring-ring, ring-ring.....doubt crept into his thoughts momentarily.

She answered. It was the voice he had instantly

liked, she picked up and said, "Well, hello Jarrod."

His face was turning red and thankfully he was at home alone. "Oh, hi Lorrie. I'm just confirming dinner tomorrow." Did he say it too fast? Was there any feeling? Did he sound like a robocall?

She obviously appreciated the call and her voice warmed up immediately. "Yes, of course and thanks for calling."

She was waiting for him now. There was that awkward pause; like after a first kiss or dance. Was he slow or what? Was it right to ask how was your day, when he didn't have a clue what would comprise her normal day? Think brother and then he said the only thing he could think of through the fog crowding his brain, "Great, um you're welcome. Uh, I'll wait out front for you, but not in my bike kit." He laughed and tried to recover real quick, "Bad joke, anyhow I'm sure I'll relax by tomorrow and now that I've said way too much I'll get off the phone before you cancel on me." And he laughed at himself.

Lorrie snickered in a cute, short laugh. "I'm not cancelling. Sounds like we're both going to need a glass of wine. Thank you again, Jarrod and I'll see you tomorrow—and not in your bike kit." She said, and he could hear the smile in her voice.

"Alright, see you tomorrow Lorrie. Bye."

"Night." And the phones disconnected.

Good Lord, he might need more than a personal shopper to pass this date test! He was not going to overanalyze that conversation. Geez Louise. Maybe this was the reason he didn't date much. What did his granddaughter say? "Awkward!"

He heard his doorbell ring and this was the part of tomorrow night that would be correct. It was his personal shopper, Lynsay Crawford. He'd met her years ago at a Business Networking International meeting. She did it for a living and he didn't have an eye for it, nor the time. So he hired her two to three times a year, she'd update his wardrobe, even shoes! This had been a rush request, but he had given her the particulars of the date night. He had told her as much as he could about Lorrie and here she was with her choices.

Jarrod opened the door and welcomed Lynsay inside. "Hello Lynsay and thanks for picking things up on such short notice."

"This is so exciting Jarrod, ah ha! A date and almost a blind date with some princess who has caught your eye. I must say, this is going to be a magical dinner."

Jarrod laughed, "Not if you heard me tripping over my words a few minutes ago. You'd have brought a clown suit for sure."

"I daresay. Women are looking for honesty and if you're a little nervous, no worries. If it's a match, it's a match and you'll both become more comfortable after a few sentences. If it wasn't meant to be, c'est la vie." She said it nonchalantly.

"Here let me help you with the clothes. Please sit here," as he offered Lynsay a seat in the front room and motioned to the couch. Lynsay was about ten years younger than he, which made him more comfortable with her selections. She was a striking blond, always perfectly fashioned, though perpetually 30 pounds overweight. She always asked how long he rode his bike to stay in such great shape. He always replied, it's nutrition Lynsay. 80% if not more. Exercise only impact about 20% of your health and waistline.

"You've been in the sun I can see. Not to worry, I half expected that and let's see, we've got an evening dinner, great Italian food, plenty of daylight left. Princess Lorrie prefers lighter colors to accentuate her complexion. Give her my number and I'll make you the most smashing couple in LaMorinda."

Jarrod loved Lynsay; she did all the talking. In fact, he felt quite certain she could carry the entire conversation and make the choices. But she was actually an excellent personal shopper and represented a hundred or more clients in the Bay Area.

Lynsay continued without hardly taking a breath. "You're nearly the same complexion, wears white like a virgin bride. Oh no, you said she was divorced, and it couldn't have been from no sex. She had kids you mentioned. Ok, white because she might be a little or a lot OCD. White at an Italian restaurant!" It was a constant stream of words as she began assembling the outfits.

"Here you are Jarrod. These are my top three choices for tomorrow evening and I won't tell you which I prefer the most on you, but I already know which one she'd like the best. Yes, you would like to know. Now go try them on and come out and let's have a look. He had 3 sets of shoes, socks, slacks and shirts.

"There are eight pair of underwear as well. Time to get rid of what you have in case you haven't recently. Don't worry about those right now, just try on the ensemble."

Jarrod replied, "Yes, mommy dearest." Dripping with sarcasm. "Give me a minute since I don't have to match up the underwear now."

"Go, go. Do you have a same-day dry cleaner? Use Fiona's over on 1st Street, she's the best."

Jarrod normally didn't take the time for the modeling of outfits for Lynsay. After his confidence grew in her choices, he would typically buy sight unseen. She would snap a photo for his reference of which shirts, slacks and shoes would go together best and send the clothes along. This was different though. Princess Lorrie, yes indeed. I need to at least look like a Prince and at some point my mouth will catch up with my brain. I'll just be quiet until then.

He looked at the three combinations for Friday's dinner. He could see himself wearing any of them. The question was, which would he feel the most confident wearing? He heard her yelling, "Come on prince charming, get some clothes on for Lorrie and show me." He laughed out loud. Jarrod could see Lynsay planting herself at the restaurant just to see him and Lorrie, colors, clothing, etc... "Be there in a minute Miss Impatient!"

Jarrod went with outfit number two and it took only one step and Lynsay half shrieked, "You picked it, we're so like-minded. Yes, that's the one. Turn dear Jarrod. My, my look at your beep." She censored her thought. "Those pants fit perfectly. Dear Princess

Lorrie, you can thank me later for picking out these pants."

"Ding, ding! Looks like we have a consensus. I'll go with these tomorrow night Lynsay. I really appreciate you fixing me up on such short notice. Should I wear a watch? She had one on; white gold or platinum."

"Yes, but let's not get all matchy-matchy with it. Hers had a rectangular face, right? Roman numerals or what were they? Show her some money sugar daddy J. What do you have in white gold or platinum? Rolex, something Swiss? Anything over $5k?"

"You mean I can't wear my red GShock that matches my bike? Just kidding Lyns. I have had my eye on one down at Davidson & Licht. It was a Brietling Avenger II. Traditional steel with black face, waterproof and 43 mm. Want me to pull up a picture on my phone?

"No, I trust you on this one."

"So I'll take all the clothes and shoes of course. Any first date tips from Madame Lynsay?"

Cologne…

In typical machine gun style and very succinct, Lindsay said, "Sure be REAL and open yourself up a bit. You don't have to bare it all, but relax and be transparent enough so she can see and feel what a good person you are. Be interest<u>ed</u>, not interest<u>ing</u>. Family, Women are more interested in family than anything else. Keep your ex-wife and girlfriends out of every conversation. Don't compare—enjoy discovering who Lorrie is. Figure out what you want. Girlfriend, wife, lover? What do you really want? No playing around."

"Ok, that helps. I appreciate you Lyns; especially for your honesty."

"Hey, you had the gumption to ask her out. Be REAL and pull down those huge walls for 2 hours. If she's right and it's the right time, she'll do the same. Gotta run before you start asking me sex-ed questions. Hahaha!" She laughed hysterically at herself and got up from the couch.

They gave a big, tight hug and Jarrod thanked her again. "Drive safe and talk to you soon."

"You better let me know how it went Mister. I'm expecting a phone call next week or a selfie with you two on an exotic beach in the South Pacific."

He walked with her to the car and she repeated one more time softly, "Be real Jarrod. Goodnight."

"Goodnight Lynsay."

CHAPTER 10

FRIDAY, JUNE 30, 0545 HOURS

Simon had attacked this mission from every angle and when it came down to it, he didn't view it much differently than the wars he had been in for his country. He had sworn to defend and protect the United States of America; some of the orders he had received and carried out had not been easy. Of course, he could walk away from this mission, but he saw it as an extension of his military service. Why not take care of a few more scumbags on this earth who were bent on ruining people financially? These cyber criminals were attacking the most susceptible people in society.

He would meet with Bravo team at 1900 hours to fill their wallets for the expenses and their labor. However, more importantly, Simon would be examining their mental condition and commitment. A formal test wouldn't be applied, but he would know based on their reactions to the plan and the look in their eyes if they were ready. He had a few backups in mind, but time was slipping quickly and this team had to move out.

Simon had begun compiling a list almost immediately of supplies they could take and those the team would need to purchase once in Botswana. There wouldn't be any residential building these teams couldn't access and kidnapping a pair of terrorists was something they had experienced overseas. Typically, the mission wasn't to bring people out alive and for this mission it was requested that they not be injured before the event. Simon had explained to Jarrod they would do their best, but sometimes more force was required to subdue the criminal.

1900 would come soon enough. For now, Simon's mind would have to disengage from the virtual battlefield, so he could enjoy the late afternoon with his wife and kids. He pulled into his neighborhood on the San Ramon ridge. Simon was pretty sure he was the only one driving through with $400 grand in a knap sack. He laughed out loud at the thought. You could create quite a bit of financial or real estate leverage with this kind of money.

Simon preferred that the men not meet their benefactor, Jarrod, and vice versa. These men had an extremely important plan to execute in less than a week and Bravo Team had to leave the country at least before tomorrow evening. The flight alone would take 28 hours from the States, over the Arctic pole, down into Europe, then to North Africa and maybe a quick puddle jump to Botswana.

These four soldiers had worked side by side in Afghanistan and then again in Iraq. After leaving the service, he knew each had done a little private work and in fact Simon had them take care of a job for himself. Simon had reserved a room for the day at a Regus business office. He had used the offices in the early years of incorporation and business ventures. He knew the management well enough that they would allow him to hold meetings at odd hours.

This suite of offices that Regus sublet were on the 14th floor of a 20 story, glass framed business office, right next to the 680 corridor in Walnut Creek. There would be moderately heavy traffic and they would all leave plenty early to arrive on time. Coffee, tea, restrooms, a private meeting room with comfortable chairs; all made for a more expedient pre-mission brief.

When he arrived at the Regus center, he parked as he normally would down in the parking garage. Parking was easy to find this night as many of the employees began clearing by 1700 and 1800. He expected very few people to notice the five men in non-business attire who were meeting this evening. If a stranger were to open Simon's black leather billfold, it would have made an easy conversation starter. There were flight confirmations to Botswana, hotel reservations and sight-seeing brochures for South Africa.

The thick envelopes of money would have grabbed their attention. Each soldier would receive their money up front and likely they'd be placing it in their personal safe or a safe deposit box. Everybody needs a stash for their cash—married or not. You don't fly under the government's banking system radar by depositing $40,000 and that was another reason why they were getting their money the night before their early morning flight.

As Simon got out of his car, he maneuvered his body, so he could scan the entire parking garage floor. The garage had sufficient lighting to keep it well lit, despite being underground. Parking spaces were easily three-quarters empty and he didn't spot any movement. He pushed the power lock button on the driver's side door and closed it shut with a solid *whoomph*. He walked at a moderate clip towards the elevator. He felt for his pulse and commanded it to be 120/75.

The cleaning crew put in a major effort with the parking lot sweeper running nightly, to the immaculately polished marble interior of the elevators and the rest rooms. Maybe that is why Simon appreciated this business complex; it was maintained with incredible standards. He wasn't certain what brand of cleaner they were using here, but he liked the light industrial scent.

Simon pressed the button to the 14th floor and it rode uninterrupted to his destination. The elevator doors slid open nearly without sound and he headed to his right towards the open reception area. He often wondered how they treated him - with such gratitude and kindness even though he rented office space less frequently than ever. They were either really nice people or their occupancy rate wasn't meeting the standard. The evening receptionist with her standard issue, post 2010, medium width, black, oval shaped eyeglasses greeted him with a stunning smile. If she smiled that way at every man, she would never lack for dinner dates.

"Hello Mr. Delgado. How was your day today?" She said with a personal, yet professional, tone.

"Thank you, it has been a busy week of planning. We haven't met before. What's your name?"

She stood up and with her hand outstretched said, "I'm Selena" as their hands shook quickly. It was pronounced with both E's as short vowels.

"Nice to meet you Selena and how was your day?" Simon tried to find a friendly tone in his voice and not make more eye contact than appropriate for a married man.

"Pretty non-eventful, but that comes with the job," she said with a little disappointment in her voice.

"I'm expecting four more business partners in the next 30 minutes. I'm still assigned to the Tahoe room? Can you please point the gentlemen back to me?"

"Yes, Mister Delgado. You do have the Tahoe room and I'll send them back as they arrive." Selene added with a wicked smile, "Let me know if you need anything else tonight." Her lips curved enticingly as her voice lingered on the word tonight.

Simon just smiled and waved as he turned to the right and walked down past several empty cubicles. The thought was not going to cross his mind, what she could have been alluding to with her final remark. Then his life flashed before him with an image of his wife and a smoking .45 in her hands. She had said she'd only get angry once with him! As he walked along the cubicles, the uniformity disturbed him. Simon appreciated tidiness and order in life, but these empty, redundant, bland office spaces were misery. The last place he'd ever want to spend 40 hours a week, let alone a few hours of a day.

With his billfold in one hand, he walked up to the last room along the corridor and found the Tahoe door placard. He opened the door and the motion detector sent the signal to the overhead lights and illuminated the room. He set the black billfold at the head of the oval, mahogany laminate table. It did have a nice finish, but looked nothing like real solid wood. It was almost too polished.

There wouldn't be any fancy PowerPoint presentation or slick sales pitch in this room tonight. Just the balls to the wall plan. They had a little over 4 days to complete this job. Fly in to Botswana, locate the target, cover their trail and back out. Just complete the mission and wipe one piece of scum off the planet. Dirty Deeds, but not done dirt cheap. The song reverberated in his head. *"Concrete, shoes, cyanide, TNT, DONE DIRT CHEAP!"*

They would not be receiving printed instructions. They would receive two items tonight in their folders. The first thing they would see in the left inside pocket of the folder would be their plane tickets. These were the tickets that could only be linked to a cash buyer. The buyer had walked into the Premiere Travel downtown office in Walnut Creek, handed the young travel agent a typed letter of instructions and cash. It had been a bit mysterious to the agent, but she wasn't one to turn down a 20% cash tip on top of the easiest, walk-in sale ever.

The illegal border crossing was the riskiest. Crossing at just the right spot and undetected. This is where the scouting and timing had to be perfecto. Ideally, this crucial segment in the plan would go off without a hitch. The return crossing would be just Bravo Team; hopefully all of them and without pursuit and gunfire.

Simon had laid out the four black folders. Two on each side of the table in the seats closest to his own. He had left the door open and heard two pairs of shoes walking towards the room. Bravo Team was arriving. Entering the door first was Richard Chew, squad leader. Following right behind him was Rob Roman. He gave each a firm handshake and greeting. Richard sat at the right-hand seat closest to Simon. Bravo Team knew he was running this op. Kendrick Daniels and CJ Lee arrived just three minutes after; the equivalent time to wait for the next elevator drop off and pickup.

Bravo Team was seated, and Simon closed the door to get the meeting started. From a standing position, Simon began the meeting with a quiet yet intense voice, "Bravo Team." He let that sink in for a long second. "I'm glad you're here, ready and able to complete this mission. This is not your government or General giving you orders. You are each contract employees, yet a team responsible for each other's lives. You are bound by your word and being paid 70% in advance; cash.

We have one target, who may or may not have protection. You will find your airplane tickets inside your folders and you can see this is a quick hit and run. I want you back stateside by Thursday morning July 6."

"Your target is Mr. Raul Soares." He took a breath and continued. At the very least, Soares is a cybercriminal. He works and likely lives at the same address: Gaborone/Metsimothabe, address: Lot 1941

Mogoditshane. The intelligence is less than 24 hours old and we are accelerating the time to make a statement. You will have another strike team working in parallel, in another country."

Simon had their full attention. There was no fiddling with airline tickets, no one checking their smart phones. These men knew what was at stake and, for the next 4 days, they would be laser focused.

"You will be in pairs for the next 96 hours without exception. Botswana is not a friendly country, though you will need to hire a few locals. I am going to outline your mission and once Bravo Team has left U.S. airspace, Chew is your ranking officer."

Richard Chew sat up a little bit straighter and took a visibly deeper breath in his lungs. Everyone looked over and he quickly nodded his head. He was comfortable being a field sergeant and had lived through many fire fights for his country. As a contractor, he'd only done this once and it was for Gearhardt. The adrenaline was something else. Not only were you fighting for your life, but if caught, the government wasn't standing behind you. The government or police would be chasing you down.

"This is how I see it going down." Simon continued on with a steady, intense voice. "You fly out of SFO tomorrow at 2045 and it's an 11 hour 20 minute flight from SFO to Munich with a four hour layover. Munich to Johannesburg is another 10 hours and 35 minutes and a nearly 5 hour layover. Then to Botswana is another hour. Arrival is 1330 local time. Adjust your sleep and body clock accordingly. You are tourists, ha." Simon let out a small laugh. "Stays less than

30 days, you are not required to have a tourist Visa. You must have six months of validity remaining on your passport, one blank page on your passport and there are no special vaccinations required."

"You have a print out for the Big 5 Safari which are held in Zimbabwe and Botswana. You will be staying at the Lensmore Hotel, which is five clicks from Soares. Recon in pairs, it will be a Saturday strike, so his movements may change accordingly. There is a problem with police corruption, especially among junior officers. So you might have a chance to buy yourself out of a situation. You will need to acquire weapons there."

Not a peep from Bravo Team yet. "Everyone's passports good?" Each man removed their passport, opened them up to a blank page and passed to Chew. He scanned them quickly for the expiration date and cleared his throat, "All good here sir." He handed them back to each soldier. Customs and passports weren't a problem in the Navy. You were brought in and you were legal, done; courtesy of Uncle Sam.

"Once Soares is subdued, you will be transporting him to the kill zone. This is where it gets interesting; listen real closely." Simon placed both hands on the table and leaned forward. His fingers were curled under the lip of the table. Each member of Bravo team sat up a little straighter and leaned slightly forward. This is what they'd signed up for, but didn't have all the details. Taking a life was taking a life, but Simon had said this would be out of the ordinary.

Unlike war, they would not want this to look like your average war casualty. Bravo Team would be setting up an execution which would be seen as a horrifying accident. Though it may not make the mainstream news worldwide, the intention was to shake up the cyber-criminal world. A majority of these cyber punks felt untouchable, hiding behind their firewall or country's border. Their crimes were typically targeting Americans and Europeans and they wouldn't face extradition for these seemingly petty cyber thefts. A slap on the wrist, maybe a little time in jail and then they'd be out phishing again.

Once in a while, as these cyber criminals were going to discover, you picked the wrong target. In this instance, the ultimate penalty of the criminal life would devour them. When you steal, you risk stealing from someone with resources, desire and highly skilled friends.

Half an hour later, Simon was wrapping up the debrief. "Papa Team. Chew is your command. Senoren number two, Daniels three and then Lee. Bravo Team. Neilsen is your command, Peterson number two, Loomis three and Roman. Absolutely no unnecessary risks, stay in pairs, come home, pick up your 30%, lay low and go back to life." From the two inside pockets of his windbreaker, he pulled out four envelopes with the $40,000 cash. He opened each envelope, pulled out the cash so each member could thumb through it. Payday. Rarely in life does one get paid in advance and here each soldier had just picked up $40,000 in tax-free dollars with one, heavy string attached to it.

It wasn't just a matter of someone taking a risk. The risks were deathly real. In order to even be considered for this risk, these men had been trained by the best Navy Seal officers for years and had successfully executed mission after mission. They had honed their craft, maintained their mental and physical disciplines and were now ready to jump back into the fray.

Chew's response was a slight nod as he raised his eyebrows slightly. Kendrick let out a quick, "Yo, cash-money. Come into my wallet." Neilsen and Roman both let out simultaneous, short, quiet whistles under their breath when handling the cash. They were all acutely aware of the risk-exchange-value, but this could shave years off their time in corporate America. These stacks represented years of take-home pay at their civilian jobs and it also clarified the highest level of risk they were taking for a few short days of their life.

Simon handed each soldier a box cutter. They were brand new and millions of them sold every year for general use in warehouses. These cutters were 4 inches in length and about 3/16" wide. A standard razor blade dropped down into the holder and protected the user by sliding the inner-frame into the handle. The handle was nothing more than a flat piece of metal folded over at an inch with just enough room for the frame to slide in between.

The expense money was in a fifth envelope that Simon handed to Chew. "$50Gs for incidentals and you will account for it." He looked at the others, "Gentlemen, extra protection for this guy; he's got the money bag and you might need it to get out of a bind and back home."

Chew took time to fan through the $50,000 in unmarked bills. U.S. dollars were the best currency anywhere. Especially good for bribes, guns and transportation in foreign countries." Yes sir. All will be accounted for by me." Then he looked up with an innocent face to add, "Receipts?" They all got a laugh out of that to ease the tension. Talking about a job and saying you'd do it were measured precursors; this was now officially show time at T-minus 10 hours.

Very rarely would Simon F-bomb, but he felt with these soldiers now was the time. "No fucking around at all! This is just as serious as any of the fights we've been in together against enemies of the U.S. There could be booby traps and you're just as likely to be up against fully automatic weapons as not. Do not. I repeat, do not, for one-minute underestimate Soares or who may be protecting him. We could only peer into our U.S. watch lists and he isn't a target, but that does not clear him elsewhere."

The level of intensity just shot up to Defcon 1. The momentary elation from the cash had slid to an abrupt halt, just as the actual cash had at the bottom of their pockets. This was the instant before your jump instructor positioned you to jump out the open airplane door at a low elevation 8,000 foot jump. It was the same feeling when your entire abdomen locks up and your muscles tense for the jump out of the plane. The moment in your mind where you notice everything in slow motion and your brain captures it for recall later. There are no other thoughts other than you are about to leap out of the plane's safety and into the sky of no handholds.

"Any questions Bravo Team?" Simon looked to each soldier and held their gaze.

In unison, they said "No Sir."

"Then, this meeting is over, and you are all free to go. Stay paired up and I will see you all Monday evening." Simon felt the tension drain from his body as they walked out the door and down the hallway. These few moments, he would replay the meeting, ensure everything was communicated. He would not receive another communication until tomorrow at 0400, when they were all due at the airport to fly out. Chew and he had already set up their blacked Wickr encryption messaging. Both of their phones had a kill command which would physically wipe the memory and then destroy the internals of the phone.

This could be done remotely as well. They could not risk the phones being compromised if something went wrong. In fact, each soldier had it installed on their phone. When they touched down late Sunday night in JFK, Simon would notify them their phones were going to be destroyed and activate the kill process. They would have ten minutes to get to a restroom. The phone would begin to incinerate and once they saw the phone finish smoldering, they would simply drop them in the toilet and flush. This was for everyone's protection.

Each phone would have a strip of thermite adhered to the back of the case and a magnesium strip fuse laid in between the phone case and the length of the thermite. Industrial pyro technicians would understand the capabilities of the brief bursts of high temperatures. It was essentially a pocket micro-thermite bomb with a magnesium fuse, which would completely destroy the cell phone. Thermite is used for both military and commercial uses. Thermite contains its own supply of oxygen and does not require any external source of air. Consequently, it cannot be smothered and may ignite in any environment with sufficient initial heat. It can even be used for welding underwater. Once they were on U.S. soil, they could almost consider themselves in the clear.

Each man rose out of his chair, pocketed the cash and box cutter, grabbed his folder and shook Simon's hand as they exited the room. Daniels was the last man out and Simon closed the door behind him. *Whoooooosh* was the exhale he let out and he could feel some of the tension leave his body immediately. What he wouldn't give for a massage right now. Selena, NO! Stop that thinking right away.

Refocus, Simon told himself. Had he communicated everything clearly? Had it been received, and would it be retained? Yes, and yes, they were all professionals and although this was short notice, there had been enough time to create a solid plan, tear it apart and build it again. Neilsen and Bravo Team were four of the best Seals he had ever worked with and they'd have plenty of time in the air to mentally gear up for the mission. He had learned a long time ago that you could not plan every detail because your enemy was thinking at the same time; offensively and defensively.

Many times, it came down to not only who followed the plan the best, but who could ad lib and mitigate risk when unexpected situations arose. All these soldiers had fought and lived through enough skirmishes that he had confidence in their abilities. Four men had just walked out of here, in pursuit of a different kind of free enterprise. They were personally filling a gap in law enforcement, so to say.

Simon knew it was time he left the Tahoe room himself. Five minutes had passed, he would chat with Selena for a minute. This would be enough lead time for the four soldiers to be well on their way home or someplace to lock up the stacks of C-notes. He scanned the room one more time as he walked the perimeter and looked underneath the table. Clean. So he grabbed his own billfold, locked it in his hand and focused on slightly easing up his grip with each step down the hallway.

Selena was bored out of her mind in the quiet of the empty, morgue-like cubicle arena. She brightened up and looked his way when she heard him walking towards her. She was definitely a people person and this job must eat her up at night, practically alone. "How was your meeting Mr. Delgado?" she asked inquisitively.

"I'd say it went well Selena. Thanks for having the room ready and sending everyone down."

"You're very welcome. Our commitment is to make your space a great business environment." Then she asked innocently; looking up through the empty space between her glasses and eyebrows, "When will we see you again? I don't have you on our calendar the rest of the month."

Simon admitted, he did like the attention and he kept a straight face while replying. "Meeting went good. I'm not sure when I'll use a room again." Ten years ago, he would have been asking what room she'd like to see him in... Time to get out of here. "Well, have a great 4th of July weekend."

She kept a smile on her face, but she sounded somewhat disappointed, "You too Mr. Delgado. Hope to see you again soon."

He smiled and waved, then turned to walk back to the elevators. On his way down 14 floors, he sent Jarrod a quick text.

> Wickr Meeting with Bravo finished and they're heading home.

Jarrod's reply came a few minutes later.

> Wickr Excellent. Thanks for the update.

Simon was in his Suburban and pulled out of his parking spot, checking the mirrors and followed the Exit signs to pay for his time. Business was taken care of for the day and he really wanted to get home see his wife and spend a little time with the kids before bed. The speech activation in his car turned on and he said, "Dial home." Immediately the phone was ringing.

His wife picked up and in a playful tone, "Hello Mr. Delgado, this is your lady in waiting, Mrs. Delgado. When will I see you?"

He was grateful for his wife's long-suffering with the kids. He had warned her; these next five days were going to be non-stop and she hadn't so much as given one derogatory remark. "I'm on my way from Walnut Creek. How's your day been? Have the little maniacs been tolerable?"

"Well you know dear; they're perfect angels," she said with a tone of sarcasm. Then she said "They've been pretty good and can't wait to see you. Me too by the way."

"I'm about to break every speed limit I see." He said with maniac smile. "Are you up for a massage to-night?" There was no better way to ensure a massage, than by giving one first, he had found with Karisa.

"I think that's the question I should be asking you," she said devilishly. "How about it big guy? Are you up for a massage tonight?"

"Absolutely! I thought you'd never ask."

They both laughed and then heard the kids ask, "Is that Dad? Mom is he almost home?"

"Yes, kids. Dad is on his way and he'll be here by the time you're finished with baths tonight." She add-ed to Simon. "These kids ... always distracting me from my hot hubby thoughts. No speeding tickets or accidents. I'm getting these kids cleaned up and we'll see you in a bit."

"Ok, love ya."

"Love ya, bye"

CHAPTER 11

FRIDAY, JUNE 30, 0730 HOURS, LAFAYETTE, CA

Jogging sucks, running sucks Jarrod thought. That's ok, he loved his bike, but today he would run for Dad. Running all day would be a small price to pay for Dad. It would be an interesting time, jogging with Super Athlete Simon and scouting out the neighborhood where Dad's oppressor lived. He found some running shoes in his closet. Hadn't used these much. A few years back, he had the wild hair to compete in triathlons, that's when he discovered his true dislike for running.

Every triathlon finishes with running 26.2 endless miles and hours. He found it more exciting to compete with a triathlon team as a cyclist: screw that running business. The beauty of man and machine; powering through 100 miles was so much more appealing. Running was one of the times he had opted out of working on his weakness. He was fit and would rather save his knees the pounding punishment a runner endured in the daily training for a tri.

Simon would be here shortly, and he was ready. The weather would be ideal, Palo Alto at 10a should be in the upper 60s and might warm up to mid-70s by noon. They'd be on their way home by then. He had his power breakfast, oats with cinnamon, apple fiber and pumpkin spice protein powder, egg and egg whites and 3 oz of blueberries. Green tea and he was ready to rock n roll. He'd put together a drink that would work before and during the run. Man, he loved to eat and drink!

Jarrod took his drink concoction and went to the garage. He hadn't driven the beast in, it seemed like, a week. Just starting those 840 horsepower was good for his soul. The mechanical firing just before the throaty, supercharged V8 rumble blasted out the tailpipes. This was definitely what he'd be driving tonight. He depressed the clutch, shoved the shifter in reverse and backed the Corvette out of the garage, left it running and hit the button to pop the back glass. He wasn't certain if Simon needed to throw anything in the back or not.

The Vette gleamed in the morning sun that filtered through the oaks. This would put a smile on Simon's face as well. They had both been Chevy guys since their teenage years. Mid to late 60s: Novas, Chevelles, Malibus and Camaros because no one had money for a Corvette; let alone to race it out. He saw Simon's Suburban coming up the street and went back to set the alarm and lock the front door.

"Hey, let's not be subtle today, right Jarrod?" Simon said in half jest. The Corvette wouldn't be out of place in Palo Alto. Maybe not your average neighborhood car in the vicinity they were scouting out, but still not out of place. Simon had his black on black on black running attire. Actually, there were a few silver, reflective Nike swooshes, but that was it for color. Jarrod had gone with navy blue shirt, black shorts and his silver and volt green Asics.

"I knew you'd want to pick up on some Stanford girls after, so yeah we're bringing the Vette." They both got a kick out of that thought and laughed. "You ready?"

"Yep, let's roll out."

Simon brought a small, soft backpack along with a liter water bottle and slid in the passenger seat. Jarrod closed the back glass, slid in his seat and closed the door with a solid whunk. He pressed the garage door button to close it and backed the beast down the driveway. Shifting into first and letting out the clutch, the Vette let out the most fantastic V8 note on the planet. The neighborhood dogs barked, and he grinned from ear to ear shifting into 2nd gear.

"Tonight, Bravo Team is flying out, they'll have 30+ hours of beauty sleep or Halo play time on their flights and will touch down Saturday afternoon local 1330 hours. Chew will set up the reconnaissance on Soares' building, pick up weapons and secure their transportation. They'll pick up Soares Saturday evening and transport him to the kill zone. Sunday morning he'll go for a little dip and meet his maker shortly thereafter."

"Yes, and sending a poignant message to the cyber hacking community. The slap on the hand first offense punishment you thought was a joke is only if you're lucky. If someone other than law enforcement gets ya, your last minutes on earth will be filled with excruciating pain and helplessness. Your family and friends might even see you on the news. Who knows, maybe the cartels and mafias will copycat this style of capital punishment?"

Simon said ruefully, "Enemies of Jarrod be forewarned. This guy has a devious and creative streak."

Both men were comfortable with the lapses of conversation, there wasn't any need to fill every moment with spoken words. Traffic was moderate by the Bay Area's standard and expected. Out of his peripheral vision, DeBoy was pretty certain he'd seen another city bus with a Shark Week advertising on the side. Traffic did thin out a little on highway 880 South, once they were past the San Mateo bridge. In all, it only took an hour, point to point, and Jarrod was parallel parking half a mile from Papa Team's target: Sarmento.

Simon looked at the map on his phone one more time, passed it to Jarrod and showed him the route they'd be taking. He shoved his bag under the passenger seat and they got out to stretch for the run.

"What do we stretch to run, our knees?" Jarrod asked jokingly.

Simon had heard about his experience training for triathlons and quipped back. "Maybe this is your second calling to man up and become a runner. Ha-ha."

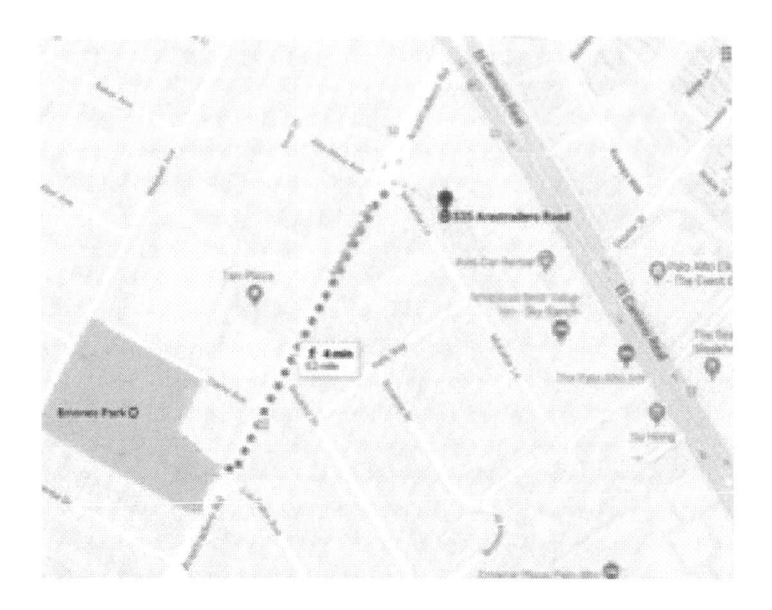

Jarrod had parked the Corvette on Clemo Avenue, at Briones Park. They jumped out of the car and began stretching for their run. They jogged for a minute to relieve their bladders at the soccer field bathrooms and headed out. There were quite a few walkers and joggers out this morning. The moms had already taken their kids to school and they were out with strollers or on their own. From here they were less than a block from turning left onto Arastradero Rd. Then a third of a mile to Union Square where the Sarmento family lived.

Simon set the pace at about an 8-minute mile. They were both looking at terrain, traffic, road construction, anything that would help them avoid delay or pick up a few extra minutes. In a quarter mile they turned left onto Alta Mesa Avenue, a residential neighborhood and it looked to have been built in the 1960s. It was a short street that made a T with Irven Court. This dead-end street was certainly one to avoid.

El Camino Real runs north and south, and was another quarter mile east down Arastradero. Interestingly, there were a McLaren, Volvo and Tesla dealerships in this small area. So far, nothing out of the ordinary. In the other direction, west bound on Arastradero from Sarmento, was Alta Mesa Memorial Park and Henry M. Gunn High School. These were not only good to know as landmarks, but also potential places to escape on foot if things went extremely wrong.

The western edge of Alta Mesa park was Foothill Expressway. Simon led them south on McKellar Lane and Union Square was on their left. There were shops, a few small restaurants/delis and an Avis car rental. A Hilton also stood out between McKellar and El Camino Real. That might be an emergency place to hold someone. They jogged down the eastern side of McKellar for half a mile till it dead-ended and they headed back up on the western side; both their eyes scanning the streets, shops and houses. Lorabelle Lane was a western facing offshoot from McKellar and literally just 3 houses.

Jarrod felt a little funny, scouting neighborhoods and pretending to be a jogging duo. Another 20 steps and they came to Kelly Way, which ran perpendicular from McKellar to Suzanne Drive. Suzanne Drive was more of a U-shaped street. One end of Suzanne dead-ended into Kelly, while Kelly dead-ended into Suzanne, which continued up to Arastradero. Picture a number six and Suzanne was the entire shape of the six, with the exception of the top part of the loop which was Kelly.

This would all make sense when Simon wrote down their observations on the drive home. They would also be driving the same loop to gain the perspective from a car and traffic. In Jarrod's mind, Kelly would be the best place to park. He asked Simon, "Will Papa bring a van, car and a van or two cars?"

"Good question. For this type of extraction, a van and a car. It will take two people to get them in the cars, even if they're knocked out. You want the other guys to bring the van, open doors, lookout, etcetera."

"Are four guys going to be enough? Worst case scenario?"

"Any four common people, no. But these four Navy Seals, just right."

This pace was pretty easy and compared to the hour up Mt. Diablo, no problem. Their breathing was fairly relaxed, and conversation was easy. "What do you think about Senoren?"

"Senoren will likely be the best choice for the trail car, but we want the van right there on the street outside their apartment building exit. It will likely play out like a few friends helping a drunk friend to their car on a Saturday night. College town, no problem. I'll talk it over with Chew and ultimately it is his choice because it's his operation."

The Union Plaza apartment building sat on a corner and was built in 1960; it had 37 units on two stories. There was a parking garage below the building at street level. The exterior was brick on the lower level with wrought iron bars making most of the cars visible. There were 3-4' tall hedges 20' long spaced along both streets. As they jogged the street, Simon slowed the pace down as they approached the street access door to the garage. He really wanted to take a look in the garage from the inside.

Simon whispered "Stop, I hear someone in the garage." Sure enough there were voices and Simon stopped to bend down and untie, then retie his shoe. Jarrod took the opportunity to stretch for a second as they waited to see who might be coming out. It sounded like at least two or three people coming out of the parking garage. With such a small complex, strangers would be easy to spot. Simon really wanted to get in the garage this morning.

They heard the clunk of someone pushing the door handle from the inside and the door opened. From the looks of the 3 younger men, their backpacks and their proximity to two college campuses, they assumed students. Recalling the photos they had found of him online, neither of them recognized Mr. Sarmento. From the sidewalk to the door was only 3 long steps where Simon was adjusting his shoes. Jarrod took a half step as he made another big stretch with his arms fully extended to the right; he was only a step and a half from the door.

All three students got through the door and the door had an arm piston which slowed the door from banging shut. The students deep in conversation weren't paying the least attention to either of them. The door began its decelerated close. Jarrod quickly took a low stretch of his right quad while watching the three backpacks continue to walk down the sidewalk, not noticing him at all. He stood up and grabbed the handle as if he walked into the garage through this same door every day. Glancing at Simon, he got the approving nod and stepped into the doorway.

Simon finished tying his shoes and casually looked up and down the sidewalk. He stood upright and performed a torso twist, nothing a jogger would need to do, but it served the purpose. Coast was clear and he advanced three steps as Jarrod held the door open for him. Walking into the darkened garage, their eyes took a few seconds to adjust and it appeared Simon was going to use hand signals. He pointed at Jarrod and then himself, motioning that they were going to walk the perimeter of the underground parking garage together.

Hondas, Toyotas, a few hybrids, a newer Ducati sport bike and a really nice Porsche 911 were the remaining cars in the garage. Simon snapped quick pictures of each license plate. Jarrod wondered which, if any of these cars, were owned by Sarmento. This was definitely a no-frills apartment complex, reflecting the era in which it was built. The building was L shaped and the garage offered two staircases, one on each end. The fluorescent tube fixtures all held just one bulb, leaving the second empty. There was just enough light to make out your car, but good luck spotting someone hiding in between cars.

Simon examined the open concrete joist ceiling. There were plenty of cobwebs, but no sign of any security cameras or fire sprinkler system. Jarrod wondered if Simon would venture up the stairs and try to enter the complex. His question was answered just then as Simon motioned to him to stay put at the bottom of the staircase; he was going up. Apartment complex managers were most likely to be found on the 1st floor, which was the same floor as Sarmento.

There were 8 stairs, then a landing where the staircase shifted 90 degrees left, another 8 stairs and he was at the entry door. Each 8 stairs had a single low wattage, LED bulb hanging with barely enough light to keep yourself from stumbling. The door had a simple master door lock that Simon defeated in two seconds. He was in and closed the door quietly behind himself. Jarrod felt his heart pounding as if he had just run up 20 flights of stairs. No need to check his pulse, he needed to measure his breathing and relax his mind.

He decided to put his focus on the noises outside the garage. In the event someone came walking through that door, he'd at least have a few seconds' warning. What would he say? "Hi, I know you don't know me, I'm just hanging out in your parking garage." Or "Hey, was going to see how many laps inside this garage would be a mile. Wanna watch?" Or "Hey, my buddy went in and he has the keys. Would you mind letting me in?" What fabulous creativity he had. Not.

Thankfully, in the 3 minutes Simon was gone, no one came through the garage door. He was definitely out of his element. Jogging and pretending to jog, no problem. Trading stocks and commodities; pretty confident in that arena. But breaking and entering; very uncomfortable. He was listening so hard, his heart sounded like it really was going to explode. *Dadum, Dadum, Dadum* his heart beat harder and harder. Where was Simon anyhow?

At last he heard the click from the door and saw

that familiar shadow. Jarrod's heart was beating just as loud, but it did slow down just a bit. All he could think of was "*let's get outta here.*" Simon signaled to follow, and Jarrod was nearly in his back pocket. A few steps and they'd be out the door and back to jogging. From their vantage point and looking out to the sidewalk, through the bars, they noticed those same 3 students walking back.

Simon immediately stopped and squatted down in a low position. They'd have to wait and hide until these guys went back up into the building. Silently, the two trespassers slid over to the right between a silver Prius and a dirty Corolla.

"No wonder you're on academic probation," one of the students jeered at the other.

"Shut up, man. I'll graduate and I've already got business flowing. I'm just getting through this college for mom and dad. Keeps me outta their house and they think it's the only way to make it in this world."

All three students stood at the rear of the Prius and the alarm chirped. The rear hatchback popped open. "You think I'm dumb? Look at all the kids who get their laptops ripped off while they're out of their apartments. No one's stealing this old Prius, ha-ha and nobody's even interested in a donut, much less the spare donut of a Prius. Take note and learn boys."

Simon and Jarrod could hear the students lifting the carpeted pressboard which covered the spare tire. There was a slight rustling and they could hear the cover being pushed back down into place. Then the loud thud of the hatch being closed. Double chirp and the car was locked.

"Any secret, magnet, crypto key holders under the wheel? Where's your X-ray glasses bro?" The two laughed a bit harder. "Yeah, good hiding, but you still forgot it stupid and we had to walk back." They all laughed weakly.

"C'mon, let's go to class." They shuffled off towards the garage door exit. "Forget anything else...." Their voices trailed off as the door began shutting behind them.

Jarrod must have been holding his breath the entire time and slowly let it out. They had been less than 10 feet away from Papa's target! Simon signaled to him with all ten fingers, indicating 10 seconds and they'd get up out of their crouch. Jarrod rose when he saw Simon begin to move. They both stepped out from behind their cars and took the dozen steps over to the garage door. Doing their best to look casual, they pushed on the door-bar to let them out and went right back to where they had been stretching less than 15 minutes ago.

Under his breath, Simon said, "We're going to jog back real slow, double back and then back to the car."

The only thing racing as fast as Jarrod's heart was his adrenaline. He hardly noticed the fact that they were running. Jarrod was bursting to say something, but knew better and just focused on throttling back and keeping an even pace with Simon. They looped back and he guessed Simon was looking for any suspicious people and cars.

Simon broke the silence and said, "Very well worth the time to check everything out. I've got plenty to give to Papa team. Let's pick up the pace, we've both got big nights ahead of us." They sped up to a 7 minute mile pace and Jarrod was thankful to burn off some of the energy and adrenaline. There were 2 stop lights where they had to wait for the crosswalk light to give them the signal. It seemed to take 20 minutes, rather than the 20 seconds waiting for the cross-traffic.

Finally, they came around the bend where they would be able to see the Vette. Simon had picked it up another level for the last half mile. "Might as well get our heart rate up," as he smiled at Jarrod. Approaching the car, they could see the activity had picked up at the soccer fields. More kids out playing, toddlers running in a funny motion with their pants stuffed by diapers. Both men quickly stretched on the grass nearby and then Jarrod popped the rear glass.

They both grabbed their water bottles and took a long, refreshing swig. Jarrod poured the rest into his shaker cup, dumped in his protein concoction, shook it up and downed it without stopping. Simon smiled and said, "Always got something in the car. You should sell supplements, man."

Jarrod ignored his comment and they both got in the leather wrapped custom Recaro seats. Firing up the V8, he pulled out of the parking spot and went up into 2nd and 3rd gears; keeping it quiet and under 3,500 rpm.

"I'll cover the map and what we saw running with Papa team tonight. Bravo team should be heading over the arctic cap pretty soon and halfway to Munich.

I'm going to take Karisa and the kids to the Aquarium tomorrow. Do you want to tag along? There's a few exhibits and exits I'd like to check out."

"What day are you going?"

"Tomorrow."

"Sure, I cleared my calendar, except for tonight anyhow."

"Well, I haven't had any time to do advance recon work for you there buddy. But I'm sure you'll find some charm to turn on. Try to keep your hands off the goods at least on the first blind date, ha-ha. In fact, I wouldn't even kiss her. Make her want it on the second date."

"Sure, me the tease. Hey, Lorrie, I'd kiss you good night, but my good friend who didn't marry till he was 35 said to not kiss on the first date. I'll be sure to ask Karisa next time I see her whether you kept your hands to yourself or not." They both laughed at the thought. A fifty-one year old talking with a forty-eight year old about first date advice and lies. It took the edge off their nerves. Then Jarrod dropped it into second gear as they got on the freeway and threw their heads back with the 862 horses wailing away under the hood.

CHAPTER 12

FRIDAY, JUNE 30, 1645 HOURS

Well, it was pretty simple with his clothes picked out. All he had to do was shave, shower and get himself over to Il Fornaio. He was supposed to be real, so no time spent mulling over the perfect series of first date questions. "What did he really want?" Lynsay's question rang in his ears. He said it aloud as he looked at his reflection shaving in the mirror. "What do you really want?" The biggest emphasis on the words: What—you—really—want.

A meticulous shave, both directions and most importantly not a single cut. Jarrod clipped his fingernails, toenails, double checked the nose hairs and he'd get Q-tips in his ears after the shower. He felt a little extravagant and turned on the regular shower head and the overhead shower head as well. He liked his showers hot and he double scrubbed everything with the loofah poof in less than 5 minutes. Twisting the knob a little more to the left, another 10 degrees and his skin was jumping. He stood directly beneath the water and just let it soak in for a few more minutes.

He turned off the water and wiped some of the excess water off with his hands; then reached for his towel. In an hour, he'd be sitting directly across from the stunning Lorrie. His first date in 13 months. He mentally reviewed what Lynsay had said:

> "Sure, be REAL and open yourself up a bit. You don't have to bare it all, but relax and be transparent enough so she can see and feel what a good person you are. Be interested, not interesting. Family, women are more interested in family than anything else. Keep your ex-wife and girlfriends out of every conversation. Don't compare—enjoy discovering who Lorrie is. Figure out what you want. Girlfriend, wife, lover? What do you really want? No playing around."

With a sky-blue terrycloth towel wrapped around his waist, he passed by the mirror again and said, "What do you really want?" "Qu'est-ce que voudrais-tu?" Recalling his high school and college French. The question of the day. Actually, the question of life. He had desired many things and had achieved or purchased them. What now? There was a void in his life of deep companionship and commitment. He also knew there was a trade-off. He'd have to be less self-centered with his time and energy. Jarrod knew in the ideal relationship, both of them would be giving up pieces of their individual selves in order to build their combined-self.

"Hey, lighten up and relax. It's a first date. She'll sense your stress and who needs more of that?" Ears, check. Eyebrows, check, Cologne check. Nostrils, always recheck. He was putting his money on ensemble #2 from Lynsay. Clothes on and zipper up, check. 4:15p and it's time to get on the road.

He had an extra hop in his step down the three steps to the garage floor. Should he have triple checked with Lorrie? Nah, she would have thought he was a psycho control freak. It's all good. He would find a parking spot, walk off a few nerves and then see the ebullient maître de, Philippe. His reservation would be confirmed and he would go wait, cool as a cucumber in front of the restaurant. Lorrie would approach like a runway model, one foot confidently in front the other on 4" heels and instantly smile at him.

Then what? She was closing with each step. Handshake, no chance; too formal and they'd already been introduced, and this wasn't business. She'd jump into his arms? No, this wasn't *Gone with the Wind*. He could offer both hands, she could grab them and he could kiss her on the cheek? Too aggressive, he hardly knew more than her name and Simon says.... What would be chivalrous? He could take two steps towards her, closer to the street, make a half-turn and offer his arm to her. Just as if they were heading to an evening formal event. Arm in arm and she could choose how close to walk next to him.

There's the plan and the rest should be real, relaxed and casual. It had been a high stress week and day; he was ready for a relaxing 60 or 90 minutes at dinner. I'd like a side order of light banter, main order of great conversation, some laughter and dessert will be Lorrie saying 'Yes' to a second date, please. If he could place an order from the secret, Il Fornaio menu, that is exactly what he'd order.

He parked his gleaming sunburst orange Corvette at 4:42pm; just one short block from the front doors at Il Fornaio. One glance into the rear-view mirror to check the teeth and he popped two peppermint Altoids into his mouth. Car traffic and parking were always busy in downtown Walnut Creek. He glanced in his side view mirror for traffic and quickly opened the car door. He barely nudged his car door as the curvature of the street helped gravity close it. Walking in between the front of his car and the car in front of his, he caught a wave out of the corner of his eye. It was Lorrie.

She was runway model. Don't forget to wave and close your gaping mouth dufus and smile back. His body complied, and he hoped he didn't look like a robot. Ok, he would have to skip seeing Philippe and relaxing before Lorrie. She was right in front of him, 12 feet and closing. Her intense copper hair was done in a simple, smooth blow out. She was wearing white cotton drop-shoulder summer dress which was ran just across her bare, suntanned shoulders, with three-quarter sleeves. The tunic stopped a few inches above her knees. She would need to be careful sitting down and he would need to keep his eyes from wandering. The sleeves and hem were lined with small, white bell-shaped tassels…who cared what she was wearing! She kept her smile and eyes locked on him. Jarrod took two steps towards her and now there was just one more step till they were side by side. He made his half turn, offered his arm while keeping his eye on her. She took his arm very naturally and they continued in stride without missing a step.

What a relief! "Well, hello Lorrie." In as friendly a voice as he could muster.

"Well, hello there Prince with your little sunburst orange Corvette. Thank you for being a gentlemen with your arm." She placed her other hand lightly onto his and pulled him just slightly towards her. "I'm going to watch you now that I see the car you're driving. Can't say that anyone has ever matched my hair with their car's paint job." Lorrie said with a little laugh.

Jarrod blushed slightly, smiled and looked over arching his left eyebrow, "I guess you wouldn't believe me if I said it was a loaner on my eco-friendly Chevy Volt?"

"Not a chance. I actually like the matchy-matchy color of your bike and car. Though, if you pull out your phone with a matching orange case, I might have to call this date off." She said with a smirk.

The short walk to Il Fornaio, along with the fun conversation, had relaxed him. She let go of his arm as he reached to pull open the door for her. As she took half a step in front of him, he automatically touched the small of her back to maintain the physical contact. She looked over her shoulder at him with a bit of a surprised look on her face. "Whoops," he said quickly with a little blush and pulled his hand back.

Lorrie just smiled and let him offer his arm again. She took it as they approached the host station. Phillipe greeted them both and smiled immediately, recognizing a newfound couple. "Ah, I see your reservation for *Signore* and la *Signorina* at 6pm *tavola alfresco. Solo un minute per favore.* I will get your table right away. Just one minute, please." He hurried off and before he could return, Philippe came out from the kitchen.

Clasping his hands in front of his heart, he sung their names, "*Lorr-ieee and Jarrrr-od Volare! He immediately broke into La Donna e Mobile, by Giacomo Pussini.*

La donna e mobile

Qual piuma al vento

Muta d'accento

E di pensiero

And with that, Philippe bowed slightly. In his famous, accelerated sentences abounding in emotion he said, "Il Fornaio and Philippe are here for your *occasione importante*. You have come to *un Quattro stelle ristorante premiere in tutto la Bay Area*. We put an extra measure of love in our pasta this evening. I knew this Friday would be *notte speciale*. Your table is being prepared? *Si, certo*! And here is your host now."

"Thank you, Philippe," Jarrod spoke first; finding a brief gap in Philippe's stream of Italian-English proclamations to what felt like the entire restaurant.

"Of course, and *Signorina* how have you been? You find yourself in the arm of the second coming of Gino Bartali, our cycling champion. You are both going to have an incredible dinner and I will stop by to see how your dinner has been prepared." Philippe quickly kissed Lorrie on the cheek "*Signorina*" as their host took them to their table out on the veranda. About half-way down and to their left was their table and Jarrod pulled her chair out for her.

She looked up at him and said, "Thank you for being so polite. Most men, it seems, have forgotten their manners."

"You're welcome." He said a bit too quickly and business like. Is that all you can think to say? He thought to himself. This is a date, not signing docs with a notary. The waitress jumped right in and asked what they would like to drink and went over tonight's two specials: Cannelloni Al Forno Casalinga Style and Piatto Smeralda.

"The Casalinga style Cannelloni Al Forno has a combination of pork and veal baked with butter, Parmigiano-Regganio and a few other select house herbs. Finally, the fresh Beciamela is added to complete this gastro masterpiece"

"The Piatto Smeralda is a tantalizing dish of perfectly marinated scallops mixed with calamari and shrimp. The chef has sprinkled garlic and red chili flakes to accompany the braised tomatoes, wild arugula, sautéed organic spinach and cannellini beans. Of course, it is matched beautifully with a grilled ciabatta rubbed in garlic and our unique extra-virgin olive oil." I personally ordered this last Friday—incredible!"

Each looked at their menus for a minute and Jarrod set his down first. "You've already decided?"

"Sure, the Cannelloni special sounds great and good odds I won't spill any in my lap." Jarrod said with a smile. “Take your time, no rush. I’ll look at the desserts.”

Lorrie made a decision as well and placed her menu on the table about the time their waitress returned with bread, olive oil mixed with herbs and spices and their drinks. The waitress asked if they were ready to order and Lorrie ordered the Capellini Al Pomodoro and Jarrod selected the Cannelloni. She collected the menus and said she’d be back shortly.

For an instant, Jarrod wished to see Philippe and have him start the conversation. He couldn’t imagine the maître de ever being at a loss for words. Here we go Lynsay; interested, not interesting. Smiling at each other, they had each other’s undivided attention. He leaned forward just an inch and said, “I’d like to hear about your family. I’ll start, if that’s ok? My mother passed away 3 years ago, my father is still alive, I have a sister in L.A. and both my children are grown. My son and his wife have 2 kids and my daughter is finishing up her last year of college. Can you tell me about your family?”

With feeling she replied, “I’m sorry to hear about your mother. I’m fortunate both my parents are still alive and they are retired in Arizona.” Brightening up a bit, Lorrie said, “I’ve got three sisters; one here local, one in Washington and the youngest in the San Diego area. I’m the second oldest and like you, I have a son and daughter. I’m really excited because my first grandbaby is due at the end of September. They aren’t finding out, which is annoying. It’s my daughter and son-in-law who are expecting.“

"My son just graduated from Cal and is interviewing. He has a degree in Finance, like me, and he wants to stay in the Bay Area. I see my parents 4-5 times a year. They'll come here or I'll go there. I wish they'd move closer to me or one of my sisters, but they are still very independent and love their community."

That was a pretty fair exchange; like for like. Before Jarrod could ask a follow-up question, Lorrie asked him about his Dad. Be open and honest, real. Though a first date would not be the best time to choke up on the emotion of Dad's Alzheimer's. "Well, my Dad is 81 now and mom passing three years ago…really took a chunk out of his heart and soul. They'd been married 57 years." He paused, it had taken a big piece out of his sister and him as well. You've only got one mom. Share - be open.

"It took a lot out of all of us" his voice trailed off a bit. "You've only got one mom." Was this going to be an hour of emotions up and down? So, so different talking with women than men.

"I'm sorry, go ahead." She said with empathy and you could see the pain on her face.

"I moved Dad into a tiered care facility last November about ten minutes from me. I get to see him 2 or 3 times a week and we spend an hour or two, walk the reservoir, go out for lunch and generally keep it local. When the kids come over for a BBQ, he'll be over as well. He's early on in Alzheimer's, so his time is pretty important right now." Well, if he felt comfortable enough to share this on date one, at least there's an early level of trust.

"Thank you for sharing Jarrod," she said softly. "I admire you for taking the time with your Dad. Where do you work and how long have you been there? Do you like it?"

Dang, how come she was getting to ask all the questions? Well, at least these were more in his comfort zone; work related stuff. She had certainly lined up all her questions. Hey, at least she's interested. He immediately thought of F.O.R.M. Family, occupation, recreation and *Muuhh*. What was the 'M' for? This was something he'd used when building his client base and work relationships. M, money? He was slipping, but he was certain she'd ask him in the next few questions ha-ha.

His old-self was ready to turn the tables, take control of the conversation, throw a curve ball back, but not this night. That wasn't just anybody and if he was going to spend 2 hours with a quality woman, he was going to make sure he was the most serious and the most fun. Change it up buddy since we're not looking for anyone to just fill a relationship time-gap.

With her background in finance, he assumed his number cruncher persona. "I've had my own business for 18 years and am an investment advisor. Currently, I manage investments for 84 clients with accounts ranging from $200k on up. I invest in real estate and hand-picked a team to oversee my portfolio: 24 condo units, 48 single family homes and 5 apartment buildings with a total of 175 units. Occupancy is at 93%, with 4% of units in various stages of renovation. My attorney advised I make you sign an NDA before we proceed any further into my financial life." He ended with a laugh. "Just kidding, well, not really. He has told me that before."

"Ok, that's part of what I do and yes, I do enjoy it. How about yourself?" It was interesting to watch her face as he was going through the numbers. She had a finance background and he had seen her mentally cataloging and calculating. There had been a hint of disbelief as she looked for any hint of exaggeration in his face. It was just a snapshot of the entire picture. Real estate, more so than every investment outside of commodities, could rise and fall like none other. You could have a large RE portfolio, however, that did not mean you were cash flow positive or even have any equity.

Lorrie had a minute to think because the waitress had brought their food. He could see she had wanted to inquire further, but he had squeezed in the question and now it was her turn to share. He was genuinely interested in her occupation or business. They both enjoyed a few bites, asked how each other liked their food.

"To answer your question, I worked for DeLoitte for five years, saw a need for temporary accounting and built a company. In 7 years it was quite profitable and had acquired many high tech key accounts. I was offered," She paused slightly considering how much detail to provide, "a very lucrative price along with 6 months of paid transitional consulting. I took 3 months off to travel, got bored and built my second temporary accounting practice. I had grown it for the last 4 years and when you saw me, I was signing the transfer of ownership contract."

"Part of my negotiation was the lease of a new Range Rover every year for 5 years and this one they pay off and I keep." Another delicate bite of a scallop from her Piatto Smeralda and sip of wine, then she said, "I manage my financial investments, have a quarter share in a gold mine, a half dozen mixed use properties and will have a PI check you out before our second date. Just kidding, not really." And to top him off, she added, "And you can't propose to me until we've worked out all the pre-nuptial details. Just kidding, not really. Or if you like, we could use the one from my first marriage."

They both laughed, and then became serious at the same time, asking in unison, "Were you joking?"

Lorrie answered first, "No, but I wish I had."

"What? The PI or the pre-nup?"

"Both" and they laughed together.

"Yes, the best financial lessons are learned personally," Jarrod quipped in after.

"At least we can laugh about it now. Ugh."

"Um, my dating advisor recommended I not talk about ex's or past girlfriends on this date."

"Your dating advisor? I won't tell if you won't. C'mon who's your dating advisor? Don't tell me it's your cycling buddy." She said with light-hearted ridicule.

"Simon, no. Well, he did give me one piece of advice, but that's not for another 20 minutes."

"Don't even think about that mister." She said with a hint of an edge in her voice.

"Not what you're thinking Mademoiselle. Guys think and talk about more than one thing."

She looked at him out of the corner of her eye as she was taking another bite, nonchalantly said, "Ok, I'll reserve my judgment Mr. Good Intentions."

They finished up and their waitress asked about another glass of wine or if *Signore* would like one now. *E dolce?*

Jarrod looked over inquiringly at Lorrie.

"We'll have the Tiramisu and raspberry-chocolate cheesecake. And if you could please put a half serving of each on our plates." In a lower-tone she said to the waitress, "You know how men are about sharing food." The waitress agreed, and they laughed together.

Jarrod was a bit amused himself. Women were always sharing plates, taking bites from the other, acting like every restaurant was a fondue bowl. Men on the other hand were territorial with the opinion, if I ordered it, I'm eating it all thank you. Sharing only came into play with babies, toddlers or a special someone.

"I'm guessing you don't order much dessert. Tell me the truth Jarrod."

"Ha-ha, you're right. I'm a bit vain about my waistline and desserts."

"I saw that when you were having lunch. I'm sure it was a few thousand calories you burned going up and down Diablo. And you only had, maybe 700 for lunch?"

"You're right, but I had a thousand for breakfast and during the ride. I'm a little fanatical about my nutrition."

"And conservative in more ways than that." She added knowingly.

The waitress brought the dessert and dropped off the check. He couldn't figure out which one was more amazing. Tiramisu or cheesecake? Cheesecake or Tiramisu? He felt the sugar dump instantaneously into his bloodstream. This was definitely not something he had on a regular basis. "Wow, that cheesecake. How often do you have dessert like this?"

"Most definitely two or three times a week, if I can fit the calories into my meal plan."

"Now we're talking; meal plan. I love when women talk about meal plans." He said jokingly and then added the perfunctory "Just kidding, not really. You'll have to sign up with my personal trainer before we can talk any more about nutrition."

They laughed and finished off the final bites of dessert. He had put a hundred-dollar bill in with the check and handed it to the waitress. She looked at it and Jarrod said he didn't need change. A $26 tip, why not.

"So, let's get this PI thing out of the way so we can have our second date, ok." He was feeling much more relaxed.

Matching him, she agreed and said, "Yes, let me write this down for you and you write down your info for me." She spelled out Lorrie Ann Williamson. L.A.W. Accounting Temps is the agency I just sold.

That should give your PI enough to start on his research.

"Oh no, *she's* a great PI." Emphasizing the *she*." I discovered a woman is the best person to research another woman."

She didn't know whether to take him seriously or not and he wasn't giving anything away on his last comment. Jarrod was busy writing down his information. Jarrod Lee DeBoy, JL DeBoy Holdings is for my real estate and JLD Investments will get your PI started.

"Are you divorced, single or married? No joke." Lorrie watched keenly for his response.

"Divorced for a little over 8 years. You?"

"I'm divorced as well now and for 6 years."

"So, on a more serious note. How does next Friday look for you?"

"Well, pending a green light on your report, I'd say 'Yes' and I get to pick the restaurant."

They laughed and took their napkins from their laps and deposited them on the table. As they were Jarrod helped pull out her chair as she was getting up from the table. Philippe rushed over to them. "Oh, I saw the *brillante* and *con una risata* and I could not bear to interrupt. How was your dinner? *Fantastico*? Yes, of course it was. You must remember Il Fornaio was your first date. I am so happy for you both. This is almost as exciting as when *mi acara figliola* became engaged to Roberto."

They both rolled their eyes.

"Oh, my wife will beat me as I say too much already. You must come back and very soon. *Vorresti fare una prenotazione Si? No?*"

"Philippe, it was a fantastic dinner and the food, staff, you were all amazing." Jarrod said as Philippe shook his right hand and then held his shoulder with the other.

He then turned to Lorrie. "You were satisfied, yes with the Il Fornaio de Romance? Lorrie, your life will never be the same after a dinner like this night. You must come see me again soon" and he reached over, kissed both cheeks. "*Ciao, ci vediamo presto.* I've got to check on my kitchen."

With Philippe rushing off, Jarrod offered Lorrie his arm again. She pulled him noticeably closer and actually bumped hips before walking. What a date. Would he be able to replay any of it in his mind? All he knew was it felt great and from the look on her face, he thought she felt the same. He hadn't played out the good night scene in his mind, but now he knew he'd be walking her all the way to her car.

As they reached her car, he released her arm and took both of her hands in his. She leaned back against her car, their hands and arms almost fully extended. She tilted her head slightly and said, "Thank you Jarrod for sharing a piece of your heart, being interested in mine, being a gentleman, blushing, and most of all for asking me to dinner. I really had a great time with you."

"You're very welcome and thank you for taking a chance on a sweaty guy walking around in his bike kit. I appreciate you creating a space where I felt completely comfortable. I'm really looking forward to next

Friday and learning more about you. And," he paused briefly "Friday… why don't you tell me what you really want in life?"

She looked as if she melted just a little inside and said quietly, "Yes, we can both share what we're really looking for in life."

He smiled and then began to let go of her hands. She held on, took a step forward, pulled him a little closer. Moving her head to the side of his face, she kissed him lightly on the cheek. He blushed, his eyes half closing and said, "Thank you Lorrie." Their lips were so close, but he relented and said, "Good night." They held hands just for a second more and then both simultaneously released their grip.

Jarrod stepped back as she opened her car door. She got in very lady-like and he closed the door for her. As she started the car, he waved and walked away towards his car. Aha, even at 50, a great first date felt fantastic! What's with the blushing? He could do without that next Friday. Walking on air, he hardly noticed the steps to his car and he was there. Find his keys, where were they? He was numb and tingly at the same time.

He started the Corvette and began speaking to it as if it would respond. "What a date brother! Did you see Lorrie? I mean, what? Can you imagine her sitting right here in the passenger seat? Yes, we got another date set up for next Friday!" He banged the steering wheel. "And did you see? *She* pulled *me* in for a kiss!"

He held the power button down on his cell phone and pulled away from the curb. He glanced at it as he was driving northbound on Main Street. When the power cycle completed, his phone immediately flashed green with the message indicator light. He resisted the urge to check messages while driving or even at a stop sign. What people needed to tell him or find out could wait ten minutes. The only number he cared about was from Dad or the facility. Strike that; there was a third phone number now: add Lorrie Williamson.

Couldn't get much better than that? He couldn't get over how comfortable he felt, chatting, laughing and joking around. They were very nearly strangers, but in less than 90 minutes that had changed completely. Where had she been his entire life? He was over the moon and couldn't tell if it was from the lack of recent dating with any purpose or because she was such a great find. He pulled into his driveway and pressed the garage door button. Home sweet home.

He was somewhat curious who had messaged him. More importantly, he was thinking of when he could call Lorrie. He wouldn't bring up the 'what do you really want' question. Jarrod just wanted to talk and hear her voice. Wonder, does she have Skype and then he could video call her. He'd pull Skype up on his phone and check if the tool found her number listed. Good chance? He couldn't get a real fix on how tech savvy she was or not. No matter, her voice would be enough to hear Monday. No Sunday. Sunday he would call her and see how her weekend was going.

CHAPTER 13

SATURDAY, JULY 1

Flying over the Arctic North Pole during the summer time was an interesting prospect. You might leave the airport in the middle of the night, but during Summer Solstice, there is fully daylight all day long. The only exception would be if there were clouds. This is why many people refer to the Arctic as the land of the Midnight Sun. You can find the sun above the horizon at the North Pole and during the summer, you will find it at its highest point in the sky. As the season changes to Autumn, the sun will move closer to the horizon, until it sinks below for the Fall Equinox.

Thus, all the passengers were instructed to have their window shades pulled down.

Bravo Team were sitting in pairs on the first leg of their trip from SFO to Munich. Team Leader Chew got the window seat 12A, Neilsen was in 12C. Daniels and Roman were further aft in 41d and 41f. 11 hours and 20 minutes and there would be time for shut eye. Without the middle seat being filled, there was a bit more room to stretch out.

Peterson was a light sleeper in a quiet bed, so on a plane he figured he might get a couple of winks. He had brought along a book to read, headphones and there was a pretty broad selection of shows and movies. There was a show on MotoGP, which caught his attention and he figured he'd kill the first hour or so with that and some light snacks.

Neilsen had no problem falling asleep on planes and it was just a matter of whether he'd be the loudest person snoring on the plane or not. He should look into those snoring procedures he'd heard on the radio. Wonder if they were legit? Time for some shut eye.

Loomis was a workout junkie and brought along several Muscle & Fitness type magazines, he was going to reread the book Nutrient Timing to see if he could squeeze a little more information from it. He was always looking for an edge in the gym and with his supplements.

Roman brought a copy of the Shotgun News. He was definitely doing some gun buying after this gig was over. Reading Shotgun News generally limited the small talk from whoever was sitting next to you, he laughed to himself. He also picked a few outdoor adventure type movies and queued them up for this long flight. He doubted he'd sleep much more than an hour straight. Just didn't like flying all that much.

In theory, South African Airways figured everyone

would be sleeping or at least attempting to within the first hour. So there wasn't any food or drink service and all the cabin lights were dimmed. There were a few reading lights on, scattered throughout the plane. The heavy breathers had been identified and if you were smart, you'd be asleep before they really started making some noise.

SATURDAY, JULY 1 10:30

Simon and Jarrod were the ultimate tourists and had some fun with their 30-something disguises. Simon was sporting a faded olive green, with a white lettered Hollister hoodie, camo Vans and Khaki cargo shorts. To complete the look, he had found a San Francisco Giants baseball cap which also had the camouflage background and orange lettering.

Jarrod went MMA style. He decided on the short-sleeved, Kimbo Slice, black background, with white lettering T-shirt. Underneath was another layer of black; in a long-sleeve, tight fitting LYCRA shirt. The black with white Converse Chucks seemed appropriate and a loose-fitting pair of black sweat pants to signify he would be training at any minute. Finishing his gear was a TapOut bandana wrapped around his head along with a pair of TapOut rectangular wrap sunglasses. For kicks, he'd have to wear it again when Lynsay came over for a clothing consultation.

The Monterey Bay Aquarium was an incredible engineering feat and most visitors shuffled through it oohing and aahing only at the sea-life behind the glass. The mechanical support systems behind the 100+ exhibit tanks pumped 2,000 US gallons per minute, 24 hours a day. Filtering was done during the open hours to provide clearer viewing for the visitors and at night it was turned off to bring in the raw seawater with its nourishment.

Monday afternoon with the kids in Monterey. What could be more unassuming? Simon, his wife and their two kids; plus, Jarrod the lightly employed, MMA bachelor friend with nothing else to do. This place was packed during the summer. Nearly 2 million people visited the Aquarium last year and to Simon it felt like every single one of them was here. He did not like crowds and especially all these moving bodies around him.

They walked through the first floor and saw the Kelp Forest with its 28' tall pane of glass. It was the very first place in the world where live California Giant Kelp, Macrocystis pyrifera, was grown. The sunlight filtered down through the seawater and glinted off the smaller sea life, swimming through the kelp in an endless game of tag. The kids were in awe of the height of the plants and the fact it could grow 2 feet a day!

The kids had to hold hands with the sheer number of people and blind stroller pushers, errantly bumping into everyone's shins. They were shouting, "up there, can we go up the ramp?" Sure thing and it was one of the two primary reasons Simon and Jarrod were here in this body-to-body pedestrian traffic - to see the largest tank in the aquarium, the Open Sea gallery with 1.2 million US gallons. It also happened to be where MBA was housing their latest Great White prize.

In an effort to be more interactive and connect via social media, the Aquarium had a contest to name this 16-foot beast that had been rescued from fishermen's nets. Bruce; aka the shark in *Finding Nemo*, had a narrow lead of 32% over *Moby Dick* with 29%. There were three more days before the popular vote would win and of course you must be at the aquarium to vote using their Wi-Fi app. Initially, all the names were scrolling across a nearby reader board. That was until a few teens discovered there were no filters on the names that could be submitted. Now only the top ten vote getters scrolled across, once approved by the marketing department.

Everyone, including Simon, was astounded at the size of this shark. It was estimated he weighed between 3,400—3,600 pounds and could swim upwards of 25 miles per hour. This animal was 100 percent pure and unadulterated predator. He had years of battle scars and you could also see the fresher wounds from the recent net encounter. Imagine the strength of an animal that weighed as much as his Corvette, 3298 pounds, and decades of hunting skills. This behemoth shark had the utmost respect in the tank as every turn it made created a clear path several feet above, below and side to side. Outside, the visitors had a hard time not watching it.

The Open Sea exhibit had an undergraduate Marine Biologist who spoke for 20 minutes, and although it was scripted, held the attention of all but the youngest. Simon's kids were fascinated with the school of sardines, asking how they all knew to turn at the same time. They appeared almost like a blanket being waved and pulled through the water by some unseen marionette's fingers. It had taken a little maneuvering and the kids had managed to squeeze into the front row with an unobstructed view.

The Open Sea feeding time was at 11am while the Kelp Forest was at 11:30am and they thought they might swing by again, knowing it would be the biggest attraction. It was almost time for the Behind the Scenes tour, so Jarrod and Simon split off from his wife and kids with a quick hug. They'd see them in an hour, meeting for lunch outside Bubba Gump's. The tour, of course, was the real reason they came to Monterey and this is where they expected to create the take pictures and measurements for Papa Team's entrance and exit.

A small crowd of 10 people had begun gathering for the tour. Hopefully, a few more would join and make it even easier to slip away. The tour guide was a pleasant gal named Chris and that was the biggest compliment she'd receive all day. Not funny or engaging or very interested in guiding the tour. She was clearly putting in time, but these were volunteer guides, which made it even harder to understand why she was a guide. Her monotone voice reminded Jarrod of a female version of the Economics teacher in Ferris Bueller's day off. "Anyone, anyone."

They heard comments like, "Good Lord, shoot me now to hear her voice for 30 minutes." "I thought your snoring was bad, but this woman makes my ears bleed." If he had earplugs for sale, he knew 40 people that would pay top dollar right now.

They had created a mental blueprint beforehand of the two floors at the Aquarium and their objective was to recon the perimeter of the Open Sea exhibit. Chris' monotone began to lull people to sleep and everyone's burning questions fizzled out with each subsequent minute of the tour. The visitors' eyes began to glaze over and Jarrod thought the sound from the water pumping through the pipes was more interesting than her monologue. She led them down to the lower level.

At last they were going to see the feeding tanks associated with the Open Sea exhibit. The exhibit was oval shaped and under a large, Plexiglas dome which allowed sunlight and some UV rays. From the surface of the water, Simon estimated there was 25 feet to the top, center of the dome. They were on a walkway that ran the entire perimeter. It was 6 feet wide and 12 inches above the pool. There was an aluminum railing of 1 1/2" diameter round tubing, with horizontal tubes spaced 7 inches apart vertically—not even a toddler could slip through this accidentally. The railing rose a full 6 feet high.

At the south edge of the pool, a locked gate and door frame had been built to provide access for the divers who cleaned the tank. They had a small, 4' x 6' platform which was 6 inches above the water with a small set of steps below the surface to aid the divers in getting out. Of all the cleaning jobs in the world, you had to be out of your mind for this tank. There were several 100-pound plus sharks and Bruce swimming around; from any point in the pool, he could reach your slow, sorry ass and bite you in half if he wanted. No thank you. He wondered if there was any hazard-duty pay when that beast was dropped off.

In addition to the gate, there were six holding tanks for the various types of food. Chris explained the staff used carts to bring measured amounts of fresh food to the appropriate tank and showed how they worked. The tanks were about twice the size of a large truck tool box, with a single large violin hinge running along the edge. There was a single lever on the right-hand side, which would open the door, and the food could run out. He assumed the floor of the feed tank was sloped slightly towards the pool allowing gravity to spill its contents.

Simon knew they were looking for doors at the southern edge of the pool. This was closest to the service access parking and most likely where Papa would enter the building Saturday night. Everyone in the tour was looking at the water or any direction other than Chris and her droning. Jarrod and Simon had hung towards the back the entire tour and now the group was reversing direction, heading towards the diver's gate and the southern edge of the pool.

By the time on Simon's watch, he knew they were close to the end of the 20-minute tour. Jarrod would rendez-vous with him afterwards at the penguin display. Simon knelt down to tie his shoes, behind the fish food locker, closest to the door he would go through. Jarrod straggled behind and looked towards the pool. The water was much clearer than the ocean and he could see the fish as they came up close to the surface.

As the group left the Open Sea feeding area, they were funneled down a much narrower walkway which led back to the main public area of the Aquarium. The walls had the same dark blue rolling wave simulation meeting the light blue 'sky.' Chris wasn't the least bit interested in counting how many tour participants started and finished with her. Everyone shook off their sleep walking and rushed past her to escape the torture of her voice.

Jarrod had made a pit stop at the restroom, hoping to kill five minutes. Simon had expected his recon to take 10 minutes, maybe 15 max. Jarrod would hang around the penguin exhibit and maybe check email for a few minutes. He was a little nervous for Simon, but not really. He could handle himself and they'd find themselves at Bubba Gump's before he knew it. Checking his phone, the great American pastime, was uneventful and filled the time waiting for his partner.

Seeing Simon amble towards him, Jarrod felt a sense of relief almost like he had been holding his breath. Simon winked and said, "Good to go." They turned towards the exit sign at a casual walking pace, Converse and Vans, keeping in step together. Heading towards the exit, they'd be out of the constricting space in just another 100 yards. Simon's backpack now held five employee shirts. It was a good thing they only checked bags and such for those entering.

SATURDAY, JULY 1, TWO HOURS BEFORE LANDING IN MUNICH

Chew loved to see how people reacted to information and he loved placing disturbing facts into casual conversations. He could see his neighbor was getting close to dozing off. They had already established the flight friendship; man-style. A few complaints about the work they did, the seats in the plane and several other inane, shared commonalities.

"Psst. Hey, Ralph. Check this out." Chew arched his eyebrows for an extra theatrical emphasis.

Ralph looked over at him yawning, "What's up?"

"They didn't tell us this when they sold our plane ticket," his voice took on the conspiracy tone.

"I'm looking through Wikipedia and they say that jet fuel can freeze. Did you know that?"

Ralph sat up a little straighter and said, "Well, I guess it could."

"It says here," looking at his phone screen and his voice increasing in pitch and intensity. Maybe a few other neighbors would hear him. "Jet fuel can freeze between negative 40 and 50 degrees Celsius. And get this; that is the temperature frequently encountered on these flights over the polar cap! If our fuel freezes, it's all over baby. We're going down and we all get to be on the 11 o'clock news. Either a week later as popsicles for our relatives to claim at the morgue or some crazy rescue attempt. Do you know how many helicopters it would take to rescue us?"

By this time, Ralph was sitting completely upright, and his eyes were a bit buggy. "How cold is it now I wonder?"

"We're flying 30,000 feet over the coldest part of the planet. It's already negative 40, just on the ground." Looking back and reading from his phone, "Did you know the FAA only requires two cold-weather suits? You know the pilot and co-pilot already slipped those on!" Then he said almost apologetically, "Hey, you know I'm kidding right? I didn't actually see those guys put them on, but I'm telling you if I was the captain that would be the first thing I did once this baby was on auto pilot."

Now it was time for one more fact and then he'd close his eyes; leaving Ralph to ponder life as an icicle. "The plane only alerts the crew when fuel temperatures reach 3 degrees above these levels! 3 degrees, are you kidding me? Like what are they going to do, go rub their hands on the fuel lines? They don't even have to tell the passengers! And 3 degrees later the jet fuel is frozen solid!"

Ralph was already worked up and stammered, "This is unbelievable. I would have never taken this flight. 3 degrees, you say?"

"You can bet your unArctic ass, they aren't going to say jack if those alarms go off. And what can you do anyways except put your head between your legs and get ready for a crash landing? I heard in a crash, you're better off if your body is relaxed. I'm going to fall asleep and I'll either see you on a sheet of ice when we crash land and become otter pops or at the airport! Two freaking cold weather suits and three degrees—we're screwed!"

With as much dramatic feeling as he could muster, Chew finished his doomsday report. "And I'm not even going to get into this article I found on radiation during Solar Storms! Your polar patootie is flying through the thinnest layer of the M-A-G-N-E-T-O-S-P-H-E-R-E. Do you even know what that means? It means you're getting radiated now like never before. We're in a freaking, flying microwave! You're getting nuked with 12 percent of your annual radiation limit right here on this flight!"

And with that Chew closed his eyes, leaving Ralph and his mind spinning at 500 miles an hour. He smiled contentedly and said to himself, "My gift to you Ralph. Sleep well."

The flight was more turbulent than the flight crew would have liked, but it was expected on the Arctic route. Only the soundest sleepers could snore their way through the jostling and shaking of the flight. The rest of the passengers slept in bursts; interrupted by the Arctic atmosphere shaking them awake and then the challenge of falling back asleep amid the cacophony of what sounded like an entire plane full of bears snoring through the deepest winter hibernation.

As the flight path edged towards the northern most points of Europe, it became much smoother and if you were to peek beyond the window shade, the sky had darkened as you would expect at 3:00am. Breakfast wouldn't be served until 8:00am, somewhere over Northern Africa and the restlessness of the flight made Loomis hungry. Well, for that matter, he was always hungry and this flight had just made him *hangry*.

Rummaging through his knapsack below his feet, he selected a bag of salted peanuts, apple and protein bar. This should keep his stomach from growling until they served breakfast. He sipped sparingly from a water bottle because even on this ridiculously long flight, he hated climbing over people to go use the facilities and he cherished his window seat. Once he paid a lady $30 for her spot next to a window. Why not?

Crunching on his apple while listening to music in his ear buds was disturbing; so he paused his music. The amplified sound of his chewing was too much.

This apple was a perfect example of how a red delicious apple should taste and almost as importantly, crunch. The brilliant red hues, with a shiny, thin wax coating and juicy enough to make you use a napkin to catch the juice. Of course, he knew why Eve said 'Yes" in the Garden of Eden. Eat something this delicious and know everything like God. It was a no brainer. Too bad she didn't have parents to tell her don't believe what everyone is pitching. That nasty devil knew exactly what she had wanted to hear and the rest is history.

The peanuts came next and all that sodium was a treat he allowed himself. Normally, he would have plain, boring, raw almonds. But for this mission and the possibility of not returning, his mind said go ahead, have the salted peanuts with the 400% markup at the airport concessionaire. He would definitely need a few gulps of water with all these peanuts.

Mentally, he was always calculating his macros. An apple that size would have been about 3 1/2 grams of fiber, some natural fructose sugar. Peanuts would inflate his sodium, but it wasn't a macro and he could be dead in the next 48 hours. Got to quit that train of thought he commanded his mind. Peanuts, ah yes, 2 servings in the packet with 4g of protein per serving, so that was 8g. Oh but now, the dessert for snack time. A Citrus Lemon Deluxe protein bar. He had to tell himself to take 4 small bites and savor the deliciousness.

He could finish this smallish bar in 2 bites and not even remember what it tasted like. This was his absolute favorite and he brought an entire box of 14 for this trip. The bar was surrounded in a thin layer of milk chocolate and inside was a light, fluffy lemon filling. Not like those nasty lemon pies, but a similar consistency that you would find in the most decadent truffle. He slowly bit into the bar and managed to turn off every physical sensor that was not involved in tasting the bar. Now this was pretty close to heaven he thought to himself.

The remaining 2 hours of the flight were uneventful. People who were awake were constantly fidgeting to get their bodies out of the crimped position from the airplane seat. Unless you were 2 years old and flexible like an al dente noodle, your lower back was screaming by the end of this flight. He would have paid double for a plane equipped with bunk beds. Anything horizontal was better than being fixed in a 45-degree seat. He was sure first class was worth every penny. The rest of the passengers would be unfolding themselves, seeing chiropractors and the first yoga studio they could find.

Where they were headed, there were no yoga studios or chiropractors. Even third world countries had their own internal tiers. Botswana had transformed itself into one of the fastest-growing economies in the world. In the late 1960s, the Gross Domestic Product per capita was around US $70 and it had climbed to $18,825 now. For reference, the poorest countries in Africa were still well under $1,000 per capita GDP. The development of mining, cattle and tourism have been the biggest contributors to the economic boom!

Living well north of the equator his entire life, normally Neilsen would be intrigued about the weather pattern differences as they were flying below the equator. But that was not the case on this flight. There was a mission to accomplish and then getting out alive. The higher the risk, the higher the pay in this case. They would earn almost double the members of Team Papa. He didn't know all the details, but taking down two people in the San Francisco Bay area was a much different prospect than flying to Botswana, kidnapping and illegally crossing the South African border with this hacker, chumming for Great Whites and then making it back home alive.

Eighty thousand dollars. It wouldn't buy you a house in the Bay Area; heck, it would be a nice down payment though. Eighty Gs! He could practically buy a house in some states. Eighty grand, tax free. He was determined to be smarter this time. It was the equivalent of two years take home pay at his current job. He'd put his life at risk for a week, use every skill he'd learned on the street and honed while serving with the Navy Seals. He might even have to lay low for a while; hide out. That was ok in his book.

He'd determined that of the $80,000, he was only going to blow 5%. He would carry it around until he spent it -no receipts and no guilt. That would leave him with $75,000 to invest. He'd need to funnel it back into his life slowly. Cash is king, and he'd be paying cash for his gas and groceries and all the other incidentals in life. This would really add up over the year and he'd slowly be pushing money over from checking to savings. He didn't want any alarms going off at the bank by foolishly depositing $10,000 or especially the full $75,000. He didn't want to be on any list.

In Botswana, the life expectancy was improving dramatically, but it was still a hard life. In 2000, life expectancy was a low 48.69 years. By 2014, it had jumped to 64.43 years. Though it would seem a great accomplishment, world-wide, Botswana did not keep pace with the rest of the world. Life expectancy measured for 191 countries dropped from 145th in 2013 to 147th in 2014.

The landing on Botswana's dilapidated airstrip was pretty standard, with a little extra bounce under the landing gear. One more bounce than any of the passengers would have liked. The timing of the breakfast meal had been good, though not very satisfying. Unlike all the major airports, this smaller airfield did not have a mechanical gate to connect with the plane. There was no forced, temperature controlled air. When the door opened up, the passengers would be walking down a portable stairway. One of the flight crew would ensure it was latched and secured to the plane properly and then test it first themselves.

The most notable difference though was on the ground. Soldiers with airport security armbands all carried a sidearm and machine gun. Those who were accompanied by a dog only carried a sidearm and held a leash tightly. Most of the security dogs were imported: German Shepherds, Rottweilers and Dobermans. Not all were fully trained and there were not many moments where bursts of barking weren't heard across the tarmac.

This immediately put the passengers on edge, unless you lived here or were familiar with the heightened security. Soldiers didn't like it when their enemy used dogs. An encounter would almost certainly end the dog's life and it was rare to get out of the exchange without being bitten. If there were two dogs, there would be a lot of blood spilled and the soldier better be extra proficient, or they would be the one losing out. Well trained pairs of dogs would place themselves on each side to split the focus of the individual. The individual's goal, of course, would be to have the dogs near each other in front of him so as to only protect one side.

The lead dog would attack an arm or leg, while the second would look for an opportunity to lunge at the neck. This was the most successful strategy for a quick kill. If the goal was to maim, then each dog would take a limb from each side of the body; bite, tug and twist. Bravo team wanted to be as casual as possible and get out of the airport without any incidents. They were simple tourists having an adventure week in a run-down country.

Neilsen was interested to think about how their profile would appear to Botswana authorities. In addition to the obvious tourist label, what other flags would be tripped? Travelling from the U.S., each with a different ethnicity, summer traveler, one member of the party was still in the Navy reserves, 2 single males with no children, 1 divorced man with 3 children and 2 ex-wives and 1 married man. How detailed would their profile be in the database?

In most countries around the world, there was active profiling and in fact, you would be sorted just like a vending machine. As they came down the portable staircase from the plane, they were being watched by the tower and from the ground. The head of security would radio his ground sergeant on who should be funneled into an extra thorough security check line. The men had taken odds and $20 on who would get selected. The unanimous vote was Roman, 'you always look guilty.'

Whether the dogs could read the guilty look on Roman's face or more likely, sense his trepidation, the all-black German Shepherd started a low growl and eased back on his haunches, slightly arching its back as if preparing for a jump. This started a chain reaction with the 4 other dogs nearby and they all began growling. Roman was pulled immediately from the line. All the passengers in line around him were tense with the dogs in such an agitated state.

With the 60 remaining people who arrived, nearly two dozen were selected for additional screening. This country was highly suspicious by nature. There was a variety of ages and ethnicities, but by and large white males between the ages of 30-45 made up the largest part of the group to be screened. As they shuffled off single file, Roman didn't even attempt to glance back at the rest of Bravo team. Their rendez-vous point had already been selected with this probability in mind.

The group was escorted by four soldiers in a diamond formation around the line with a dog on either side. Even though the passengers weren't ordered to place their hands behind their heads, it sure looked that way. There was no presumed innocence here. They were led to an outbuilding, which must have been a remnant from the original airport, was adjacent to the main terminal. The building was a combination of cinder blocks with a corrugated steel roof. A heavy gauge steel door with grey chipped paint was the only entry point from the airfield and there were 2 smaller windows equidistant on either side of the door. The windows were at least 10 feet off the ground.

He couldn't tell if this was really meant to scare and intimidate a confession out of the selected passengers or the airport security team just happened to stumble across the perfectly sinister interrogation room. As they walked in, there was just the one heavy steel door to go in or out. The room was quite large and empty other than the 4 evenly spaced tables in the room and their chairs. Each table had 3 chairs; two interrogator chairs opposing the accused. Not that anyone had been formally accused; just profiled and selected.

The ever-present dogs were in the room as well. Two handlers and their Doberman pinchers remained directly outside the door. Yes, they were the fastest of the three guard dog breeds here, but no one was going to outrun a Rottweiler or German Shepherd either. Inside the room were two German Shepherds, one at the door and the other at the far wall. The still air of the room was rank with fear, sweat and dogs which was exactly how they wanted it.

Groups were equally divided into each corner and the least likely guilty person was pushed towards the table first. First, the interviewee was asked to remove shoes, socks shirt or blouse and hand them to a third guard. The guard ran a metal detector over them, inspected the soles of the shoes, pulled out any insoles. They expertly felt along the lining and seams of the clothing looking for contraband.

Thankfully, it didn't appear there would be a body cavity search here. The first four had all kept their pants and shorts on. It did seem like they were being monitored and closely watched through the eyes in the sky. This was setup just like a Vegas casino; except for the wild carpet, free drinks, hot waitresses and the fact that getting caught doing something illegal here could mean being buried in a road-side ditch late at night.

They all arrived at the prearranged meeting point - a very touristy pub in the heart of Gaborone. Each soldier had a light backpack or duffel bag with some clothing and personal hygiene essentials. The group's meeting was not one where they were going to sit down and be seen in each other's company. Rather, Bravo team leader Neilsen would position himself where he could monitor who was going in and out of the bathroom. If anyone went to the bar, they felt they were being tailed. If not, they would use the men's room and leave for another walk to the hotel.

Neilsen, as the leader, was there to knock anyone off their tails. As he sat there nursing his imported beer, Peterson came into the pub and walked back to the wash room. One down and two more to go. His eyes constantly swept the room; watching the staff and clientele. This was definitely a tourist spot and set up with an English pub feel. Precisely 3 minutes later Bravo 1 emerged from the wash room hallway and left the pub without so much as a glance in his direction.

Peterson and his wiry frame stepped into the entrance, acted as if he was looking for the restroom, spotted them and walked quickly towards it. Two down and just one more so the Team Leader could exit himself and make his way to the hotel. Like clockwork, 4 minutes passed and Bravo 2 was headed out of the bar.

Internally, Neilsen was feeling a little tense and his mind focused just a little hard. You couldn't begin to let your guard down because the first two had come through clean. It was a little harder to look around casually with the neck muscles tightening up. Bravo 4 had been pulled at the airport just because he looked guilty and anxious. He came through the doors and hesitated briefly before heading to the men's room. Apparently, Botswana authorities were convinced he wasn't that big of a risk and let him on his own.

Neilsen's neck muscles loosened slightly and his heart rate backed off slightly. Step by step the plan could be checked off. This was a more significant milestone; to not have anyone trailing the team gave them freedom in the city. They were all heading back to the hotel, which would be less than 2 klicks from the target.

After waiting another five minutes for Roman, Neilsen would stop in the restroom now to relieve himself and then be on his way to the hotel. Flying into Botswana had triggered one alarm, but now that they had cleared that alarm and had all walked freely within the city for an hour, it appeared they were in the clear.

Bravo team's cell phones were set up on an international plan and had been darkened as well with software to encrypt and erase messages. Loomis and Peterson had checked into their room and messaged their roommates with the room number. Adjacent to each other, rooms 141 and 143 was the new home base. They figured Gaborone Travelodge would certainly draw other U.S. tourists from the name alone.

The pictures online almost hurt your eyes with the garish, ultra-neon green front counter. It looked as if there had been paint left over from a 90's kids program. Even brighter were the employees' polo shirts. In fact, the only brighter shade of green that any of them had ever seen on clothing were the Nike Volt Green shoes. The exterior paint scheme of pea soup green coupled with a dirty, off-white would make this building easy to find.

Loomis and Peterson had each swept their rooms for any types of hidden video surveillance cameras. As Neilsen and Roman joined them in their respective rooms, they went through their own methodical room inspection. One could never be too cautious in a hotel, much less in a 3rd world country. Not a word was spoken during the sweep until the all-clear signal was given.

Their bodies were ten hours ahead of the Pacific Standard Time Zone they had flown from 16 hours ago. Their sleeping patterns would need to adjust, though not completely, because they were going to be in action mainly from dawn to dusk the next 2 days. In order to begin the sleep cycle adjustment, they all took a 2-hour power nap just to clear their minds and relieve the muscle tension from the flight.

The sound of two alarms were immediately shut off. The soldiers had all woken on their own a few minutes before the alarms sounded, so there were no startled thoughts or motions to address the sleep alarms. Their first order of business was to steal license plates and a Land Rover. In their advance scouting, they had designated two car rental yards within ten minutes of easy walking distance.

This was going to be more of a brute force operation. Sure, there would be finesse, but somebody getting grabbed on the streets or from their apartment wouldn't raise more than an eyebrow here. They were directed to not harm others, unless their life was at risk. But they were not going to steal a car through force; rather with stealth.

CHAPTER 14

Many of the Botswana neighborhoods had become desensitized to certain criminal activity. Those with a high crime rate were more a result of lack of officers and resources, not because they cared less. It is a truly unfortunate state when citizens being taken from their homes and beaten is commonplace. Most neighbors would turn a blind eye and justify it by saying, "they must have owed a debt or stolen something."

There was also the matter of protection. Just as in the States, certain groups had syndicate or protection by association and others simply paid for the muscle. It was no different here. Raul Soares, computer criminal, had inherited protection because of his association with the tightly knit hacking team in Botswana. They paid for their general protection, but not for a personal security guard. Most hackers felt untouchable, living in their faceless, Ethernet worlds. Syndicates couldn't really control them, because they were at risk to have them on their network domains. It was a convenient, but enforced relationship. The hacker paid for protection and that protection was ensured with the stipulation that their systems would not be compromised.

The best protection was supplied by the most ruthless organizations. However, hackers had seen what had happened to hackers who had thought about black mailing these groups or had inadvertently taken something from one in their group. In Botswana, getting caught meant a long painful death and maybe some of your family members as well. The murder rate in 2009 was about 14, but in just three short years it had climbed to 18.4 out of 100,000 Botswana were murdered.

In 2015, the Botswana Crime and Safety report noted that the biggest crime threats were confrontational thefts like residential burglaries or smash-and-grabs. In fact, a steady increase in home invasions occurred the previous year, with many occurring in the daytime, nighttime or even while dinner parties were happening. This unconceivable brazen behavior had even led to the occupants and house staff to provide safe combinations, credit cards and bank account numbers.

Raul Soares lived a fairly low-key life. He lived alone and most of his neighbors couldn't tell you anything more about him other than the clothes he wore. Raul had become very proficient at phishing and as a result his income and confidence had swollen. The FedEx and UPS drivers would tell you he received more packages internationally than your average Botswana. He had considered moving to a newer apartment complex or purchasing a townhome or condo, but for now he was satisfied furnishing and accessorizing his current abode.

He knew the neighborhood had protection and was making a six-figure, tax-free income. He maintained a reasonably quiet life for fear of attracting attention. Showing the flash and bling to the outside world was not worth the inspection by the authorities. He enjoyed the phishing, luring and looting of the U.S., U.K. and European people. If you weren't intelligent enough to protect your identity, accounts or passwords, Raul would gladly swipe those from you.

Raul had online associations, but in the physical reality of life he had almost completely disassociated himself from humans. He viewed them as tools, suppliers, retailers, servants or income streams. Raul was quite satisfied with the pace, direction and trajectory of his life. He worked when he wanted with no boss, paid his bills, paid his protection, bought his gadgets and toys. He was a part of a growing industry, which had a seemingly limitless income potential.

Raul was happy. Raul was fat. Raul was lazy. Raul was overconfident.

Bravo team had split into two groups of two: Neilsen with Roman and Loomis with Peterson to walk the blocks surrounding the car rental facility. Southern Off-Road was a 4x4 hire and rental company in Southern Africa which serviced both Botswana, South Africa, Mozambique, Namibia, Zambia and Zimbabwe. They offered comprehensive insurance and they'd be stealing one of their Land Rovers, either a Defender or Land Cruiser. They had a few bags to carry and wanted some elbow room for the five of them.

This was a full-service company. They would even bring the car to the customer. There were 4 rows of 6 vehicles and it appeared that 4 or 5 more were out on rental. July 1st is when the peak tourist season begins, and rates are effectively raised 25%. It appeared gouging and capitalism were alive and well in Botswana. With few exceptions, they'd be just another white 4x4 driving through the back country. There were a few other colors in their inventory, but those had all been rented.

The apartment complex where Raul Soares lived was more of a long-term hotel. Most rooms were rented by tourists for 7 to 14 days who were trying to save a buck. Raul was there because it offered air conditioning, which was a must in the summer; especially with his computer equipment. He had converted the smaller of the two bedrooms into his computer room. There was a small kitchen area and living room. It was all he needed. The neighborhood was familiar and the looped barbed wire, on top of the concrete block wall surrounding the property, gave him a sense of security.

When he offered 3 month's rent in advance, the manager had quickly modified the lease agreement and placed him in the most up-to-date apartment. Raul's apartment was one they used on the website with a refrigerator, flat screen TV and nice clean linens. His bed linens were changed every Sunday afternoon and it was not happenstance that was the only day his bed was ever made. He also received fresh towels on Sunday and had worked out a deal with the housekeeper to do his laundry once a week for the equivalent of $3. This was the good life.

Their plan was pretty simple. Under the guise of a late package delivery, Bravo Team would be able to enter the apartment grounds compound, approach Soares' door, and upon asking for signature, deliver a skilled, brute force submission. There were several contingencies, but in life there were very few heroes who were prepared for a home invasion; let alone capable of defending their house and family. Soares felt powerful in his cyber dominion, but he was about to come to terms with the non-firewalled side of life.

Each member of Bravo Team had brought seemingly everyday items with them in their luggage. While the items were common and certainly wouldn't be allowed in the cabin: wire cutters, scissors, duct tape and some fishing gear, they didn't arouse any suspicion for U.S. tourists traveling to the southern region of Africa. The only items yet to acquire were the guns and knives.

Botswana had laws similar to most regarding gun control: the mandatory age of 18, background check, limit of 3 per person and 100 rounds of ammo. In Botswana, the maximum penalty for unlawful possession of a firearm is 10 years in prison. Though, for non-citizens, it was a little unclear what would happen. Botswana had not signed the United Nations Protocol against the illicit Manufacturing of and Trafficking in Firearms, their Parts and Components and Ammunition.

All firearms had a unique identifying mark that was required by law and the state authorities used arms tracing and tracking procedures. Citizens were only allowed possession of rifles and shotguns; private possession of fully automatic weapons, pistols and revolvers were prohibited. An interesting ratio of firearms was maintained in the country. The number of privately registered guns in 2003 was 30,984. The number of law enforcement firearms in Botswana was 2,598 and the military defense forces had 17,100. In Botswana, police officers on routine patrol do not carry a firearm.

Game wardens, otherwise known as wildlife agents routinely encountered armed subjects and thus, carried their own firearm as would the border station agents going into South Africa.

The unmistakable mechanical double cycling of shotguns could be heard as Bravo Team made their final checks at the hotel room. Four Remington 870s and four boxes of shells had been delivered to their hotel room in a Cello instrument case which had been modified. A smaller Viola case had accompanied it and was filled with four 9mm P90s, black. Two clips per gun and a box of ammo. The handguns had been broken down earlier; clips unloaded and reloaded. The springs were checked and rechecked.

It was dusk and the final task for Roman was to wipe down his room. Loomis was going through the same process in his room. They had barely been there for 24 hours and it was time to get the wheels rolling on this mission. Neilsen and Peterson reviewed the plan again. Earlier they had found an eager dry-cleaning clerk to buy two brown khaki UPS delivery shirts, one was embossed with Moswen, which meant Light in color and the other was blank. "When they look under that hat and see those baby blues, they'll know you're not a local. Light in color." Neilsen laughed out loud.

"When they get close enough to these baby blues, that'll be the last thing they remember." Peterson stated plain as day.

The two men would be travelling on foot, covering the 7 kilometers in a leisurely 45 minutes. Roman and Loomis would finish the cleaning, load the instrument cases and drive the stolen Land Rover to the target's apartment. The neighboring rooms wouldn't have noticed any noise over the next two days coming from rooms 141 and 143. If there had been a security camera on the hallway, no one would be seen entering or exiting the rooms either. And the cleaning staff would find beds that had been slept in, but would only recall later that the room had been remarkably clean otherwise.

Loomis was driving and Roman was in the front passenger seat; they were not your typical delivery drivers. Hats pulled down low, the vehicle moved at the exact pace of the in-town speed limit. The other two Bravo Team members would be hot, sweaty and dusty from the walk. They had memorized the route and some of it would be along rough sidewalk, while other parts would cut across fields.

Their timing was impeccable. Beginning one kilometer out, the foot soldiers had time to circumnavigate the perimeter of the apartment compound. Peterson casually made his way in a counter-clockwise route, scanning every car, house, building and person. Neilsen took the clockwise route and he too, was looking for anything out of the ordinary. Was there any physical protection in place? Escape routes had been established in advance, but being there on foot cemented the path in his mind.

Anyone in Botswana who purchased items through Amazon could expect their parcel to arrive within 22 to 30 business days. Expedited was 12 to 15 and the fastest available priority shipping would be 5 to 7 business days. Needless to say, there was quite a bit of anticipation when those brown packages, with the Amazon embossed charcoal tape arrived. Soares loved his retail therapy. He could not have cared less *who* was delivering the package; it was all about the gradual build up and surprise of the packages arriving at his apartment.

Neilsen's phone buzzed twice in his front pants pocket. He was expecting a separate 'all clear' message from both Peterson and Loomis. They were very close to Soares now and the air in the Land Rover shifted from hot and dusty to an energizing field of sensory data. Every car, every person and every shadow needed to be assessed. Was it friendly, neutral or a threat? Was anything erratic in behavior? In evaluating people, the hands and eyes were the most crucial focal points. At a poker table, detecting a single physical 'tell' could finish a hand in your favor or let you fold to play another hand.

Slowing down time truly felt possible in the moments surrounding an intense event. Bravo Team were aware of the passage of time right now. However, the rate at which their brains were processing input through their senses made it seem as if time could be counted in half, quarter and eighths of seconds. Checking his cell phone for the 'all clear' messages was a necessary evil. They didn't have a secure radio system to transmit audible instructions and confirmations. These dark phones provided something more valuable for this mission: communications that were automatically erased.

Neilsen quickly opened his phone and scanned the 2 messages. His scouts had given the 'all clear' message and it would vanish from his phone after 30 seconds. He didn't comprehend the technology, but it was the end result that mattered most—their bits and bytes were secure and then chewed up and spit out. Just as Wickr was the cell phone app to turn their cell messages dark, Bravo Team was the Wickr for Raul Soares' worthless, cyber-criminal life here on the planet.

Neilsen would be sending five status messages to his senior in command, Simon. Any additional messages would mean that something had gone awry.

1. Bravo Team in Botswana hotel.
2. R1 in their control.
3. R1 enroute to shark alley.
4. Bravo Team on flight home.
5. Bravo Team out of U.S. terminal.

Simon, of course, would be relaying that information to their benefactor along with team Papa's milestones. Serious professionals didn't chit chat about work with their bosses. There was no impressing the boss; they were paid to get a job done in which a high level of skill and risk were mandatory. There were no brownie points, no timecards, no customer surveys. Just get it done while staying alive and out of the authorities' reach.

CHAPTER 15

SATURDAY, JULY 1ST, 1100 HOURS,
PLEASANTON, CA

"Don't forget the duct tape" yelled Chew. They had met up at Chew's house and the van was in the garage with Neilsen checking off his list. The crew always played poker before a job was going down. It helped relax the nerves, got them joking around and their minds off the task at hand. Two targets added more variability of course. Each man partitioned out the fact that one was a woman. You're on the list, now make your final wish. All the preparations had been made and there would be in-the-moment variables that no one could account for now, but they were damn ready.

They had to make several loops around the neighborhood until an appropriate parking space became available. Their unmarked cargo van backed into the space, nearest the stairs, leading up to the Sarmento's apartment. Nobody would give it a second glance because it looked like any other van a subcontractor would use to haul tools and equipment. Roman and Kendrick had the van while Daniels and Chew drove the second vehicle.

Kendrick had confirmed Sarmento's Porsche and Prius were in the garage. Chew had confirmation that Miguel was online and on the router in their apartment. Iovita was connected, but on her mobile via Wi-Fi. It was Friday and like most students, neither was in class. Two wireless video cameras were in place at each end of the hallway. Daniels and Roman each had laptops and could control the camera zoom remotely. "$10 says they order pizza tonight" Roman challenged Daniels.

"I'll put $50 on Chinese delivered" Daniels replied, having looked very closely at their banking transaction log.

"I'll take your $50."

18:18

The Chinese food delivery taxi pulled next to their van and Daniels gave a big grin. Roman handed him a $50. They both zoomed in with their cameras to watch the transaction. "Double or nothing on who comes to the door. I say the wifey."

"No thanks, I'll keep your money. She's probably more of a servant than wife and he won't get off his lazy butt to answer the door."

Sure enough, Iovita answered the door. Her dark, thick hair was pulled back in a ponytail. Deep, dark eyes with rounded eyebrows. She was wearing a light pink tank and running shorts, and actually looked fairly toned. Eating dinner at home was a good sign for them. It didn't look like they'd be going out. Not that it mattered, they always got their target. The Sarmento's had no idea what would go down tonight around midnight.

20:50

From down the street, perpendicular to the Sarmento's, Chew and Neilsen were keeping a watchful eye on the window for light and movement. They'd been online for hours; ugh, what a life. Huddled in front of a computer hacking through the internet and taking advantage of others. "Payday. Today is the day until death do us part…" Chew's voice trailed off.

Neilsen had found God and Jesus on his last tour in Syria and ever the comedian, he began singing "Goats go to hell and sheep go to heaven. Go to hell, go to hell, go to hell..." his teeth clenched a little more with each 'go to hell.'

Chew looked at him and frowned. Neilsen looked back and said, "What? You don't think there's a hell and heaven? A reward and punishment for what we do here on earth?"

"C'mon Neilsen. You think you're getting bonus points tonight for effing these two?"

"I figure if I'm good at something and it accelerates the sorting process, that's ok."

"What if they gave all the money back and became nice, honest sheep? Pun intended."

"You mean like Zacchaeus the wee little man from

the Bible song? What if they kept stealing and hurting more people? Hey if you wanna bail on this scene, the three of us can handle these two punks. The way I figure it, they've done enough damage and I'm here to make sure, after tonight, nobody else's old man is ripped off by these two."

"I'm not quitting, just thinking how some things you can't undo and the permanency of what we were asked to do for our country the last 12 years."

"I'd stop thinking about that. Sounds like you need my Jesus, though."

"That's enough Neilsen. What I need is some quiet. They just killed the lights. Message our guys."

The live band could be heard throughout the plaza. The cover songs were pretty good and ranged from "Lola" to "Love Shack" to "Roar". Daniels and Roman got the message and Kendrick said, "She was in pretty good shape, but he isn't. I bet he's done in 5 minutes, but she'll be tossing and turning for another fifteen minutes. Band stops at midnight and Chew says we're going in at 2240."

"Got it"

Every 2nd song, the band managed to turn up the volume just another decibel or two. The whole plaza and neighborhood would be rocking by the last song. This was not part of the neighborhood charm Chew figured, but it would certainly help them.

Baseball caps pulled down low, Chew and Neilsen skirted the crowd listening to the band. There had been a slight break and the band's manager was handing out business cards. Now they were back at volume

9, cranking out Party Rocking, LMFAO. Chew eased by the van and tapped lightly on the side. He knew his guys were ready. Roman would make sure the van was ready to receive its two new passengers. Daniels would be coming with them.

Daniels exited the van and they had all agreed a ball cap wouldn't work with his Afro. He had a beanie with a small brim, pulled down tight. He'd be responsible for the Sarmento's electronics, helping Neilsen as they helped walk their drunk friends down to the van. Roman would be strapping Iovita to the cargo eyelets while Neilsen and Daniels brought down Miguel. The instant they were secure, they'd leave the area and head down to Monterey.

Inside, Chew would be taking care of the electronics and staging the apartment. Neilsen would be done before Chew so he'd be on the watch for the apartment. They had played it out in their minds dozens of times. Entering, subduing and putting them in the van. As carefully as possible, there were to be no cuts, marks or bruises—at least before Monterey. The three were ready to head up the stairs with Neilsen and Daniels removing the cameras and dropping them in their inside pockets.

They knew they'd be working close range and had H&K P30s with silencers. They did not expect to use them. If they did, Chew hoped it was only to knock them over the head. At no point would they ever jeopardize the mission or risk being caught, so if it took a few bullets to do that, they were all comfortable with the task.

Daniels hadn't spotted a chain on the door or any electronics on the doorframe, so this would be pretty straightforward. The noise of the band was a double-edged sword. It disguised the noise they were making, but it would also become louder the instant they opened the Sarmento's door. Masks down. Daniels picked it, looked back to Neilsen and Chew. They were ready to enter. All three slipped in and the only light was coming from the outside through the opaque blinds.

The layout of the apartment was very simple. Kitchen, half bath and laundry on the left. Directly in front of them was the combination living and dining room with a midsize couch extending from the corner right wall in front of them towards the sliding glass door. The bedroom was on the right and they could see the door was open. Miguel was a heavy sleeper and mouth breather.

Silently down the hall Neilsen and Daniels crept in a low crouch. Chew stayed back near the entry way. Every nerve on their bodies was on full alert. Hearing, smelling and vision all acutely heightened. Time slowed down in these moments, they were in the target's house and each step brought them a second closer to looking down the barrel of a shotgun or finding two people soundly asleep.

Daniels looked into the doorway, the closet and bathroom were on the right. In the far-left corner was the bed and a double dresser was on his left. Directly across was the bedroom window which was cracked open and the music was coming through it with the cool night air. It was quite amazing how the brain could segregate and filter out noises. The music was definitely noticeable, but in this state of awareness, they could hear the quiet breathing of Iovita.

She was lying on the left-hand side of the bed, her body spooning up against Miguel. Their breathing was in rhythm and Daniels was a second away from giving them both the scare of their lives. He signaled Lee to go around on Miguel's side of the bed. They both leveled their guns about 12 inches from the faces of the two. Daniels signaled with three fingers that they would pull their hammers back. 3, 2, 1 and click, click followed by a loud whisper "Don't move an inch."

The clicks and voice had an immediate impact and the couple's eyes were as big as saucers. You'd only wake up like this once and if you ever had the chance to sleep again, it would be months or years before you would be able to sleep deeply. Neilsen spoke next "Do not even think of moving. Nod for yes, shake for no. Are you dressed?" Miguel nodded his head very slowly.

Daniels then said to Iovita, "Very slowly and quietly pull your left arm out and raise it over your head." She obeyed as tears began to well up in her eyes. "Now, your right arm. Cross your right wrist over your left and roll over on your stomach to the left."

Lee pushed his gun a few inches closer to Miguel and said, "Raise your left arm very slowly over your head." He did, as realization swept through his eyes and mind. "Your right arm. Cross your wrists and roll to the right on your stomach." Now they were both face down and instructed to slowly put their hands behind their backs.

They put their guns to the base of their skulls as Chew stepped in and zip tied their hands behind their backs. Iovita was rolled over first and began sobbing quietly. Her mouth was duct taped shut. Miguel next and then they sat them up. Chew pulled hoodies over each of them. Next, Neilsen and Daniels removed a small plastic container from their inside pocket. It was a rag soaked in chloroform. They were thinking "sleep tight, you're about to take the ride of your lives."

Lee and Daniels each put an arm under Iovita and held her between them; just as any two good friends would help out a drunk friend. Her head drooped against her right shoulder as they easily carried her down the hall towards the front door. Chew held the door half open and with his ball cap pulled down low, he was looking for neighbors and listening for any potential visitors. He gave the signal to Senoren and the back door to the van was unlocked.

Chew turned around to make sure the men had their first package ready. He would walk a step ahead as a shield to any onlookers and open the van door. 'All clear' and they quickly stepped in unison from the apartment. Four slow, measured strides down the hall; at just the pace you would need to help a friend walk. Daniels and Neilsen each grabbed a handrail while supporting Iovita as they stepped down the first eight stairs. At the landing, they adjusted their grip and pulled her down the final 8 steps. Chew stayed one step below and his height, combined with Iovita's short stature, effectively blocked the view of her wobbling head.

They paused with Iovita on the last step as Chew checked left, center and right for any potential witnesses. He rescanned and it was clear to move. He slid open the side van door and then waved them to bring her into the van. They deftly maneuvered her lithe body into the van and placed her on the floor, face down. Chew slid the door closed as quietly as he could and then stepped over to the rear of the van to watch the stairwell and look for anyone who might be walking around the parking lot. Daniels zip-tied her ankles together while Neilsen strapped her down at the waist and torso.

The moment Neilsen opened the van door, Chew headed back up to the apartment taking two stairs at a time. Daniels was the last one out of the van and locked it behind him; then he and Neilsen quickly followed after their field Sergeant. Chew reached inside his jacket to put his hand on his gun as he reentered the apartment. Adjusting his eyes to the unlit interior he could hear his team coming up the stairs.

It was risky leaving Miguel while they carried Iovita down to the van, but the size of the team was suited for the mission. Guns drawn, Daniels first and Neilsen second, they made their way quietly in a crouched stance down the hallway. Kendrick peeked into the room and saw the silhouette of Miguel lying where they had left him 5 minutes ago. He rose to his full height and silently walked over to check Miguel. He extended his H&K and ever so lightly touched Miguel's right ear lobe. No movement other than his light breathing. So Daniels holstered his gun and waved Neilsen in the room.

There was at least a 60-pound difference between Miguel and Iovita, so more effort to drag his limp body between them. Not difficult at all when you had adrenaline pumping through your body. They followed the same exact movements as before and ushered Miguel to the van. It was more awkward hoisting him into the van and they unceremoniously half-dropped him on the painted steel van floor. As before, Daniels zip-tied his ankles then he checked the pulse of Iovita. Neilsen strapped down Miguel and hopped in the driver seat.

Chew had stationed himself at the inner corner of the building near the stairwell and pulled out his phone. Senoren had been watching and he texted Lee to have them come over. As they approached, Senoren started the van and pulled out of the parking spot. Chew headed up the stairs to stage the apartment and take a few items for some post-op work. With the blinds drawn, he pulled out his penlight and quickly found both laptops in the family room.

He went back into the bedroom and grabbed both their cell phones. Those went into his knapsack along with the contents of Miguel's wallet. He didn't find Iovita's purse or wallet in the bedroom and opened all the dresser drawers as any thief would do in a typical burglary. He quickly ran his hands through the clothing in the drawers and found one jewelry box. He dumped it out on the bed and grabbed two watches, several gold bracelets and a very nice gold necklace with a diamond pendant and some diamond studded earrings.

The top right dresser drawer was their junk drawer and he dumped it out on the bed as well. That is exactly what it was—junk. All the miscellaneous trinkets and items people never dispose of over their lifetime. Nothing of value to take, but it did make his robbery staging that much more convincing. The room was moderately trashed. He checked the small closet and under the bed, but didn't find anything a crackhead thief would take. Chew finished in the bedroom, he went back down the hall to check the kitchen for her wallet.

On the counter, he found her purse and dumped everything out. He took her wallet and left the rest spilled on the counter. Next, Chew walked over to the sliding glass door and opened it. The sliding glass door had been locked, so he unlocked it and opened it about 3 inches. He opened a few kitchen drawers and cabinets as any burglar would have done. He had everything he needed now. All surfaces had been wiped down and he was going to exit over the back patio overhang.

His heart was pounding, the drop was only ten feet, but this was where you could twist an ankle or someone could spot him, a neighbor could be walking their dog… He cleared his mind, silently opened the slider and listened for a full 30 seconds. The sounds of the street floated up to him, though nothing out of the ordinary. The volume from the live band had been lowered to a much more civil volume. It was time.

Looking down on the ground to scan the left and right it was clear, and he expertly bellied over the half wall, lowered his body and quickly released. His ankles, knees and hips flexed with the impact to distribute the jolt. Thankfully, the ground was fairly level on the backside of the building and his ankles were fine. He walked briskly towards the laundry room side of the building, peeled off his face beanie and stowed it inside his windbreaker jacket.

As he approached the corner of the building, he began to jog. In two minutes he'd be on the street, make a right onto Kelly Way, jump in his car and leave the area to rendez-vous with his team. This piece of the mission had gone off as planned, but there was no elation yet. After the night of the 4th, when he was home listening to his wife and kids sleep, then he could begin to relax slightly.

They had rented a beach house near Cannery Row for the 4th of July weekend and that didn't come cheap; $3800 for the week. This pale sea mist green Tudor in particular was selected because it had a garage and was less than 3 blocks from the Aquarium. The day before, Papa team had run down to make sure everything was in place for their stay and extra guests. Everything had checked out and the three security cameras at the garage, front door and back deck had been temporarily disabled.

The delivery van with Neilsen and Daniels arrived just before midnight and driving through town there was still quite a bit of activity. Upwards of 3,000 visitors would be arriving to stay in a rental or hotel and twice that would come in and out for the Independence Day fireworks show and to visit the local attractions. This holiday week was a real financial boon to the surrounding area and if everything went as planned, there would be an unexpected event worthy of media coverage.

Kendrick had removed the front license plate from the cargo van and the back one had been covered by an

Auto Nation used car sales placard. They eased down Monterey's main drag, past the Aquarium and made a right on 7th street. Left on Central, three more blocks and they'd have another layer of seclusion by parking in the big, detached garage of the rental home. At least from the street, it appeared this neighborhood had tucked in early and nobody would see them driving up to the house.

Simon's family would be coming down to occupy the rental and any nosy neighbor would remember that a family had stayed there for the 4th of July weekend; boy, girl, mom and dad. Just another black SUV, play on the beach with the kids. Simple.

CHAPTER 16

SUNDAY, JULY 2, DUSK, BOTSWANA

Peterson was the best at hand-to-hand submission, so he was chosen as the delivery person. It wasn't that the others were slouches by any stretch of the imagination, but seeing Peterson in action on the judo mat or any hand-to-hand engagement left the audience and opponent in shock. Peterson would have his 10mm hidden in the waistband, but this submission and control should be handled with his hands only.

At 16 inches wide by 12 inches deep and 12 inches high, the first package was wide enough and awkward enough that it wouldn't be simple for Soares to hold and then sign the digital package tracker. They knew, from his purchasing history, Soares loved to shop. Straight up shopaholic now. So a second tube-shaped container was added, which was certain to roll off when Peterson handed him the packages. There would be several opportunities for an off-balance exchange and that was the time to strike.

On the quarter hour, for the past three hours, they had been monitoring Soares' computer activity. He was up to no good again. A quick, one-word text was sent to Neilsen, which indicated whether Soares was surfing, idle or hacking. After they left the hotel, Bravo Team leader had replied to one of the texts, asking for the text frequency to be reset to every 5 minutes. As they made their final checks, Neilsen sent a text 'countdown.' It had been prearranged to reduce the cycle every five minutes and the texts would begin coming every 2 minutes and then decrement by another 30 seconds until it was almost a real-time status.

Idle

Idle

Surfing

Surfing

The Surfing messages continued and Neilsen thought there was no better time than now. He responded with the text Green; then he and Roman took their flanking positions for the entry team's protection. Neilsen was 10 feet from the Land Rover, leaning up against the warm, dusty, brown cinderblock wall. Despite the confidence they had in each other, there would be a natural rise in tension; a heightened level of awareness to execute the mission and get out alive.

Roman was positioned at the corner of the same wall about 25 feet from Neilsen. He too was leaning and listening at the car entrance to the apartment complex. Loomis walked over to the exterior wall in between Soares and his neighbor to the right. When you opened your front door, the human eye's immediate inclination was to look out the opening door on the same side as the hinges. Loomis was on the opposite side so as not to be in Soares' peripheral vision.

Loomis pulled out his phone as if to casually take a look at the screen as Peterson approached. Loomis was more excited to watch Peterson's package delivery and more critically the delivery of his first punch. If Soares leaned over to pick up a dropped parcel, then Peterson would come from the top with an elbow or fist. It would be close quarters, so there wouldn't be enough room for a kick and a knee was chancy when your opponent may catch a glimpse of it coming and tilting his head could avoid the impact.

There was no doorbell and Peterson deftly knocked while holding the tube-shaped package in his right hand and balancing the electronic package scanner on top of the other box on his left side. The visual cues of a brown UPS logo shirt, Amazon boxes and a scanner should lower Soares' defensive guard. There was movement and steps in the apartment and a slight pause as he looked through the front door peep hole. When he answered the door, Soares opened the door wide to accept the packages.

Peterson's brain slowed time as he saw every movement as separate still picture frame in a shuttering film. He marveled that his mind could slow down time, yet when he spoke it wasn't in the same, slow speed. "Here are your packages," Peterson mimicked a slight Botswana accent he had practiced the last week. He didn't necessarily want to take the packages inside and lose the close quarters with Soares. One step in the door was fine, but only if he didn't take more than one step back.

With the packages in hand and common courtesy, Peterson would control the boxes and the handoff, thus ensuring they would not be more than an arm's length apart. If he were motioned inside, Peterson could always play off that he didn't want to intrude, the boxes were light, blah, blah, blah... Soares was keenly interested in the packages because it was such a delayed gratification when ordering anywhere outside his local community.

"Thank you," Soares hurriedly replied and then paused knowing he must sign before accepting the packages. Peterson helped convolute the transaction by handing him the tube first and asking him to sign on the device. The abductor continued to hold the larger box under his left arm and handed him the signature device as well.

Soares had automatically grabbed the tube with his dominant hand, not thinking he needed it to sign. With the handheld device now in his left, he looked up at Peterson a bit confused as if he should have known he couldn't sign and hold the tube at the same time. Peterson gave a half-hearted, fake customer service smile and looked back at him blankly. Soares, wanting to get these packages inside and opened, bent over at the waist and turned slightly to his right, to set the tube down.

The ex-Navy Seal had played out this motion in his mind and felt as if he had choreographed Soares' movements. It couldn't have been any better. Soares had looked down to see where he was placing the tube and had lost eye contact with probably the most lethal hand-to-hand combat individual breathing in his country. Peterson shifted his weight slightly to his left quad and turned 30 degrees at the waist. His right arm had already been bent at a 45 and in an instant, he had cocked his arm up and come down viciously with his elbow to the base of Soares' skull.

Soares let out an 'oomph' and crumpled to the floor. He was knocked out cold and would have a nice goose egg begin to protrude in a matter of seconds. Peterson quickly set down the box on the other side of the prone body and in one motion closed the door as he was stepping over Soares.

Loomis winced when he saw the blow delivered by Peterson. Perfection: speed, force and an instant KO. He had knocked others out in fisticuffs, but they were always long, drawn out bloody brawls. He would keep his lookout post while Peterson finished wrapping him up for delivery. They had a 3-hour drive ahead of them, an illegal border crossing and a deadline with a shark tour.

Out of instinct, Peterson felt for Soares' pulse and registered a slow beat. His intention was to deliver 70% of his maximum force. Just like a golfer shortening his backswing, he had compacted his own motion. This guy should wake up in 15 minutes with excruciating pain at the base of his skull. Peterson quickly put duct tape over his mouth, zip tied his wrists behind his back and his ankles were zip tied as well. Everyday items that would pass through any airport security or could be picked up at any local hardware store.

Next, Peterson pulled a small, rectangular shaped black box out of his backpack. It was the size of a small backup drive. He found Soares' laptop and plugged an RGB cable from the modem to the black box and then into the laptop. This new internet connection would establish automatically because the laptop was already authenticated by the modem. Then the box would send a request to its handler to establish a VPN connection. Hacking the hacker would begin

The upload and download speeds had been monitored for the last week, so they conservatively estimated the process of retrieving all the data on the hard drive, logons and passwords would take less than 20 minutes. Peterson would be administering a shot of Seconal to Soares' upper arm. It was easily purchased on the street and would keep their hostage sedated for at least 12 hours. Afterwards, he'd be staging a few, pre-selected items in the apartment; including the needle used for the Seconal.

The final sunrays had shortened on the horizon and a dusky sky took its place. The insects were chirping, buzzing and hunting in the evening sky. The download had completed, files had been replaced on the hacker's laptop and Peterson shot off his text to his field command: Ready.

Neilsen gave a brief whistle for Roman, who immediately spun towards the Range Rover. They were going to drive quietly to the front of Soares' apartment and open the rear, swing-out door. Roman and Neilsen would block anyone's view who happened to be looking out their window as Peterson hauled out Soares' limp frame. Neilsen would stay at the wheel and watch for any signs of movement. He quickly flipped a U-turn and the loose layer of dirt crunched on top of the hard, dry ground. Neilsen backed up slightly and the back of the Range Rover was just three feet from the door.

Loomis swung the rear SUV door open and then stepped over to position himself near the front door. Roman had jumped out of the Range Rover to stand next to Loomis. Peterson heard the double tap door knock and eased the door open. He squatted down to grab Soares' 170 pounds of dead weight. He rose and lifted him from around the chest and drug him from the apartment entryway to the rear deck of the SUV. Loomis grabbed Soares legs, just above the knees and helped Peterson hoist him into the cargo area of the Range Rover.

With the legs clear of the door jamb, Loomis closed the SUV door with a metallic clunk and simultaneously Peterson turned the door lock on the inside of the apartment door knob and eased it quietly shut. Not a sound was heard from the entire apartment complex. Everyone was in the transport vehicle and they were on their way to the city limits. The quicker they could get off public streets and out onto the dirt road the better. Their route was planned beforehand and now it was only a matter of 15 miles to get out of town and into the bush, the last place and underpaid game warden would want to stop four men in an SUV late at night.

1500 kilometers was a long time to travel with a hostage in your back seat; at least Neilsen had thought ahead and brought his iPod. There was time when they'd need shut eye and quiet and other times when some pounding heavy metal would reenergize and focus them. It might also be a fantastic distraction if they were pulled over.

Botswana to the SSW coast of South Africa. Their destination would take 16 hours at least. Like his buddy Simon always said, "You can sleep when you're dead." Simon and Neilsen had discussed it thoroughly, weighing the pros and cons of driving along the border in Botswana or in South Africa. Flying or driving? Landing in South Africa and crossing into Botswana or vice versa? Better to be in the bush, on common tourist back country roads or on the interstate? They decided to hug the Botswana border using a combination of back roads and they would cross the border into South Africa just north of the city of Mahikeng. They wouldn't be stopping at a border crossing; that was for certain.

Neilsen remained in the driver's seat for the first hour leg of the trip. The constant jostling on the rutted roads put Roman to sleep in the front passenger seat. Peterson also slept while Loomis kept his eye on Soares' lying figure in the back. After the 3rd hour, they would be well into South Africa and refuel, then change out driving teams. It would be a quick refueling with one pair stretching while the other two watched for any signs of unwanted company. They had four extra 10-gallon cans for gasoline. There wasn't a 24-hour AM/PM Arco gas in every city like back in the States.

As they made their way south, towards the city of Kimberley the gas gauge dropped into the last eighth of a tank. They would stop and fuel up from the cans. The terrain was rough, but not a lot of elevation so gas mileage was poor, but fairly predictable in the V8 guzzler. Kimberley was the capital of the Northern Cape Province of South Africa and the populate was around 225,000 people, best known for Apartheid and the discovery of diamonds in the mid-1800s. They hoped to find a late-night gas station open here.

Their path was basically parallel to interstate route 12 from Kimberley, to Hopetown, Britstown and Victoria West. They would need several stops for gas, water and anything decent they could eat from the gas stations. Crossing the border, each stop carried a threat of discovery. One of the South African Police Service requirements for rental vehicles which were travelling from out of the country, was a border letter from the rental company authorizing the driver to take the vehicle out of the country and the dates of travel.

If it came to a roadside check, a curious enough police officer would undoubtedly check the vehicle and occupants for passports. They'd be cooked. The two choices were bribery, which was not as likely to be successful in South Africa as Botswana, or threat of force. The second option always worked. However, there could be serious ramifications depending on time of day, witnesses and the condition you left the officer. The threat, if given properly, could be enough and when given enough money to take a nice family vacation. nearly all took a blind eye and called it a day.

There was an electrified fence built in the 1980s along the northern border of South Africa and interestingly it could be set at alarm or lethal modes. Up until 1990, it was set at lethal and over 100 fatalities occurred to those who came into contact with it. The fence consisted of two razor-wire barrier fences flanking a pyramid of coiled razor-wire containing a series of 3,300 volt, one-amp electrified wires; they will get you every time. After 1990, it was adjusted down to alarm mode to warn border patrol agents of attempted crossings.

The fence, while effective in many areas for a number of years, could not be maintained. There were large gaps to accommodate migrating elephants and so many illegals dug under or cut through it, that it was found ineffective. The fence bordering Zimbabwe and Mozambique does continue to receive maintenance on the 140km electrical deterrent. For many other areas where the border had been fenced, funds were shifted into more border patrol agents rather than continue to maintain the electrified fence.

All the soldiers' phones were charged and they carried an extra battery next to the spare clip in their waistband. Neilsen's phone was lit up and mounted so he could see the GPS. He had sent off a three-word text to Simon: *Driving with bait.* On another continent, before Simon could read the text and grin, the message had already dissolved from the phone screen. Neilsen thought to himself, 'Man, I love this freaking technology.'

Visibility was clear, though jumpy with the rough roads. There were eyes darting about, but none followed in the turbulent cloud of dust kicked up by their tires. It was easy to be lulled into a comfort trance; not one vehicle seen in the last hour. Just their Range Rover and the evening bugs splattering the windshield. There were some pretty juicy creatures flying around out there as evidenced by the inch-plus, colored globs on the pane of glass.

The powerful V-8 engine, transmission and exhaust combined to give plenty of warning to the animals to clear out. As long as they didn't startle a herd of elephants or wake up a sleepy border patrol, they'd be just fine. None of Bravo team could hear much of anything after the first 30 minutes of road noise. It all blended together, fondling their eardrums in an attempt to coax a quick cat nap. All the men felt pretty good the first hour or two. With the lack of outside stimulation and the pending driver rotation, it was easy for Peterson and Roman to catch a little shut eye.

CHAPTER 17

SUNDAY, JULY 2, 2345 HOURS

They were nearing Ramatlabama and approaching the area to cross the border; everyone was on edge. It wasn't so much what might be following them and, really, would Botswana border patrol care more about who was leaving their country versus South African police worry who was entering theirs? They were both going to be plastered all over the international news within 48 hours. Neilsen veered left as he was right on top of the dry riverbed waypoint to cross into South Africa.

Bravo Team didn't have to worry about the legal semantic differences between the countries. Every action they were taking from kidnapping, to buying, purchasing and carrying handguns, to illegal border crossing was definitely illegal. The cumulative guilty verdicts would amount to a few lifetimes in prison. "Why we get the big bucks, ay Sarge." Loomis suddenly cackled to his own amusement.

Neilsen replied in agreement, "Yep, trained by the best and how we make it happen."

There was an urgency to put some miles between them and the border. At this time of night, with the nearest border crossing station closed, they were highly suspicious. Four tourists at almost midnight and not anywhere close to a touring destination. Neilsen pushed just a little harder on the accelerator and each rut, root and rock was accentuated by the increased speed. The team knew the reason and were all on a heightened level of awareness; looking for any lights on their side of the vehicle or overhead.

They had maintained a parallel route to highway 18 and roughly twenty minutes after the crossing, Neilsen headed west to intersect route 18. This road would lead them to Mahikeng and hopefully an open refueling station with gas. In their preliminary online searches, there were three gas stations open 24 hours in a 4 km area. As they travelled down the flat, worn asphalt, highway 18 would intersect and merge with Route 49 West. This was where the first of three stations were located.

The heavy foot on the gas pedal had dropped the fuel gauge below the 1/8th mark as they entered the outskirts of Mahikeng. Mafekeng was the historical name that most African historians would use. The Siege of Mefeking had an important piece of history during the Second Boer War. It was a 217 day-long battle for the town of Mefekeng. Neilsen hoped to spend 217 seconds there and get them back on the road. The clock was ticking and he knew above all else, the odds of being discovered would continue to climb the longer they held onto this hostage.

The Total Mefekeng gas station looked like it was uprooted from any Mid-American town, rebranded and dropped onto a slab of concrete. The overhead aluminum roof spanned to cover four, single-lane gas pumps and there was a matching convenience store. Surprisingly, it was fairly well lit. As the dusty Range Rover pulled up to the outside lane, a trained eye would have picked up the simultaneous opening of the four doors and how the men scanned the area, spread out and rotated stretching.

Neilsen pulled his baseball cap low and grabbed for his wallet as he strode to the storefront. There was a set of double sliding glass doors and, at eye-level, someone had placed a hand drawn sign with an arrow pointing to the right. For the late night safety of the cashier, a barred window with a slide out money tray was as close as a customer could get to the cashier. The Bravo Team leader kept his head down as he was counting South African Rands(ZARs) from his wallet. Yesterday, he had looked up the conversion and $50 US was approximately 684 ZAR. He pulled out seven R100 notes which bore the picture of Nelson Mandela on them and the inscription of South African Reserve Bank across the top left of the bill.

His head rose just enough to spot the money tray and see the hands of the cashier. A few dime sized holes had been drilled to help facilitate conversation, but Neilsen could barely make out the muffled, "Hello and welcome. How many liters would you like today?"

He simply slid the R700 into the tray and watched the hands quickly count the seven bills. "700 on pump 1, please come back for your change." Neilsen spun around and saw that Peterson was at the ready with the nozzle in position to pump.

Pump number 1 hummed and Peterson squeezed the handle and locked it in place. They wouldn't be picking up any snacks or water here; though each soldier did use the facilities. Soares should be coming out of his medication induced sleep soon. They'd find a private spot off road to pull him out so he could relieve himself. Peterson topped off the tank and replaced the nozzle on the pump as Neilsen walked over to get his change. The cashier was curt; quietly saying as the money door slid out, "Your change. Have a nice day."

Bravo Team had fueled up, stretched out and pissed in less than 6 minutes. "Try that on any family road trip," Neilsen thought to himself and let his mind slip back for a minute to his wife and kids at home. It took longer than that just to get the kids to pee before they went out. Ha-ha, he couldn't wait to get back home. "Snap back to this South Africa situation, Shawn", quickly reprimanding himself. Losing focus could cost him any chance of enjoying family and another minute of life.

MONDAY, JULY 3RD, 0900 HOURS

The last hour AC/DC had been wailing through the speakers, covering most of the tire noise. Bravo Team were two-thirds of the way to their destination. If this mission went sideways, they would still execute

Soares. Bravo Team knew the objective of this mission was more than that; it was to send a message. Each member, having served numerous tours with the US Navy Seals, understood that sometimes they had been directed to send an impactful message and this was one of those missions.

Soares received a few sips of water through a straw whenever they stopped off road to fuel up using the gas cans or to take a whiz. Very few words had been spoken directly at Soares from the outset of the trip. He remembered the flat, serious tone from one of his captors, "Bang your head if you gotta pee. Don't move much or I'll knock you out. You'll get a little water every few hours." All he could do was nod his head, with the duct tape over his mouth and eyes blind-folded.

Driving fifteen hours anywhere was ridiculous. Driving fifteen hours through this God-forsaken land in a bouncy Range Rover was crushing his spine and nobody could get comfortable!

Roman was thinking Neilsen's iPod selections were interesting, especially now. These guys in Rage Against the Machine band were pissed at everything. But it sure did help with the vibe and you couldn't hardly not bang your head a little. They were on a mission and it could get mean and nasty, might as well have some heavy metal running as background noise on this endless road trip.

"Killing in the Name" came crashing out of the speakers next. Wasn't this a little early? Maybe they were getting amped up for a potential encounter with police?

This lead singer was screaming at me now—wonder what Soares was thinking.... Wait till he hears "Bullet in the head." Neilsen laughed aloud at his own joke.

They hadn't seen a single helicopter during the daylight hours of the trip. Other than letting Soares out under cover, there didn't seem to be much purpose continuing to venture off road and reconnecting to highway 18. The city of Kimberley had come and gone in their rear-view mirror and Beaufort West was the next major city along the highway.

White, dirty Range Rovers were somewhat common and with the active tourism business in South Africa & Botswana there were a lot of reasons to overlook the vehicle occupied by these four men. It was the American's Independence Day weekend and with so many tourists, the South African Police department had been asked to relax a little and not pull over and harass those believed to be vacationing in their fabulous country. Why would they ever come back if they felt there was a bias or profiling against them?

Travelling at the speed limit or with the flow of traffic, Roman was now driving and keeping a steady three car lengths between him and the delivery truck in front of them. To Bravo Team's benefit, there wasn't an effective and fast communication between Botswana and South Africa, especially regarding lesser crimes like stolen vehicles. Both countries had enough crime and civil unrest to keep their police and military occupied. At some point, stolen vehicles were either taken back to the originating country or found abandoned and dealt with accordingly.

Both countries were full of tourists wishing to live out a little Indiana Jones and rent their own vehicle. Many wanted the well-advertised guided tours, but some first-time visitors thought they could just rent a Land Rover, drive off road for a few miles and video a lion cleaning her day-old cubs. Certainly, Bravo Team had seen their fair share of smaller game animals, giraffes and even a few elephants, but they were here for a much different wildlife experience.

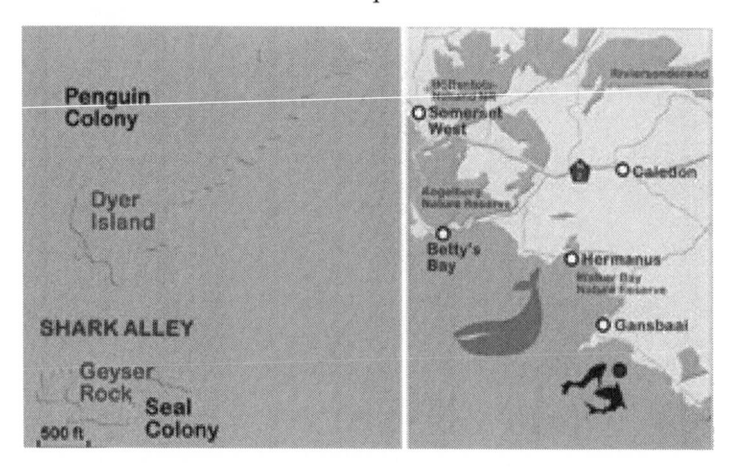

MONDAY, JULY 3, 1400 HOURS, ROUTE 43

After fourteen hours of being tenderized in the back of the Range Rover it was time to put Soares to sleep. They were an hour outside town where there were some final preparations to be made. Kleinbaai Harbor was situated next to Gansbaai Golf Course and that is where Loomis and Peterson were going to begin scouting. It is a 9-hole course with ocean views and has the distinction of being the southernmost golf course in Africa. Based on social media posts, the golf course's club house was the most likely place for the boat crew after a long work day on the harbor.

Typically, on weekdays, the companies who ran shark cage excursions made a single tour. On weekends and especially holiday weekends, they would run two tours; one leaving at 7am and the next leaving at noon. The shark cage company they had selected was no different. Neilsen had called last week and both morning and afternoon tours had been booked for months. Their 13-meter catamaran had a capacity of 40 passengers plus crew and the shark cage itself could hold 8 divers. Trips ranged from four to five hours and at R1650 per person, it was a profitable venture.

The boat was fairly broad across the beam, at 5.1 meters, with two pairs of Suzuki 200hp outboards; one on the left and another on the right. Additionally, there was room between the outboards to place the shark cage. It wasn't so much the on-board capacity that Simon had been interested in, as he was conceptualizing his plan, but rather the catamaran hull and clearance underneath the vessel. This hull would be more than sufficient.

Kleinbaai Harbor was a mixed-use harbor. There was a selection of private recreational fishermen who would back their boats down the concrete launch. The Great White tour boats came most often and almost as popular were the whale, seal and sea life tours. In the states, Kleinbaai would be considered a boat launch and not a true harbor. There weren't boat slips, per se, where owners would dock their boats overnight or for extended periods. The concrete boat launch was only wide enough for 1 large boat to be launched or two smaller boats could launch side by side.

The hook-shaped sea wall jutted out approximately 300 feet and provided some protection for the boats. It was raised concrete with worn car tires attached as bumpers. The rounded part of the hook was nearly 8 meters wide and lined with tire bumpers also, providing a barrier in the event a boat came loose , and it would not damage its hull or props on the concrete boulders below. Passengers for the larger tour ships could line up along the wide walkway for boarding and leaving their tour boat.

Boats were left on their trailers through the night which made it easier to clean and inspect. This was where Bravo team would secure their stowaway in the very early morning hours. Inspections were not as strict at Kleinbaai Harbor, nor for most of South Africa. Captains and crew were responsible and if something broke or was not seaworthy, then it would cost them money to miss a day on the water. Their reputation and online reviews were crucial to keep the flow of new paying customers.

4.3 stars was the overall rating for the Shark Cage Diving Company. The boat at capacity was a bit crowded, but as soon as people started diving with the cage, more elbow room was cleared. There were a few remarks about how things seemed a bit hectic shuttling people to the dock and getting underway on time for the early morning tours. This was just the opening they were looking for - a little unorganized and rushed getting the boat in the water. Bravo Team would ensure there were a few other hiccups in the morning for the boat captain and crew.

3am June 26th, Day 1 of the Discovery Channel's Shark Week weekend. 5 minutes from Kleinbaai Harbor.

Soares body didn't twitch at all when the twenty treble hooks were pressed into the back of his calves, both butt cheeks and along his shoulder blades. They were pressed just hard enough to get the three hook tips and cut off shank about 1/8" into the flesh. The four trickles of crimson multiplied by 20 hooks could have passed for a painting had it been on a canvas and not Soares' flesh. The tranquilizer had kept him sedated during the pin cushion exercise. If their medical calculations were accurate, he'd wake up just in time to see the chumming.

TUESDAY, JULY 4, 0430 HOURS

Neilsen and Roman had been taking care of a few things to trip up and frustrate the boat tour crew tomorrow. Now Neilsen grilled Loomis, "So Soares was still knocked out?"

"Yes sir," was all Loomis wanted to say. He knew his command had another dozen questions that would be coming rapid-fire and nothing else was necessary anyhow.

"The self-sealing screws held fast to the hull?"

"Yes sir."

"Soares body was hidden in the tunnel, Neilsen said referring to the catamaran's hull tunnel space which was in between the hull drop outs.

"Yes sir."

"Run into or see anybody?"

"No sir"

"How long did it take you?"

"25 minutes sir, just like we practiced."

"You checked his pulse?"

"Yes sir, it was 80 over 40. Breathing just fine through his nostrils."

"Anything else to report Loomis?"

"No sir. Just want to get the hell outta here."

Neilsen replied gruffly, "Once that tour boat clears the harbor with our boy, then we clear out."

CHAPTER 18

TUESDAY, JULY 4, 0710 HOURS

With no sign of the crew or captain at ten minutes past the hour, Neilsen and Roman knew their tactics had created the desired delay. They should be arriving any minute; frazzled and anxious to get their boat in the water as fast as possible. For many of their customers, this was a once in a lifetime trip and they certainly didn't want to be a negative component. The crew and captain were in 2 different vehicles and they came barreling down the road.

Through their high-powered binoculars, Bravo Team could see their excited gestures as they jumped out of the SUVs. Some of the words they were shouting could be easily made out; lots of Fs it seemed. Roman had a chance to crack a smile and laughed to himself. Those little deeds were an expression of his mischievous side. Fortunately, the boat was hosed off and fueled up every night by the two least senior crew members, so there wasn't anything else to prepare.

One crew member had run towards the harbor's tractor which was used for backing the larger boats down the ramp and into the water. Three of the crew had leaped aboard as the tractor was being hitched to the trailer. All their competitors had already loaded their passengers and started towards Shark Alley. Meanwhile, their customers were agitated and distressed not having their boat in the water or captain and crew for that matter. They might be able to make up a few minutes on the water, but they'd just focus on making it the most memorable Great White cage tour possible. They had no idea how memorable it was going to be. Bravo Team had ensured that fact.

Bravo team had a few seconds of humor watching from the hilltop as the crew was scrambling around the dock area trying to launch their vessel. The smiles slipped to serious furrows on their brows with there still being a chance of discovery in the chute of their hull. The tractor had begun backing the boat down the boat launch and into the water. Though every passenger's eye was on the boat, their view of the hull was obstructed by the shark cage and four outboard motors hanging off the stern. The soldiers let out a collective sigh as the boat met the water.

The crew had fired up the outermost engines, which belched two small clouds of blue-grey exhaust. "So we have 16 self-tapping screws into the hull," began Neilsen. "How solid did they feel?"

"Sir, real tight. Arms, legs, gut and chest were held solid. Double checked his gag as well Sir," Peterson was direct. Even with the chance to add crude, graphic descriptors in place of the word 'tight.'

Neilsen asked, but already knew the answer, "And the barbs? Pressed in and wiggled around?"

"Yes sir, a little blood for sure from each one and he was definitely coming out of his sleep."

Neilsen just nodded. Soares would either be scared shitless, nibbled on by a Great White or be torn apart by multiple Great Whites. It was out of his hands now, but if he was a betting man he'd put money on Soares' limbs ending up in the gullets of a few Great Whites. Ideally, there would be enough left of Soares for the authorities to i.d. him and they could trace down his self-employment means. Then with the speed of the ILOVEYOU virus, the hacking and phishing world would know Soares' identity and occupation.

Coupled with what would be happening in Monterey, the cyber world would be buzzing and looking for answers. These two summary executions occurring outside the judicial system meant some entity with means and possibly multiple killing squads was pissed. Somebody was aiming a statement at the cyber-criminal world, by pulling them into a non-adjudicated and very physical retribution system.

The passengers quickly boarded the Shark Cage tour boat and the crew cast off the dock lines the instant the last foot crossed the aluminum gang plank. The captain fired up the two dormant engines as he pulled out of the harbor. The engines roared when the captain shoved the throttles forward and the nose of the boat raised up slightly. With the crashing of the catamaran's hull across the waves, Soares' head banged against the aluminum hull and mashed the barbs into his skull and the other points across his body. The chumming had begun unbeknownst to the crew.

"She's underway and it looks like Soares has held underneath." Neilsen spoke quickly. "Roman, bring up their marine frequency."

"Sir, it is up." Roman acknowledged 2 seconds later with a black, handheld marine radio held to his ear.

"Loomis, what is the boat's distance and speed?"

Loomis looked like any other tourist with a camera smashed in his face. Through modern technology, a Nikon Coolpix P900 with 83x optical and 166x Dynamic Fine zoom, he would be able to watch the entire 5-mile cruise to the destination. "He's pushing 20 knots an hour I'd say, Sir, and is 400 yards from shore. 1200 yards from our position and will reach Shark Alley in approximately 19 minutes."

The Bravo Squad Leader gave a simple grunt in reply.

For at least 19 minutes Neilsen, Peterson and Roman would be scanning the horizon for any movement. They all hoped these sharks were hungry, actually they preferred 'hangry,' as the current Gen-whoever combined the words hungry and angry into hangry. We needed some hangry sharks in South Africa this morning.

CHAPTER 19

TUESDAY, JULY 4, 0900 HOURS, TIP OF SOUTH AFRICA

Aboard the shark tour catamaran, the passengers were holding on tightly. Happy to be blasting through the seas at a quick pace, but chilled by the temperature, spray of the ocean and extra wind. The captain was watching the clock and mentally kicking himself at being late. It seemed obstacle after obstacle was in his way this morning and his entire crew for that matter. Had it been a full moon the night before? Crazy! But he had to stay focused on the ocean, his boat, crew and passengers.

He knew all the other tour boats and their favorite spots so picking the most expeditious route while avoiding them was pretty easy; easier because they were already at their first destination, he couldn't help thinking to himself. "Can we get there already and just drop the cage?!" was the next thought in his mind.

The Apex Predator arrived at Shark Alley a good 25 minutes behind the other shark cage boats. The captain and crew of the SA Great White, a beat up 45-foot single hull boat, were fairly close at 60 yards to their leeward side. They gave a sarcastic applause to the Predator which made them all grit their teeth just a little harder.

The ocean temperature was a perfect 17.5 degrees Celsius, visibility was great today and the divers would get some great photos and memories with these conditions. The boat had puttered and coasted in the final 300 yards to minimize the disturbance. With the anchors dropped and set, two crew members were nearly ready to push the cage in the water. The tour boat advertised the fact that they had a specially formulated chum; that would not be an understatement today.

The novice tourist divers aboard the unique catamaran were anxious to get in the water. They too had noticed the great visibility and could hear some excitement from the other boats on the water. The crew only needed to push the cage 3-4 feet and the weight would tip it into the water. They had just begun pushing it and a rather large Great White swam towards, and then under, the stern of the boat. From reflex, they had to stop the momentum of the cage so as to not drop it on the shark.

A chorus of 'Whoas,' 'Oohs' and 'Aahs' and 'Did you see the size of that shark?' buzzed the entire length of the Apex Predator. Cameras could be heard zooming and clicking away with a few whistles added in to acknowledge the Great White. Immediate estimates of the shark were given.

"Was it 16 feet?"

"I'd say 17!"

"Couldn't have been that big, really?"

"Jump in and measure him next time" brought a round of chuckles from all aboard.

The cage went in with a moderate splash and was tied off on the leeward side of the catamaran. One of the crew had his dive suit on and was immediately approached by a second Great White. The shark twisted and dove down at the last second before hitting the cage. The passengers were eager to get in as well. Water temperature today was a brisk 58, so they'd be in and out a little faster than normal. The first mate continued to chum the water, throwing handfuls of red, dripping globs 25, 20, 15, 10 and 5 feet from the boat.

The local cage diving boats also threw out large pieces of cut bait, tied to a heavy line with a float on it. As Great Whites are surface feeders, they will chase and bite at the pieces of bait. The crewman simply pulls it in towards the cage, lets the shark take a nibble or grab hold, then the razor-sharp teeth rip it off, all the while, bringing the shark closer for the camera shots.

It seemed that it was indeed a specially formulated chum as the 3rd and 4th sharks drew nearer to the boat. Typically, sharks would swim by the cage and everyone would be happy. There was the occasional moment where a shark would bite the cage, but that would happen just a few times in the entire season. Once the cage divers viewed the Great Whites up close, there was no need to remind them about keeping their arms inside the cage.

The Apex Predator may have been late to the party, but they were certainly getting all the attention now. As the first group of six came out of the cage and got back on board, the second group was set to jump right in with waterproof cameras in hand. Jason was the crew member who was in the water for the first few groups. He was a bit bored with the job after two seasons, but the pay was good, and he wasn't looking for anything beyond the next payday.

Because the divers were only half a meter under water, all that was required was holding your breath. The 7mm wetsuits were provided along with goggles so no one had to worry about tanks, regulators and the like. Jason noted this was probably the most active day he'd had on the water, maybe ever, as far as Great White sharks were concerned. He was pretty certain he counted seven of them and they hadn't hardly been in the water 10 minutes.

As the in-water 'expert' he basically kept moving out of the way so the tourists could change spots with each other. Sometimes there was waving underwater or one friend tapping another to point in the direction of a shark or seal. Jason saw a hand flash briefly in an arc out of the water and back down to hit the person next to him. Then, that same man shot up, tried to shout something that sounded like the word shark, but ended up spewing vomit out into the ocean. He had managed to grab the man next to him, maybe as a precaution?

After a quick breath in and convulsing out another chunk of breakfast, the man screamed over at Jason, "That shark had an arm!" cough, cough "in his mouth!" The man next to him, eyes seeming to pop out against his goggles, could only nod frantically in agreement. Jason immediately thought this was some kind of rehearsed Gotcha by these two guys. Then he thought maybe some fool stuck his arm out and got it snatched off.

Jason took a quick breath and put his head under water; he'd have to count 7 torsos and 14 arms. It only took seconds and he had touched seven shoulders and counted all 14 arms. Ok, joke was on him. No missing limbs here. Then out of the corner of his eye, swimming up to the surface, he saw a Great White swimming by and it was the big one.

Everything was a bit frantic on board the Apex Predator when Jason came up for air. He was laughing at himself at falling for a prank, but upset that they had to deal with a barfer on board. Just seeing someone puke usually made at least one other person throw up. For a few seconds he remembered the time he and his 3 sisters all had the stomach flu at the same time. Man, they had those double sinks full, toilet and bathtub—so gross! Must have been a real downer week for his mom!

The sound of the first mate screaming snapped him back into reality. "Over there, the big one has something in his mouth!" Every head turned instantaneously in the direction of his pointed finger. The largest of the Great Whites had surfaced for a second, broadsided, jerked his head downward, but there was the unmistakable form of a human hand and fingers dangling by a tendon from his bloody jaws.

Lord have mercy, Jason thought and grabbed each of the 7 divers' hands. 14, yes 14, all accounted for here! The captain had ordered everyone out of the cage and into the boat. Divers were scrambling up the ladder as if Jaws himself was chasing them up. Jason had to get one more look and dove under water. A second shark was coming underneath him from the front of the boat. The shark spun around, headed down slightly and as he was underneath the cage, came back up at an angle towards the hull of the boat. There was more blood in the water than normal chumming would leave.

"What in the world..." Jason thought, "Was he going to head butt the hull?" He quickly squatted, almost out of breath so he could see beneath the catamaran's hull and the impact the shark was about to make. What he saw, he couldn't believe. In the void between the two catamaran hulls was a man! He was suspended or held somehow in the gap by cords at his legs, waist and chest, just above the surface of the water. He was spread-eagle, face down; except one of his wings, errr.... arms was half bitten off. The shark's head came out of the water, munching on an arm. The next shark going after a bigger bite seeing the blood pouring out of his Soares' decapitated upper arm.

The shark had underestimated the man being able to move as he was able to jerk his body up just enough to avoid the rows of jagged teeth. Jason couldn't believe what he was witnessing and he catapulted himself up to the surface. As quickly as he could spit the words out, he yelled, "There's a man under our boat! In the gap of the hull!"

The captain, first mate and everyone looked at him dumbfounded. How or why would anyone be outside a cage in Shark Alley water? The first mate quickly recounted heads. Had they missed someone in the rush of the morning? Was the ticket count or number of waiver forms wrong?

Jason yelled, "He's tied somehow to the hull and the shark bit one arm off, now the others are trying to finish him off!" How could anyone believe this madness? Nobody in their right mind would get in that water with all these Great Whites around, but they had to do something. Shoot the sharks? Talk about biting the hand that feeds you—that was against the law anyhow.

Think quick. The captain's mind had nearly come to a complete halt. Get under the boat to save someone? Lure the sharks away? How? Jason's hysterical voice broke through the captain's cloud of uncertainty, "release the anchors and get outta here!"

Whatever was going on, that definitely sounded like a good idea. These sharks wouldn't want to chase food all the way to shore when there was a bounty of seals and sea life right here. He yelled out the orders, cut the anchor lines. Get out of the cage Jason and we'll cut the cage loose. Everybody hang on! He was running to the wheel house as he yelled out. The crew members closest to the anchor lines cut them quickly with their knives and did the same with the cage. The engines growled with life and it took less than 30 seconds to get moving towards land.

CHAPTER 20

"It's going down" said Loomis looking at the action on his Nikon viewfinder. "Everybody's pointing at the water, people are jumping out of the cage and back into the boat. Discovered, dead or nearly dead. They've seen something, cutting the anchors and racing in. Meet your maker, Soares."

"Pack up boys, NOW!" was all Neilsen needed to yell. "Channel still up Roman? Switching to coast guard or the marina? Keep searching, they've gotta say something or maybe the other boats?"

Bravo Team jumped in the Range Rover with Peterson at the wheel. Neilsen rode shotgun with Roman and Neilsen banging shoulders as they hurtled into the middle row. They already had their new plates on, freshly exchanged from another white Range Rover in town.

The radios on the other boats were trying to reach the Apex Predator. "What's going on cap?" "What are you doing cutting your anchors and cage? Respond Apex!"

The captain of the Apex Predator switched his radio to the Marine emergency channel. "Mayday, Maritime Safety Authority commander do you copy?"

"I repeat, Mayday, Mayday anyone from Maritime Safety Authority do you copy? This is the Apex Predator. We are in need of an ambulance and emergency medical staff at Gansbaai Harbor. We have a wounded man, shark attack, bleeding heavily. Copy?"

"Apex Predator, this is Sergeant Neumann of the Maritime Safety Authority. We copied. You need an ambulance and emergency staff at Gansbaai Harbor. What's your ETA? Is the subject stabilized?"

"Sergeant Neumann, this is the Apex Predator and we are leaving Sharks Alley, approximately 18 minutes out. Subject is not stabilized. He is pinned between the hulls of our catamaran. Subject may have a limb bitten off. Copy?" As the words came out of the captain's mouth, they sounded ridiculous. They couldn't race flat out for 18 minutes and hope that this guy wouldn't have bled out and died. The beating he was going to take from the water, plus the blood loss....no chance he'd survive.

"Sergeant Neumann change that ambulance heading. There's no way subject will make it that distance. I'm heading to Dyer Island and send a rescue helicopter there ASAP. Copy?"

"Copy, calculating, 1 minute."

The Dyer island shoreline for the most part was protected with a very rough rock surface. There were several dilapidated building structures that were only used by the penguins and other habitat. A very small pier was where he'd attempt to dock the boat and loosen the man underneath. The swells were very unpredictable here, but he had no choice. A boat the size of the Apex Predator would be very difficult to dock, but if not, he'd just run it up the ramp.

"Apex Predator. We've got a medical Heli on its way back to land already, so I'll send a 2nd immediately. He's taking off now and ETA is 14 minutes to Dyer. Copy?"

"Copy that Maritime Safety Authority."

Shark Alley ran between Dyer Island and Geyser Rock, so it was a very quick sprint and the captain knew the seconds were ticking. Likely this guy was in shock at best, but most likely bled to death even if the sharks didn't take another bite out of him. He'd certainly give it his best shot. Miraculously the tide and swells cooperated, the deckhands had them tied off and they had only radioed the Maritime Safety Authority 5 minutes ago.

Jason had kept his gear on and Michel put his on quickly; they both jumped off the stern the instant their boat touched the pier. It was quite shallow and when their feet touched, they pushed up easily to find themselves face-to-face with the unknown man. His torso and head were pointed towards the bow of the boat.

There were three flat 1" wide nylon straps screwed into the inside of the catamaran's pontoons. His left wrist was held in place by a strap, looped around the wrist and secured by screws into the hull. They held the man's body into the void against the front of his shins, at his waist and at the chest. His head and right shoulder were hanging down at an odd angle because the arm and wrist had been bitten off.

It looked as if they hadn't made it in time. There was another deep bite taken out of his right thigh, the gash was so deep the femur bone could be seen. It was a ghastly wound, with the skin shredded by each of those teeth. There were no fine incisions. Sharks have multiple rows of teeth unlike a nice, neat row of human teeth. The shark teeth were bent and twisted this way and that; incredible tools for destroying skin, fur, flesh and bone.

Jason kicked forward and reached up to try and find a pulse. He dared not look into the man's face, let alone his eyes and have harrowing nightmares the rest of his life. His hand found the man's neck and then jawline. Jason pressed his fingertips into the neck to feel for the carotid artery and any sign of life. The head moved as the pressure had been applied, but it was not the movement of a living body.

Not your day mate. Jason put his fingertips against the other side of his neck. Jason thought, "What did you do, or better yet, who did you piss off to get screwed up under a boat as shark bait?" He turned and shook his head negatively to Michel. Then he ran his finger across his throat and said "Tell cap'n he's gone."

"Your last hour on earth must've been pure, holy terror with those Great Whites coming at you. I can't even imagine what it felt like to get your arm bitten off, you poor soul. What could you have done to deserve this?"

Michel came back sad and teary eyed. There was no noise coming from aboard the vessel. Jason had his screwdriver to unscrew the prisoner's bonds and Michel would keep an eye out for anything looking for another morsel.

CHAPTER 21

Bravo Team had a fifteen-hour ride back to avoid the authorities, cross the border and dump this vehicle. Neilsen wasn't foolish enough to retrace his steps. The Range Rover's tank was full and so were the spares on the back.

"Anyone want money on Soares being alive? 30-1 odds, $1000 max?" Roman doubted he'd have any takers, but threw it out there for conversation.

"I'd take 200-1 for $500," said Loomis. "It's against my nature to bet against my handiwork. Though 200-1 is better odds than the Lottery back home. Figure some of this payday is gonna get blown."

"Nah, I'm cool." Roman replied. "We'll hear it on the news soon enough. That wasn't your everyday shark attack."

Night couldn't fall fast enough for Bravo Team. They all felt more comfortable in the dark or in the water. Even though dusty, white Range Rovers were commonplace here in South Africa, they all felt as if they were sticking out like a neon green Lamborghini. They were more than 9 hours into the drive back. Everybody had their guns on them and the two pit stops for petrol and to pee were high alert events. There was no time to miss a detail or red flag now. Six more hours on the road with half in South Africa and the other half in Botswana.

Their rooms were already paid for last week. Hot meals, hot showers and laying low for 36 hours; then they'd be on the return flight home. Debrief with Simon and Mr. X., final payout, melt back into society and keep a low profile. Back to the moment Neilsen told himself, back to the moment and keep focused as he gripped the wheel a bit tighter and cranked up Metallica, "For Whom the Bell Tolls", another 5 decibels.

CHAPTER 22

TUESDAY, JULY 4, MONTEREY BAY AQUARIUM

The marketing department was really having fun with the great white shark naming campaign. The number of registered members on the Aquarium website was going through the roof! Ticket sales were always brisk for the two weeks bookending Independence Day, but the combination of having this behemoth 300 tooth Great White submarine swimming on the other side of the glass had created a draw like none other.

Godzilla, Super-Size, Moby, Mommy Dearest..... Bruce was the most popular with references in Jaws and Finding Nemo. Carchardon carcharias, the scientific name didn't fly, so the beach volley ballers had shortened it to Karch Kiraly. Minnow, King Kong, Guppy, Ohio, for the nuclear class submarines and rounding out the top ten: Sharkpedo, Sharknado from Pokémon. For the past month they had allowed children to vote using kiosks around the Open Sea tank and they had started with 5 stand-alone units. Management had quickly realized that every child wanted to vote, even the terrified ones. 5 units grew to 50 and they'd simply use them for surveys or other informational purposes in the future. 20,000 voters with all their contact information a day. If only there were this much interest in voting for a local measure or President.

Local radio stations were blasting contests all over the air waves and of course the skyrocketing band would CJ Driger would be performing at the semi-private concert just before the fireworks show. Their hit single, "Conquer", was being played every 90 minutes. Visitors had given non-refundable deposits on rental homes and hotel rooms. Couches opening up on Air BnB were snapped up within minutes.

Simon had briefly thought of using the shark dollies to transport the cyber thieves into the Aquarium, but any time these types of carriers were rolled into the dock area, there was an immediate interest by any workers on what was being brought in and of course the larger the container, the more curiosity generated.

To bring the cargo into the MBA, they had opted for 4 pallets of shrink-wrapped cleaning supplies. Two pallets would carry the bound and muzzled cyber criminals while Lee and Senoren would be in the other two. Chew and Daniels would be driving and offloading the truck while Simon would be just outside the rear, perimeter fence of the property. The delivery truck would be stolen from Hertz and three sides of the pallets were pre-stacked for their passengers. A perforated, corrugated plastic slip sheet would cover the top of the cleaning supply pallet.

The other difference between the two pallets would be how they arrived at the Aquarium. The two former-military would be there to send Miguel and Iovita to their final earthly moments, while the cyber crooks would be contemplating why they had chosen that particular path.

The 4th of July had arrived, and fireworks had been going off sporadically all week long. The city was abuzz with activity and overall everyone seemed to be in a great mood. They had the Monterey Bay coast line, clear skies in the forecast and the top ten Billboard band, CJ Driger, was in town to entertain the MBA crowd just before the fireworks show would kick off. A great throng of people had pulled into town and the Aquarium was jam-packed.

Scalpers were having a heyday, selling and reselling the 1,200 private MBA party and concert tickets. By Friday, boats had anchored near the mouth of the Aquarium's inlet and the Coast Guard was called to break up the little boating-right skirmishes. Half million-dollar yachts gently moved in rhythm with the ocean. Only those with provisions or a secondary dinghy had a chance at retaining their spot. The moment someone began pulling up anchor, a half dozen others were jockeying for the next closest spot.

The Great White was being watched 24x7 and the scientists felt he was growing more agitated by the day. Of course, all the animal rights activists had latched onto the fact and added it to the array of protest placards. The million-gallon fish tank just did not seem to be big enough for this monster. In the last week, the other sharks in the tank only ate if they weren't afraid of the Great White and could sneak a bite away. The Great White had actually flipped a hammerhead up in the air with a lightning fast flash and had gotten underneath it. Effortless, like a child tossing a tennis ball in the air. Needless to say, that hammerhead had been in hiding the rest of the day, keeping a safety buffer zone between itself and Bruce.

And just last week Bruce had taken a bite out of a smaller shark; almost as if to sample an hors d'oeuvres. There were at least a dozen parents and children vomiting; not all of them made it to a trash can. Most people aren't ready for all the realities of nature as many want the pet store version of nature. Confined, controlled, easy to handle and simple to replace a goldfish. However, the shock of seeing this fierce bite in front of their very eyes was too much. They realized what an easy target they would be if they were swimming in the ocean and on the menu that day. There was tremendous drop-off in the number of people swimming and surfing in the Monterey Bay that day!

The scientists couldn't find a cause for the shark's recent bad attitude. They knew when it had started, last Thursday, and it seemed to ratchet up. After the holiday weekend, they would begin the planning phase to put Bruce back into its home in the Pacific Ocean. They couldn't risk causing the decline or death of this celebrity creature. Well, at least until the holiday weekend was over. Every day, new attendance records were shattered, and it was the go-to 'spot' for every visitor. Many of them stopping by the Open Sea tank

2, 3 and 4 times on a single visit to admire the size and power of Bruce.

Ever since the introduction of the Great White into the tank, none of the feedings had been done in the tank. All were done from the edge of the pool with the feeding poles. Even the most experienced feeders had considered it with the unpredictability of a new shark, especially a Great White. The management team had strictly prohibited it and cleaning crews had doubled in size, from two to four cleaners and from 3 to 6 'guards' who were there to protect the blind sides of the cleaners.

When the big boy was brought in there were 5 employees who immediately asked to be reassigned to another display, any display, just to get out of that tank. There was a very eerie feeling, as if the shark could tell you he was the biggest, the baddest and, at any second mister cleaner, I could come over and bite you in half just because you are in my space. It was completely unnerving to be in a tank 30 feet below the surface and the only thing protecting you was a weaponless co-worker who might get 1 karate chop against a 2-ton shark.

With the 7 years of drought in California, the 500-gallon portable water tanks had become commonplace in California. El Nino had helped refill many of the reservoirs and there was a surplus of the water tanks which could be placed in the bed of your truck. With the massive rainfall during the winter of 2016, the water tanks were sitting around unused everywhere. They were quite easy to find as every entrepreneurial Joe had tried their hand at reselling; as if it were the gold rush and they had the last gold pans for sale in San Francisco.

The Sarmento's had been marinating for the last 16 hours in a combination of sea water, salmon and seal blood and guts. The cold entrails wrapped around their bodies and the stink was pretty strong in the garage. They were going to make this meal look, smell and taste as tantalizing as possible. Jarrod and Simon hoped the combination of one very pissed off shark, a dozen hungry sharks, blood and guts of the salmon, seal and two frantic cyber criminals would make for a potential feeding frenzy that Monterey Bay Aquarium would never forget.

They had a look of desperation and confusion on their faces. Unsure of how the next few hours would play out in their lives, but fairly certain torture or a painful death would follow. The duct tape kept all but the groans silenced.

TUESDAY, JULY 4TH, 1800 HOURS

The two pallets were sized to fit between the wheel wells of the stripped out, extended length van. The other two pallets of cleaning supplies were already in the truck with Peterson and Lee seated on foam cushions. The stolen delivery truck had four seemingly innocuous pallets of cleaning supplies in its cargo bay and headed off for the short ten-minute drive to the Aquarium's warehouse dock.

The bill of lading was straightforward and stated 4 pallets—cleaning supplies. Each pallet had a packing slip in a plastic window envelope adhered to the shrink wrap. The receiving associate was more interested in his phone than who was possibly bringing cleaning supplies to the Aquarium. The concert would begin in 2 ½ hours and he had 4 hours of work to cram in before, so he could get a prime viewing spot for the show.

Senoren and Loomis drove the truck in slowly to the loading area. Senoren hopped out of the passenger side and guided Loomis as the truck backed into the receiving dock. The backup beeps seemed especially loud to the soldiers. They were entering the final hours of the mission and the climax was coming; not trying to attract any extra eyes, but not wanting to look suspicious either. Loomis put it in Park and then cut off the engine. They intentionally arrived a little after normal shipping/receiving hours and, just as they thought, most of the Aquarium activity was at the opposite end of the site where the concert would be held.

Loomis and passenger wore their work caps down low to help hide their faces and worn leather work gloves so as to not leave any fingerprints. Neilsen rolled the pallet jack over the smooth concrete receiving dock floor, flipped it around and rammed it into the first pallet carrying Iovita and Miguel. The pallet jack wheels chunked over the wooden slat and into position where it could raise the pallet. With a half dozen pumps, the pallet was off the ground and with a grunt, he wheeled it back to the receiving dock elevator.

The doors slid open at once and he pulled the pallet in after himself. Pressing the 2nd floor button, he looked out to see the dock employee approach Senoren as the doors were closing.

"Hey, listen you guys aren't going to be long, right?"

"Nah, they asked us to start bringing these up to the 2nd level to save them some time. Be outta here pretty soon."

"Ok, great. I've got to run over for a few things before the show starts. I already signed you out."

"See ya next time" he said as he half-leaned against the pallet.

Sweat began to immediately soak his underarms and perspiration broke out on his forehead. He quickly wiped his forehead with his sleeve while taking long, quick strides back to the truck. They were finished here and in 37 minutes, they'd be back, having left a pair of new sunglasses on the receiving desk, irritated and with a nearly empty payload.

Loomis was just getting out of the elevator and was more nonchalant, even whistling a tune as he walked towards the truck. He got in on the passenger side and let out a long, low whistle. "Whew, so far we're hitting the clock perfectly and 2 minutes ahead. Let's get outta here."

Before he could finish the sentence, Peterson had started the engine and put it in reverse. All the energy and attention at the Aquarium was focused on the imminent concert and people jostling for the best view. The rear backup beeps barely sounded 4 times and the truck was slammed into drive, lurching forward. Neither man spoke, they were trying to block out the fact that in the next 30 minutes they would return to the scene of the crime, as accessories to a double homicide and pick up their brethren who had done the same. They hadn't been following orders as US Navy Seals, but rather as paid executioners.

A heavy ocean air filled the room and a moderately loud industrial fan helped hide the noise of Senoren and Lee coming out of their temporary palletized hideout. Had anyone walked in, they would have seen two pallets of supplies, like any other warehouse. One was completely still while the other looked like a baby chick viciously breaking through its shell as it is being born. Senoren emerged from the pallet with dark brown khakis and a MBA button-down shirt. He bent over to touch his toes, did a full body squat and shook himself out to get the blood flowing. Peterson stretched his arms till it looked like he would dislocate his shoulders, rose on his toes, held the position and his breath for a ten count and then exhaled quickly.

They briefly glanced at each other before Senoren went over to the double push doors. He'd be looking out for any unexpected employees. There shouldn't be any with all the buzz about seeing this band. He checked his watch, 20:15, and they would begin any minute now.

Peterson made a cut horizontally through the shrink-wrap, between the top and second row. It was just above his waist and the row of paper towels was easy to grab, squeeze and lift off. He placed the paper towel roof off to the side and began pulling off the cleaning supply boxes from one side of the pallet. He meticulously stacked them to the side and soon the water container sidewall was completely exposed.

They were tough. Neither Miguel nor Iovita had thrown up or had streaks of tears running down their faces. The blindfolds would remain on for now. Peterson and Nielsen unlatched the top of the portable aquatic holding cell. The smell of dead sea life drifted up and settled in their nostrils. They were machines executing their plan. No surprises when the lid came off; neither of the Sarmento's were Houdini and their wrists were still bound together behind their backs.

The pinkish seal intestines were draped over the shoulders, crisscrossed underneath their arms, then wrapped around their waist. It is normal for carnivorous mammals, like seals, to have intestines which are 5-6 times the length of their entire body. So, the intestines from one large seal was more than enough. When the lid came off and was lifted overhead, Miguel and Iovita immediately tried to get up which was nearly impossible in a wet tank, slippery from the seal oil and fat, no shoes and your arms manacled behind your back. Both soldiers were ready for this and a quick rap to their temple, with the butt of their handguns quieted them down.

Miguel would be first. Nielsen and Peterson each grabbed under his armpits and lifted him out of the tank and pushed him face down onto the deck near the edge of the tank. Miguel was prone and stretched out on the deck, his feet dangling over the pool. Nielsen had one knee in the middle of his lower back and the other knee on the back of his neck. He double-checked the duct tape over his mouth, because that was going to be important.

Both soldiers looked up to see whether everything was still clear in the hallway. Peterson had all his weight pressing down on the lower part of Miguel's calves. He reached in his vest and pulled out an X-ACTO knife. He nodded over to Peterson who grabbed a handful of seal entrails. Hovering the razor-sharp blade over Miguel's heel, he plunged the blade into the heel. His foot instantaneously arched from the pain and the scream was suppressed by the tape. Blood was pumping out of the slashed foot and dripping into the pool. Simultaneously, the entrails splashed into the water.

The desired effect was to stimulate all the sharks in the water. The inner ears of sharks would register the intestines splashing into the water, then the shark's paired nostrils would be hit with the seals guts, blood from the captive and then finally the big splash and thrashing of Miguel in the water.

Quickly, Nielsen pressed the bloody X-ACTO blade into the other heel and slashed down towards his toes. More blood poured out, his entire body arched at the pain and he tried to let out another scream of agony. Nielsen slashed through the blindfold and tossed it in the water. Miguel was in so much pain and all he could see was the boot of his captor and a concrete floor.

Iovita was now petrified, she could hear the struggle and muffled screams from her husband. She thrashed and twisted to both sides in an attempt to see who was hurting her husband, but she was held firmly in place.

Several of the seal's organs were tossed next into the pool. Below the surface, there was an immediate chain reaction. All the sharks had caught the scent and felt the vibrations in the water. Bruce was the first to move and reversed his clockwise swimming path. Since his captivity he hadn't been fed any seal, but the delicacy was instantly recognized and he immediately swam towards the other end of the tank.

Speed was of the essence and all the soldiers knew it. They hoped this human-seal gumbo was going to be tantalizing for the Great White. Each gulped at the thought of facing the beast in his watery home. Each soldier grabbed the lower forearm of Miguel's and pressed up hard enough to give the prisoner another jolt of pain. Nielsen cut through the rope binding his wrists together. With their free hand, they grabbed his upper arms, lifted him up and heaved him into the water.

There were a few dozen hardcore Aquarium lovers who were ignoring the concert in lieu of having unoppressed time to view the ocean life. There were two levels for the audience to view the Open Sea tank. Those who were watching had noticed an immediate alert in the water when the first drops of blood and seal entrails had landed in the water. From their viewing angle, they couldn't see anything other than the sharks all turning their attention to the left edge and surface.

Nielsen's hand shot into the water with Miguel's phone in the weighted, airtight container. He thought wryly, "This should be a first for Facebook Live."

The sharks had instantaneously adjusted their clockwise swim circle. The closest rotation to the prey was taken by Bruce, of course, and the other sharks took their position in the rotation based on their aggressiveness. Two hammerheads kept a ten-foot glancing distance below the Great White. Next came the 4 reef sharks, less confident, but hungry and curious. The blood and guts gumbo had started the tracking.

Within 5 seconds of hitting the water, Miguel's thrashing, terrified body received its first bone-jarring bump from Bruce.

Iovita had heard the splash and muffled cry of Miguel. Though disoriented, she knew that wasn't a good sound for someone who was bound and gagged. She immediately began to strain at the bindings and the soldiers found her just as difficult to handle as Miguel. Peterson expertly whacked her at the base of the skull. Not with enough force to knock her out, but certainly stunning her from more movement.

Like her husband, she was entwined in 50 feet of seal intestines as Nielsen pinned her calves down on the hard, wet concrete. They had been instructed to wait 60 seconds before throwing her in the tank, 28, 27, 26 seconds his watch counted down. The tip of the razor blade sliced into Iovita's heel and her entire body arched from the tortured nerve endings. The blade cut down her foot sole, finishing between her second and third toes. Her blood poured into the water to provide yet another scent for the sharks to track.

3, 2, 1…Peterson and Nielsen hoisted her up and as she twisted wildly, they squatted, then exploded upwards and threw her fifteen feet beyond the edge of the tank.

Nielsen placed Iovita's encapsulated phone into the water and it began to sink while rotating slowly. Her phone had be set to upload a live Periscope feed. Any of these two perpetrators' social followers would be seeing up close and personal what it would be like to face Bruce and his mates in their eerie neighborhood.

The audience observing the Open Sea exhibit was seeing much more than the rabid fans outside. The screaming had begun when the first teenager thought she had seen someone fall in the water. The lighting wasn't great at the top of the tank, but the frantic human silhouette was unmistakable. He was fighting to get to the surface, yet with his arms secured behind his back, it was an awkward and slower process.

The audience gave a collective groan as they watched the sharks zero in on the target. There were no Aquarium employees to be found as they'd all gone to listen to CJ Driger perform. Several people ran off to try and find a staff member. Many buried their faces in their hands to halt the disturbing, live Shark Week episode that was unfolding before their eyes. Others just stood there, mouths and unable to turn their eyes from the horror.

When Bruce gave his first beef tenderizing bump, the crowd inhaled deeply, knowing what to expect next. The Great White wasn't intimidated by anything this size. Miguel smelled mostly like a seal, was emitting a terrified aura and Bruce always had room for another bite. The crowd held their breath and one elderly woman passed out from the panic she felt helpless to change. This Great White's attacking pattern was ingrained from 18 years in the open sea. Smell, inspect, bump with his snout then an immediate 90-degree pivot to the right, combined with a dive down just deep enough to completely move his body around and get directly underneath the prey.

The Hammerheads and Reef sharks darted off and as Bruce came out of his downward dive, he exploded upwards as Iovita hit the water another 20 feet beyond his target. The audience was quite surprised at his speed and from the angle of his head and mouth, they all knew this - he was going to take a really big bite!

Great White sharks have an estimated biting force of 4,000 psi, 20 times greater than a human jaw. A tremendous difference even compared to a lion or tiger at 1,000 psi. In less than a second, Miguel and the audience would see firsthand there would be no tentative nibble. A moving creature that smelled like his favorite meal, though swam awkwardly, would be a treat from the salmon steaks and other sushi assortments. He could even play a little, see what kind of will to live his prey could muster.

Miguel looked down, heart racing, as he saw the shark swim down and away from him. Then as Bruce pulled out of the quick dive and made a direct line towards him, Miguel instinctively turned away to try and protect his soft abdomen. It was futile and the 20" wide mouth with over 300 life-tearing teeth bit into him. His spine was instantly crushed. The initial bite mark was so wide, it ran from Miguel's left hip all the way to his left shoulder.

The force of the bite severed his left arm and as Bruce was shaking Miguel like a rag doll, the arm squirted out of his mouth. Something for the Hammerheads to chase down. Several more people in the audience passed out as the blood began to create a small cloud around the attack area. With Miguel in his mouth and not tasting particularly like a seal now, Bruce's attention shot back to the area where another seal scent and splash had occurred.

He bit down a little harder on his prey, searching for that delicious seal fat, but only finding the intestines that had been wrapped around Miguel. Bruce cocked his head and spat out Miguel as his head and gills rose above the surface of the pool. His mouth, which was always open for a bite, was now lined up on the second seal target. One of the Hammerheads had made off with Miguel's arm and the other three had shot over towards Iovita.

The audience could guess from the silhouettes that a man and woman were in the water. Some were unsure how one person, let alone two, could fall in the most dangerous tank of the entire Aquarium. Others conjectured they had been pushed in. Or, had one slipped and the other attempted to rescue him? It was pure suicide to enter the tank, though. One of the Hammerheads hit Iovita in the face, knocking her head back.

Bruce had turned his attention towards the second splash and the Hammerheads' own survival instinct kicked in and they went to look for scraps from the original prey. The Great White didn't need much time to close the distance from meal one to meal two. In fact, with a few flicks of his enormous tail, he could cross the widest part of the tank in 4 seconds. This target was definitely moving more, though not moving much further away. No problem when you're the king of the ocean, your mouth is wide, you're one of the fastest hunters around and you have honed your skills for nearly two decades.

CHAPTER 23

It was Sven's last day working at Monterey Bay Aquarium. His boss didn't know it yet, but he was sick and tired of the crowds, smiling at hundreds of strangers every day; maybe it was thousands. He was going to stay for the concert, record it and text his boss that today was his last day. He'd recently downloaded the Periscope app to stream live video. Every employee had to sign a waiver that they would not video or audio record the concert or take any pictures.

Yet one more way corporate America created their little monopolies. He was sure they'd be doing it themselves and selling ad space on YouTube. Well, they wouldn't be the only ones with aspirations of a million hits and paid commercials. For the last two weeks he'd connected with, followed and exchanged follow-4-follow with every Periscope user who had transmitted video from the Aquarium and anyone who had subsequently watched those uploads. This is who he wanted to initially publish it for and hopefully create the catalyst to his live video. He planned to upload a raw version to YouTube, and then an edited version within 24 hours.

The concert had attracted quite a few followers. Popular band, new hit song and playing in a very small venue. What perfect timing! Sven was following the rhythm of the song with his head and drumming fingers. He looked over at his tablet to ensure the quality of the feed was excellent and saw the push notification from Periscope that someone else was sending a video near the Aquarium. Maybe some fan or another disgruntled employee had a similar entrepreneurial bent as him. He clicked on the notification to see what his competition was uploading.

It was obvious whoever was holding the phone or video recorder was an amateur. It wasn't very clear, and Sven looked at the concert stage wondering, "Where was this guy pointing his lens?" Then, as he realized it must be someone inside a tank, his brain and eyes assimilated the images and he knew someone must be shooting underwater. This was ridiculous, every employee knew that was strictly off limits. Looked like it was going to be someone else's last day as well.

As the camera lens swung around, he could now pick out the seaweed from the Open Sea exhibit tank and then Bruce swam down towards the bottom of the tank. That Great White had given him an eerie feeling. Who was screwing around making a video in the most dangerous tank? He was confounded for a split second as he tried to mentally position himself behind the camera. This angle was all wrong. It couldn't be someone at the edge of the tank. They had to be stupid enough to either be in the tank, about ten feet underwater or somehow have a remote-powered camera.

The wide-angle lens showed an apparent lack of sea life. Normally, the schools of fish swam through at least every 30 seconds and he hadn't even seen a glimmer of the schools of sardines. And then as Sven's eyes adjusted further to the picture, he saw the oddly swimming character. It looked as if someone were practicing their dolphin kick with their body undulating from their torso to the tips of their feet.

Why in the world weren't they using their arms? What kind of imbecile would be in that tank? No goggles, tank, shark feeding stick. It was almost as if they were on a death wish dare. Then, in a flash of sudden movement, Sven saw Bruce coming up and instantaneous dread came over him. This was the end of the dare for this poor soul. He'd seen the clips from Shark Week and other National Geographic shows and knew how Bruce would finish this scene.

Bruce did not disappoint. The speed, force and certainty of his gaping maw came into mash and tear this person. It looked like Bruce was going to literally bite him in half. Sven's own body twisted, his abs involuntarily tightened like they never had before. He couldn't squirm away, and neither could Bruce's victim. What a horrific scene with the blood everywhere and most of this person's body being severed in two. Who was videoing this and uploading to Periscope? They were gonna end up being sued in court. Or was this a psychotic's final sadistic act, to video the completion of their own suicidal, watery death wish?

After heaving the second prisoner in the water, Nielsen, Peterson and Senoren checked the area to make sure nothing was left behind other than the water container, relating to their capital punishment mission. The delivery of cleaning products, items the Aquarium already used, and the non-scheduled drop-off was a dead end. The steep angle of the video camera mounted on a pole to monitor delivery trucks would only show a driver and passenger with hats covering their faces.

The receiving dock worker would only vaguely remember a Latino and Caucasian man, who he didn't believe had ever delivered there before. There were at least a dozen deliveries every day and it wasn't his job to pull IDs and memorize faces. The MBA was always short-staffed in the shipping/receiving department; not many of the volunteers wanted to be lugging boxes around. They volunteered so they could be near the sea life.

In the animal kingdom, the most fat has a propensity to be stored right in the middle of the body. Humans and animals alike. Sharks love the richness of salmon and seals, so they go right after the midsection. Sometimes a tailfin or fish head will get in the way, but the target is always the decadent abdomen. The second unknown target in the tank would be no different. Bruce had grown tired of the same old diet, day after day, of 10-pound fish blocks. Plenty of it, but there hadn't been any hunting, cornering or bumping. Just a chunk of meat on the end of a stick or floating down to meet him.

As Bruce's sonar bounced off Iovita's body swimming to the surface, he shot over immediately, and those pesky sharks cleared away. The Great White homed in easily on the new target. He was pissed and this one might taste better than the last one; let's eat. The audience was screaming at the glass pane, trying desperately to urge the poor woman out of danger's path. It was a few helpless moments, as if watching an executioner walk up to the gallows pole.

The other sharks were picking and pulling at Manuel's remaining scraps. Though lifeless, there was fresh meat and blood in the water, a taste each shark was eager to try. They weren't sitting at a table, munching away. It was more of a grab and run with the sharks tearing off as much as they could and darting away to chomp, swallow and go back for more.

The tank had a growing red cloud from the pints of Manuel's blood. There was a new edge in the pool as if the inmates had been given free reign and had taken every advantage possible. The 7 sharks were extremely efficient in finishing Bruce's work. There was more of Manuel in a shark's stomach than not. The initial frenzy had slowed down now with the taste of seal being stripped away and human flesh only offering a variation on their meal plan; not the savory seal that had enticed them.

When a Great White took a bite, there was little chance for survival. The mouth, which could cover such a large surface area was lined with teeth from 1 to 2 ½ inches. There was no gentle nibbling from the most feared predator of the ocean. Biting down, crushing and tearing caused a nearly complete disablement of the prey. Without a quick release and medical attention, a human victim wouldn't survive an adult Great White attack.

Iovita was squirming with all her might, beginning with the hips and thrusting back and forth, struggling to surface her body. Bruce sensed the distress of his prey and propelled himself forward quickly. He opened his mouth as wide as possible and bit into her soft backside and legs. The force was such that it dislocated her hip. This was the least of her problems. The femoral artery had been torn open, causing a tremendous loss of blood.

This one tasted a lot better than the last. The richness of her body fat coupled with the flesh and some remaining seal entrails was pretty appealing. The best part, though, had been the simple of variety on his palate. Something different, some creature that moved and kicked and squirmed. The fact that the other sharks were fighting over the remaining scraps; all increased the definiteness of the Great White wanting to finish off his prey.

The alarm was pulled when the security staff who had only been monitoring the video feed from the cameras they had zoomed in on the concert, finally saw the hysteria of the crowd at the Open Sea tank. They immediately shouted orders for all units not assigned to the concert for a code ten to the exhibit and Open Sea pool deck area.

The emergency protocols did not include this situation and steps to follow. There was tsunami warning, earthquake, fire, active shooter and less urgent emergencies, but not for sharks are dining on someone in the tank. Nobody was going in that tank with Bruce, blood and 7 other hyper sharks. There wasn't any type of screen that could be dropped down to divide the pool and attempt a recovery. It was much too late for a rescue.

The night shift biologist, Ingrid, was rushing there now from the offices. Lighting could be adjusted in the tank and above it to help the team recover the body remains. There were fishing nets that could be placed on extension poles to drag through the water. They had to clear out the area. People were drawn to car accidents and this was no different. The video cameras had already shown people were taking pictures and videoing the mauling. He wouldn't be surprised to see this up on YouTube in the next few minutes. People had a desire to be first and especially if it was reporting bad news.

The city had provided three officers to police the concert and a dozen temporary security officers were stationed about the concert area. The concert would have to be stopped and the band's manager was going to intercede after the next song finished. Hopefully, the band had played the smash hit. The Aquarium was already crowded with news media here to report on the star show.

The major tasks were to recover the bodies, get the public out of the exhibit area and help the police figure out what happened. There was just one video camera viewing the deck area for that exhibit and the security supervisor immediately backed it up. He sat down with a computer tech and they began reviewing the recordings of the last half hour. They had better back up the entire day of security camera footage.

"Back up camera 12 and go to 8:45pm. Let's see what was happening then."

The tech used the slider bar to 20:45 on the meter and pressed play. The image was blurry, as if the lens was dirty or the zoom was unfocused. It looked similar to an image that was projected, but the opaque lens cover was still on. You could see some general colors blurred together, but not anything specific like the tank, the railing around it; nothing at all.

"Is there anything you can do with picture qualify? Zoom it?"

"Not really, this is the recording."

"Switch over to number 12 now. What does it look like?"

They both saw it was the same image, there was no sound. It looked like there was a blurred object moving; though it was so unclear it could have been anything. Bigfoot could be in the room or a super model. "Call down there to have someone look at the camera." The police chief would be here any minute and this was looking ominous.

CHAPTER 24

The delivery van was just three blocks from the Aquarium when the alarm sounded and another block further when the concert was cut short. Traffic was moderate, as most fireworks spectators had been camped at their viewing spot for several hours. Each mile they placed between themselves and the crime scene made breathing easier. There was tension in Peterson's hands as he gripped the wheel, but the soldier's training kept him focused on the task.

A delivery van with heavy duty suspension, of this size would, be in high demand. The neighborhood, they were leaving it in was ensure it would be whisked away before dawn. The E Alisal neighborhood near the 101 in Salinas was easy enough to find and Simon would be picking them up. The rest of the crew was already at their hotel showering and bagging all the clothing to be incinerated.

It was 9:32 when they parked the van. Both men rolled down their windows and began wiping down the car. Every interior surface that could have been touched was cleaned. Each gloved man grabbed a gallon bottle of chlorine bleach and dumped it on the steel floor of the van. All carpeting had been removed in advance of the mission. It was a loud ride, but the carpet fibers could collect an amazing amount of DNA.

They would use highly concentrated ammonia, NH3 to help inhibit DNA testing. Followed by BSA, or benzyl sulfonamide. BSA contains an ammonia group in it which prevents the polymerase chain reason—used to amplify DNA for testing purposes.

Nielsen jumped out first, baseball cap down low and he couldn't wait to get away from this scene. Peterson finished dumping his bleach and left it in the back of the van. This van would need a few hours before it could be driven, he chuckled. His eyes felt like they were on fire and going to burn up right inside the sockets. They both hit the sidewalk at a moderate clip, silently they strode side by side, down one block and then a right where Simon would be waiting.

As they rounded the corner, sure enough the big black Suburban was idling. Tinted windows leaving no clue whether anyone was inside. As they approached it, Simon's electric driver's window slid down and he gave the clear signal. They jumped in and sped off as the doors closed.

Each man let out a long, slow breath. Essentially, the mission was over, but they needed to get out of town. There would be on eggshells for a week and as the days passed, the tension would slowly dissolve. There was no such thing as the perfect crime; planning was crucial, but there was always the chance of happenstance or human error. In this moment, they were 60 miles away and didn't have a helicopter flying over their vehicle. There hadn't been a siren directed at them.

Every step had been executed as planned and each man reviewed the film in his mind. No missteps had occurred to their knowledge. These were confident men; professionals performing a complex and high risk set of tasks. Both cyber terrorists were in the tank, they had left the panicked Aquarium without a hitch and they had already left the vehicle behind.

Simon reached inside his black nylon pullover for two envelopes. It was payday and both men had earned every dollar. The envelopes were thick with bundled $20s and $50s. The men thumbed through the green-backs; grateful for the tax-free income opportunity. As they travelled through back roads, the firework shows throughout the area flashed, showered and boomed in the evening sky.

Peterson was the first to be dropped off. Simon was always curious to see what he was driving or riding. This guy went through cars and super bikes like Jar-rod went through supplement bottles. As they eased to the curb, Simon saw what had to be the newest su-perbike. He didn't follow motorcycles very closely, but this looked like a fairly new Ducati, with a 1198 badge. Nielsen whistled and said with emphasis, "Now that's a getaway ride."

Peterson smiled as he threw his right leg over, then put on his helmet and gloves. Putting the key in the ignition, slight twist to the right and pressing the start button created the most incredible twin-symphony through the set of Termignoni carbon fiber pipes. No need to rev it while on the stand, they both knew Peterson would let it out a little as he pulled away. Never one to disappoint, he dropped it into first gear, eased out the clutch and pulled back on the throttle.

The four Italian baritone cylinders exclaimed their cacophony through the pipes and made the men in the Suburban a little envious; contemplating a cash transaction at a local Ducati dealership with their cash windfall. The next stop was Nielsen, pretty reserved guy who loved the muscle car era. They drove over to the next drop off point; Mission Point Rd. As they eased up to the street parking, there sat gleaming under a street light, a brilliant glossy black 1969 Camaro with white racing stripes.

Simon and Nielsen exchanged a brief salute, shook hands mightily and he slid out of the Suburban seat. A few quick steps as the double chirp of the alarm unlocked the driver's side door. You could see Nielsen's reflection in the paint as he reached for the door handle. He expertly maneuvered his athletic frame into the car and pulled the door closed him in one motion. The solid *thunk* of the Camaro's heavy gauge steel door sounded and the 396 SS motor fired up instantly with a V8 growl.

Simon had to smile. Boys and their toys; correct that: single, unattached, no children boys and their toys. Gotta love it. His Suburban was all he needed for transportation. Sure, he would swap garages in an instant with Jarrod and his sunburst orange Vette, glacier white AMG Mercedes SUV and deep blue Tesla sedan. Back to the task at hand, which was driving back to the rented beach house without being tailed or picked up.

It was a little after 11:00pm and he couldn't wait to let go of the day's stress in his sleep. He was certain Karisa would be awake and waiting for him. He had sent her a few texts so only she knew it was him and he was safe.

ETA 15 minutes, Love you Kar

Simon's mind drifted to his benefactor, employer, cycling buddy and friend, Jarrod. How was he contemplating the night's events? Was there elation or regret or both for striking back at his father's cyber attackers? He mentally checked off the mission objectives and each had been completed. For the moment, there was a sense of relief. He wouldn't allow his mind to be drag him into the 'what if' game.

"What if there was another video camera?"

"What if it was a setup and Jarrod or some other group wanted all the loose ends tied up."

"Enough!" Simon shouted out loud to snap himself out of the downward spiral.

He was nearly at the beach house and if he was freaked out Karissa would sense it. It was time to chill mentally. He immediately shifted his thoughts to his kids and the upcoming birthday party. Jacob would be turning 6 on the 29th and he was excited for his little guy. He'd finished Kindergarten and done great; despite all the cautious warnings about young immature boys, blah blah, wait a year, let them calm down.

As Simon pulled up to the house, he could see the porch light on and through the front window a soft glow of light. He clicked the remote and just wondered briefly to himself what it would be like to live in a beach house in Monterey. "Need to get on that advanced investing plan buddy", he lectured himself. As the garage door rose, he saw Jarrod's Corvette already parked. Good sign, though they'd already texted about each other's whereabouts.

Simon got out of his car and closed the door behind him. He took a full stretch; reaching up as high as he could and then arching his back. He felt every muscle stretch and he needed it from subconsciously sitting tensely most of the ride back. He released the stretch and shook his arms for a few seconds as he walked towards the man door.

The door led into the kitchen and there was his Karissa, standing at the stove with a hopeful smile on her face. She quickly stepped to him and threw her arms around his neck. Simon felt all the tension go at once in response to her body. "I'm so glad you're back," she spoke into his ear. Simon had wrapped his arms around her torso, lifted her off the ground and hugged her back just as tightly while pressing his cheek against hers.

"Yes Kar, I'm back." He gently lowered her back to the ground, but held the hug for an extended minute. Karissa released his neck and grabbed his head so she could kiss his face. Releasing her hug had let out the involuntary shaking and so Simon pulled her close again to calm her nerves. Gradually, the shaking went away and the tension in their hug eased up till she felt in control of herself.

When they finally detached themselves from each other, Simon gave her another quick kiss and they walked into the front room. Jarrod was sitting there in the recliner with his nose buried in a book. He looked up upon their entering the room and gave a broad smile. Appreciative for their company as he was trying to unwind as well. He raised himself out of his chair and extending his arm said, "Thank you very, very much Simon."

Simon nodded as they shook hands and pulled each other in for a brief hug and clap on the back. "You're welcome Jarrod, we pulled it off." Jarrod didn't know to what level of detail Simon had explained their mission, but Karissa looked at him and her facial expressions flashed from fear to misunderstanding to awe to gratitude.

Jarrod wondered if she had turned the news on when the sirens had begun. There would be quite a bit of buzz in the local scene, stretching out across the world. Society loved to feed itself on the dramatic, the horror, the tragedies and in this case intertwined as a murder mystery. "What would the police find?" he asked himself? Would the CIA become involved? Soon enough, he would find out to what extent the local and national authorities would pursue this case.

"It's been a long day," Jarrod spoke with a wry smile. "I'm heading to bed. See you guys in the morning." A tension relieving yawn escaped his mouth to finish relaying his thoughts.

"Yep, see you in the morning," Simon chimed back. Karissa simply said, "Yes, good night."

CHAPTER 25

WEDNESDAY, JULY 5TH, 0530 HOURS

Jarrod awoke from a troubled night of sleep. He was a thinker and had run through many scenarios in his mind before finally drifting off to sleep. He had played out several escape routes from the U.S. if the pressure alarms rose too high. He had the means, but before he began replaying these in his mind, Jarrod pulled himself out of bed to engage his body.

He relieved himself in the bathroom and quietly walked back to his room to get ready for a quick run. Normally, he didn't like exercising without breakfast. This morning was an exception because he wanted to clear his mind, breathe in the salty air and release a little more stress from the previous days' mission.

Jarrod pulled and straightened out his comforter, then neatly folded his sleep shirt and shorts on the bed. He would normally go for a long ride on his bike, but this morning was an exception. Running was really simple and the less time to get started, the better. He pulled on some running shorts, a lightweight shirt and hoodie. This was Monterey and it would be in the high 50s in the cool of a summer morning here. He laced up his running shoes and walked to the front door.

Stretching was such an ingrained part of his life that he could begin clearing his mind as he went through the mechanics to stretch out his back, quads, calves and hamstrings. He needed this run to begin the next chapter of his life. What had he done? It was more than eye for an eye. He began running down the neighborhood sidewalk; heading north and towards the waterfront. An 8-minute mile pace felt good this morning.

What had he done? A few cars were awake with him, but not necessarily their drivers. He had elevated himself to the position of international cyber prosecutor, judge and hangman. Jarrod could feel his heart beating strong as pushed off the sidewalk with each stride. He glanced over his shoulder. Any other maniac joggers, police or unidentified cars tailing him?

What had he done? Broken numerous laws. Excessively righted a wrong? Stood up for the defenseless. Returned stolen money to their owners. Caused a stir in the cyber-criminal underground. Splashed every major news feed with a horror story. Given those with galeophobia, the fear of sharks, a sleepless night.

He had fought for his Dad.

When it was all said and done, he had fought for his Father; his only living parent. Two thieves had stolen from his Dad and preyed upon so many other Mothers, Fathers, Sisters and Brothers; he had circumvented the criminal judicial system and fought mano-a-mano representing the victims, he and team Papa had fought for them all: the underdogs, the exploited and the vulnerable.

Jarrod had reached at the Pier and his chest was heaving. He had completely lost track of time and the three-mile run had turned into a full-on run. Less than 18 minutes for 3.2 miles as measured by his smart watch. He felt great and he dialed back the pace along the boardwalk to a leisurely 10-minute mile pace. There were a few beach walkers scattered along the shoreline. Some were walking while others stared out into the rhythmic 4-foot waves.

He took the wooden plank steps down to the beach and slowed his jog to a brisk walk. Heading down to the water, he glanced up and down the shore for the biggest gap between people. He adjusted his direction and fully breathed in the clean, salty air.

Last night had drawn a stark contrast in his life. Unlike Simon, with his loving confidant' and wife Karissa to cradle in his arms, Jarrod had a book cradle in his hands. Alone with his personal accomplishments. Ever since his youth, he had been busy, productive and looking for the next adventure. Sure, he had Dad, the kids and grandkids. Though he had invested time and love to nurture them, there was still a gap in his life. That one person with whom you could intimately share life.

He looked to the bubbly surf approaching his running shoes and took two steps back. That encapsulated his relationship with women the last dozen years. He'd get close to the ocean, but not let it engulf him, or go for a swim. It might just be time to change that with Lorrie. That was a big assumption after one dinner. It was more about attitude and willingness to give it a shot. Jump in the ocean and go for a swim buddy. He let his thoughts linger on her image for a while. What was she really like? Where was she in the relationship searching process? He'd have to ask. Sounded like a good second date question; ha-ha.

Jarrod hadn't solved all of life's mysteries, but he had at least committed to taking a relationship chance. He clasped his hands behind his head and took a long, deep breath. He felt energized from the run and the new proposition. On his jog back to the house, his thoughts returned to Dad. There wasn't anything he could do to stop the Alzheimer's; he felt that had slowed it down somewhat. Dad was in a comfortable and safe environment. But that was the easy part. Writing a check to the care facility was simple.

Jarrod felt the need to invest more time into his Dad. He could do more than lunches twice a week and the walks. Living in the home, coupled with his state had fenced in his life to a 10 square miles locked perimeter from the care facility. What could he do to create a few more snapshots in his memory bank? And how could he tie in the rest of the family. Sure, everyone looked to Jarrod as his caretaker, but let's see what he could put together and his sister Janelle might have some great ideas as well.

Where he was right now; Monterey. Dad had owned a few sailboats over the years. Of course, he'd love to be here in Monterey. San Francisco, Napa Valley,

Muir Woods, and he could go on and on. It seems like his life had been narrowed down as well. To where he wanted to cycle, buy a property or vacation. There were so many places to visit from his Northern California doorstep.

Field trips! Just like Dad used to take him on field trip adventures, he could do the same. Set the goal and the minimum standard his mind automatically thought. He was practically back to the cottage and was bursting with energy. Jarrod couldn't wait to get this on paper and carve out days in his calendar. Why shouldn't he give the better part of the day to Dad?

As much as he wanted to sprint the rest of the way to the rental house, he steadied his pace at a fast jog and let his mind check off Bay Area landmarks he could visit with Dad. He had the time and financial freedom, let's create some memories for Dad. Get the kids and grandkids to join in on the quick adventures.

The early morning jog was exactly what he'd needed to close a chapter and open up the next two in his life. Cyber terror fighting citizen cape off and Dating Game contestant / field trip adventure guide capes on. Jarrod eased up as he turned into the driveway and pulled up to a complete stop. He began stretching and added a few more places to the list, box suite at a Raiders game; possible. Maybe he'd arrive with Dad for halftime and the 2nd half, but the family could enjoy the entire game.

Hamstrings stretched, calves and quads were next. Why not a symphony? Squeezing that lactic acid away. Was the 2 ½ hour drive to Lake Tahoe too far? His legs were stretched apart and he was bending over to touch the ground between his feet and then he stretched his fingers to his heels, exhaled out and he stretched even further. Bringing his hands back, he bent his left knee, raised his torso and leaned to the left. He stretched out, centered himself and then repeated the stretch on his right side.

He completed his stretches and to the two porch steps up to the house and unlocked the door. He was famished. The house was still quiet; a day at the beach running around, plus the sea air had zonked Simon's kids. He grabbed his notepad to list out some locations for Dad and relationship intentions while he was cooking his eggs.

- *Build a relationship*
- *Quality*
- *Depth*
- *Transparent*
- *Trust*

Field Trips with Dad—invite family—they need lead time

- *Muir Woods*
- *SF*
- *Napa*
- *Symphony*
- *Art exhibit*
- *Warriors / A's / Raiders luxury box*
- *Monterey*

The eggs were cooked, and he added a dash of pepper. Pomegranate tea, he laughed at himself; so rote and routine with the eating choices. Habits. Patterns. Structure and framework. Most would laugh, but he planned to live till 100 and live it actively. The smell of food and noises in the kitchen may have stirred the kids. He was absolutely certain Simon and Karissa were awake; they just weren't getting out of bed. Nothing so great as to be awake in the morning, savoring your spouse, while the kids were peacefully asleep.

Oatmeal was next on the menu. ½ a cup of dry oats measured into a bowl, heavy on the cinnamon, apple flavored fiber powder and some pumpkin spice meal replacement powder. Jarrod added hot water and stirred it in slowly. He was very particular about his oatmeal; no runny, mushy, soupy oatmeal for him. His was fairly sticky and his kids and grandkids loved theirs the same way. He tossed in a layer of blueberries for good measure.

Jarrod heard a bathroom door close, the ensuing waterfall and flush. The microwave acknowledged his oatmeal was finished and as he pulled it out, he heard Simon's voice behind him say quietly, "Morning Jarrod."

"Morning Simon. Want some tea?"

"Sure, I'll try your tea again. Man, you are always eating, huh?"

"Hey, I know morning routine isn't much different than mine; sans Karissa of course." Jarrod whispered the Karissa comment.

"Looks like you already went for a run. How's the air and break?"

"Felt great this morning and it's a fun change to run in this heavy ocean air. Want to go for a ride later today?" Jarrod wanted to ask whether there were any loose strings, but certainly not where they could be overheard.

"Yeah, let's go at 11. I want to spend some time here. Not many mornings where I get to see them rise and shine." Simon sipped his tea and as if on cue, his sweet daughter padded softly into the kitchen; rubbing her eyes and holding her infant blanket.

"Daddy, I can get to see you in the morning?" Her 4-year-old voice rose with hope at the end of the sentence. She reached up for her Dad. He effortlessly picked her up and spoke gently to her.

"Yes, Princess Jocelyn. I get to see you this morning and tomorrow and the day after that. I'm excited to have breakfast and play on the beach with you."

All of a sudden her eyes widened, "And we can make sand castles today? A really big one? Can you help me make them big Daddy?"

Jarrod found Simon's transformation fascinating. Just last night he had been the driving force behind a risky, domestic hit squad and this morning he had molded himself into a compassionate and caring father. Communicating with words and excitement for the days ahead. He laughed to himself because when Jacob woke up, it would be a whole new story.

Jacob was a miniature squad leader; cut from the same personality template as Simon, while most of his physical features favored his mother. What a little determined firecracker he was at just 5 years old. Jarrod was sure his little body was almost fully recharged, and he'd be waking up any minute now. What an amazing stage in life. There was so much work and reward at this stage of parenting.

Sure enough, Jacob's little ears had picked up on the voices and he came bounding into the room in his Navy Seal Halloween costume that doubled as his pajamas. Simon had relayed to him that Jacob would wear them to preschool, had they let him. "Daddy" he exclaimed. "You're here for good now? We get to play all day with you? You should have seen all the fireworks for Independence Day!"

Little Jocelyn was curled up on her dad, looked up and said in a hopeful voice, "Maybe there will be more fireworks tonight, Daddy?"

Jarrod left the room to go shower and shave. He was happy the mission had succeeded and financially as many of the victims had been repaid that could be traced. They had taken two less criminals off the judge's docket and hopefully created a stir in the cyber-criminal world. He was anxious; the hot shower and shave would put him back in his morning routine. Though he had imposed a 2-day hiatus from email, he still might glance at some investments after the closing bell.

1100 HOURS

Jarrod and Simon both had their cycling kits on and were checking over their bikes in the garage. Of course, the kids wouldn't leave their Dad's side for a moment.

They had been so excited to have him all morning to play with and keep his attention. Simon had given the kids a detective eyes project; find 5 things that were different about one bike from the other.

Joceyln, who was older and more experienced at the game, rattled three off, "Color, Daddy, yours is black and Mister Jarrod's is orange. You have different shaped backpacks." Both men couldn't help but smile as she was referring to the small, under seat-mounted storage for inner tubes and tools. "And your seats are different. Mister Jarrod's is breaking in half and yours isn't."

Simon looked at his daughter and replied, "Yes, that's exactly what I told Jarrod when he bought that seat for $200. He needs one that isn't broke in half."

Jacob piped up and said, "You have different words on your bike Daddy and letters."

"Very good Jacob. And tell me what else you see that is different."

Jacob got an even more determined look on his face, a miniature impersonation of his dad's facial expression as he looked from bike to bike.

Simon put his bike right next to Jarrod's and said, "Look really closely at the rims and tell me what you see."

Jocelyn spoke up and said they have a different shape, right Daddy?"

"Yes, indeed the shape and height are a little different from each other. How about this little part here

Jacob? It's called the hub." He pointed to the front hub on the bikes.

"Does it have more sticks on it?"

"No, look again; really close"

"Yours is black Daddy and his is shiny black."

"Excellent, both of you! Now we're going to go on a ride and we'll be back after lunch. So have fun, listen to Mommy and I'll be back before you know it."

As both men walked their bikes down the driveway and to the sidewalk, out of the corner of his right eye, Simon noticed a white SUV coming at a fairly slow speed. He tilted his head and made a motion as if he was stretching his neck to get a better view. His face registered instant recognition and under his breath, he spoke to Jarrod, "You really know how to pick them buddy...."

"What's that?"

Simon waved at the white Range Rover and gave the queerest smile as he said, "Your new girlfriend is a stalker and she's here."

Now that got Jarrod's attention and he looked to see what in the world Simon was talking about. He looked up to see a gleaming white Range Rover being driven by a woman...what? Lorrie and her flaming red hair were down here in Monterey? Jarrod's mouth dropped open and Lorrie had a similar gaping look on her face a half second earlier as she associated the 2 cyclists with the snapshot in her mind of Il Fornaio and then with their blind date.

The Range Rover stopped, right there in the middle of the street next to the house. Lorrie looked like she wanted to ask a question, but had forgotten to roll the window down. She fumbled with her oversized sunglasses and got her driver side window down.

In unison, they both said, "What are you doing here?"

Then as they instantly remembered their manners, each added, "Hi Lorrie. Hi Jarrod how are you?"

Jarrod jumped at the opportunity to tease Lorrie a little, "I thought you were hiring a PI to check me out? You're here personally to see where I go and who I hang out with?"

Lorrie smiled a quipped back. "I'm great doing great, thanks. How about you?"

Jarrod just laughed, "Touché. Where are my manners?"

"I'm checking up on my beach rental and you must be the infamous, last minute renter JD something-or-other business. Ha!"

Simon peered up and angled his face away from Lorrie, but where Jarrod could still see his face. The look that Simon shot over, instantly said, "How in the world, of all the places in Monterey and you rented unknowingly from her."

Jarrod briefly acknowledged Simon with a quick, quizzical lift of his eyebrows. Then replied with a laugh, "And you must be Ms. LW Rentals; I presume." He walked closer to her car and said, "Ok, let me try to rewind this conversation a little, "I really like your place. Nice interior finishes. How long have you had it?"

Lorrie played along and said lightly, "Oh, you know a few years. When you could buy them for less than half a million." Then added, "You better give my house a 5-star review on Flipkey, if you want all your security deposit back." She had started off the sentence with a serious tone, but couldn't hide her smile by the time she completed it.

"That was one of the reasons I picked the place. It had the highest security deposit. Figured it must be a great place. Either that or a landlord who thinks they're more than amazing." Jarrod was relaxing and enjoying the banter. "What are the odds…." His voice trailed off as he was practically at her car door.

Lorrie looked at him directly, "Exactly what I was thinking…., what are the odds?"

Jarrod changed his tact. It was time to nudge this relationship along, rather than wait another week for the next date. "This is a long way to drive, just to get asked out on another date." Jarrod said with the widest smile on his face; locking their four blue eyes.

Lorrie dropped her eyes slightly and said softly, "Well, I am staying one more night."

That sure was an easy opening he thought. "Well, I'm sure you know a great place to eat here. How about 6 o'clock?"

He felt like saying something extra; anything to sell himself or sound romantic like, "Aren't you slightly curious how circumstance and chance is trying to slip into your schedule?" He paused just to watch her face.

In his quick assessment of Lorrie, he thought she was very independent and confident, not easily influenced by chance or emotion. So, let's give her a few seconds to speak her mind.

For a moment, Lorrie appeared to fall back into her rigid, planned schedule. There hadn't been anything on her calendar and this certainly wasn't 48 hours' notice. She had already selected the proper time gap between the first and second date; well, maybe not the perfect time gap, but the span of time where she felt comfortable. Rather than slip back into the inflexible Lorrie schedule, and courteously say "Let me think about it." While all along having no intention of modifying her calendar, she tilted her head back up, turned on her most genuine smile and simply said, "Sure, Jarrod. Let's have dinner at the Chart House on Cannery Row." Conceding on the schedule, but controlling the locale, she smiled brilliantly at him.

She pulled her head back slightly, raised her eyebrows and reached to cover her mouth; almost as if she had tried to pull the words back. Lorrie could hardly believe those words had slipped out of her mouth. She was used to parrying with the other party and negotiating everything to a Win on her terms. Something was certainly different about the beginning to this relationship. She felt willing to give up some control, explore, concede and open up to this man in front of her.

Jarrod watched her reaction and was amused and curious at the same time. He didn't like reading people's physical cues and guessing what was going on in their brain or heart for that matter. He didn't know what to say. "Are you sure, you seem like you wanted to take that answer back." Or should he say "Or some other time if you've already got plans." Or "Great, I was thinking about you this morning on my run to the beach." His thoughts trailed off and he told himself to stop over-analyzing, ignore the responses based in fear and doubt. Stop over-thinking.

"Well, fantastic! I was jogging this morning on the beach and thinking about you..." and his voice trailed off as he took a step closer to her. There was warm feeling spreading throughout his body and up to his cheeks again. She was more than just a prize or someone who would look great on his arm. She seemed to be blushing a little herself as she bit her lower lip, then smiled. They were a little more comfortable with the other now. It seemed like circumstance was giving them a friendly nudge.

The End

ACKNOWLEDGMENTS

This book would not have been completed without CJ Driger, my accountability partner. Our check-in calls kept me on task for the necessary milestones; including the painful process of submission to book agents and their ensuing rejections.

Thanks to my Mother for her many hours proofreading this book, correcting my grammar, punctuation, over-use of words and offering many suggestions. Thank you to my Father, who introduced me to his favorite fiction authors as a young teen, supplying a constant stream of novels and demonstrating his desire to read.

Thank you to my kids giving up some family time and continuing to encourage me through the writing process.

Thank you Lena Foggiato-Bish for providing expert Italian translation and colloquialisms.

Thank you, Richard Chew, for outlining the technical details of accessing ISPs, the Internet, and tracing down IPs to physical addresses.

Thank you to Vanessa Maynard for your excellent graphic artist skills and assistance with the physical book layout.

Thank you to my friends and brother-in-law, Corey, for allowing me to use their cool and catchy names in this book:

Al Loomis

CJ Lee

Corey Peterson

Jarrod DeBoy

Johnny Senoren

Kendrick Daniels

Lorrie Williamson

Richard Chew

Rob Roman

Shawn Neilsen

Thank you to all my family and friends who gave supported throughout the process of writing Shark Alley. I wrote it during a difficult period in my life and could not have completed it without your encouragement and prayers for my complete well-being.